The ONION Peeler

Alexandra Baresova

The Onion Peeler

Tellwell Talent
www.tellwell.ca

ISBN
978-1-77370-496-8 (Paperback)

Disclaimer

The Onion Peeler is a work of fiction.

Any resemblances are accidental and likenesses coincidental.

"You don't have a soul. You are a soul.
You have a body."

~ C. S. Lewis

Hiraeth(n) homesickness for a home you cannot return to, a home which never was; the nostalgia, the yearning, the grief for the lost places of your past

FREEZING

Pete's Lunch

A biting rain tore at the east side of our faded wooden cottage. It relented briefly but started up again a few minutes later, howling and whistling like a banshee from another realm.

Why is it raining so bloody hard? It's December after all. It's supposed to be cold and snowing. A blanket of fluffy snowflakes should be covering the ground.

While mentally debating the latest buzz about the slowly warming earth, a cool breeze at floor level sent a shiver down my spine. It was time to put on another sweater. I stretched slowly, cat like, and wiggled my toes. Savasana, the corpse pose, was so damned comforting. I could have stayed there forever. Forever and ever. I felt at peace in the velvet blackness, the few seconds of nothing. Of no thought. Doing yoga asanas on our lumpy green mottled carpet was not comfortable but was better than no exercise at all.

Other than shoveling and piling the mountains of snow that eventually came down, I got little exercise that winter of 1976.

I finally managed to sit upright, roll up the grey woolen mat and stash it in my favourite wicker basket. I tiptoed into the kitchen so as not to wake my man who would be leaving for work soon enough.

As I opened the fridge and grabbed a loaf of homemade bread to make a sandwich for Pete's lunch, a deep wrenching, which started as a familiar twinge of angst earlier, quickly grew into a roller coaster ride in my queasy stomach. A sharp sword sliced into my gut. I leaned into it. It fled. This time.

Some days I feared losing my breakfast. Hitting at unpredictable moments, this nausea and gnawing felt like something horrid was about to happen. What the *something* was, was never really clear. Ghostlike and vaporous, this slimy creature fed on any of my fears and refused to solidify into anything specific. By the time evening rolled around I was wiped out, after fighting those elusive, invisible demons all day long.

Will this ever let up? I had thought for sure the yoga would help. *Damn the yoga. Damn the fucking yoga. It does not seem to be helping. I've been trying to figure this out forever. Ok. Not forever, maybe for about three years, anyway.*

Just make Pete's friggin' lunch. Focus. Focus. I slowly smeared a chunk of coarse, whole grain bread with peanut butter and cut thin slices off a juicy Mac apple. Done—a crunchy, tasty sandwich. Vegetarian option number one: anything with peanut butter.

I wrapped it in brown parchment paper and packed it into the beat- up, black metal lunch box with the worn leather handle. A great yard-sale find, it held a full thermos of hot tea for Pete's midnight break at the local sawmill. The Breaking Back Sawmill, as I called it. But never to his face.

On that chilly December morning I wondered whether this would be Pete's last day. The word was out. Old Breaking Back would probably lay off a few guys before Christmas. There was no such thing as job security in those days. A sawmill job in Twin Forks, the tiny southern B.C. town, might not have been a picnic, but it had allowed Pete and I to get settled and put some real roots down. For a while anyway. Or so I had hoped.

Pete was desperately unhappy. He was just pulling boards. Milled lumber came off the green chain belt and he had to stack it in piles—minute after minute, hour after miserable hour. Night after night and day after day. We both agreed it was mindless, tedious work and took a heavy toll on his body. Sore shoulder muscles and back pain had become the norm. He often woke in the middle of the night damp and restless, trying to shake off nightmare hallucinations of mountains of timber flying off the belts and ripping him in two. There was never enough Ben Gay, that soothing cream for sore muscles.

Restless and easily bored, I searched for meaning in the ordinary day-to-day grind of living. And had discovered Kahlil Gibran, the spiritual poet from Lebanon. I sometimes carried a small book of his poems in the pocket of my homemade floral apron. He was intense, spiritual, romantic and intelligent. And had beautiful eyes. Well, I thought so anyway.

After depositing the full lunch kit by the back door, I opened Kahlil's book and read a few lines. My rambling mind wandered toward what Pete would endure at his job and I again ended up imagining him pulling and stacking 2x4s in that dusty, noisy hellhole. Poor Pete. Guilt, an old familiar friend, tugged gently at my sleeve.

But it was a job I could never do. For one thing, B and B Sawmill stood for everything I did not believe in.

How much land has to be stripped away, how many old growth trees are sacrificed for toilet paper, how much of a tree is left wasted in enormous, chaotic slash piles off steep, mountainous logging roads? Always hidden from view. Of course we need lumber and paper, but there is way too much clear-cutting going on these days!... I finally stopped my internal rant and reopened the book.

Oh, Kahlil, if only I had lived in Lebanon fifty years ago. You might have held my hand, looked into my eyes, and said, ever so gently:

> Work is love made visible. And if you cannot work with love, but only with distaste, it is better that you should leave your work and sit at the gate of the temple and take alms of those who work with joy.

As if on cue, a loud plaintive cry brought me crashing back to earth.

Shit!

After stashing Kahlil's transformative words, I tip toed softly into the bedroom so as not to wake Pete. I picked up Ethan, our toddler from his wooden crib. He immediately stopped his whimpering and the two of us made a quick exit. We settled into the worn rocker next to the big picture window in the living room. After smoothing his fine brown hair and covering him with a blue knit blanket, Ethan nodded out. I watched the winter rain leave icy teardrop tracks on the dusty glass. In the distance mineral gray clouds spewed a wet mix across the wide valley. A lazy winter sun gazed over the outlying hills. Gently we rocked, quiet and peaceful.

But slowly, with every shallow breath, like encroaching tidal waves on a moonless night, the charcoal walls of the room flooded in. The rocking chair lurched back and forth, back and forth, no longer comforting or soothing. Nausea struck me in the gut.

As my breathing slowed, I was sucked further and further down a rabbit hole. This bottomless chasm was quickly filling with the sludge of self-doubt and a good helping of fear. Fear of the future and hatred of the past.

I could not avoid it or deny it; my own brooding angel leaned over my shoulder and whispered her discouragement. "You're such a loser. What the hell are you doing with your life anyway?"

Like it or not I was probably a loser.

Admit or not, I was so damned trapped.

An Easy Divorce

By the end of the week, I got hit with a light fever and damp chills. Hot, cold. Hot, cold. *It's probably only the flu, always going around. Everyone has it or is just getting over it.*

Baby Ethan was finishing his breakfast and the highchair was a mess with mashed oatmeal and raisins covering every square inch. I heard a quick rap, rap at the back door. Not expecting anyone and being a suspicious, introverted creature, I opened it only a crack.

A pleasant face with dark serious eyes and a neatly trimmed, auburn moustache stared back at me. *Quite nice looking, actually.* I smoothed down my frizzy red hair.

"Hi. Are you Sasha Predov?" An official looking badge on the arm of his navy jacket made me stand a bit straighter.

"Yes, who wants to know?"

It wasn't about trust. I simply appreciated a bit of anonymity—especially in a small town where everyone knew everyone, and everyone knew everyone's business.

"Deputy Sheriff, ma'am, delivering your subpoena to appear in Kelowna court regarding your divorce. You just need to sign here—if you don't mind." Tiny beads of sweat dotted the lip crease above his Errol Flynn moustache.

What a hell of a job. Delivering divorce papers.

Perhaps I was a little cranky; his appearance was sudden and unexpected, my appearance must have left much to be desired: hippie mom with long, frizzy braids, in grubby, baggy clothes, covered in porridge.

I quickly signed the official-looking documents with his sleek government issued pen and stood silently, pulling bits of dried food off my apron as he sorted his papers. My newish apron with embroidered lilacs. I used to think it was pretty earthy and cool right after I made it. But right then, I felt shabby and my apron looked simple and silly. And unwashed.

Karl, my ex and I, had discussed the matter of an easy divorce. For some unfathomable reason, and after much bickering, we agreed it would be best for all concerned if I simply said I had committed adultery, although it wasn't close to the truth. I had to leave him. He was a bit of a nut case, and after only about eighteen months, I was so sick of his straying eyes and druggie ways. I had left him in our cute trailer in a well looked after, landscaped trailer court on the edge of town and met Pete a month later, while hitching near Spokane. So, I had not committed adultery.

Why does Karl even want to marry again anyway? What's the bloody panic?

The handsome sheriff smiled awkwardly, thanked me hastily and left. Surprisingly, he didn't get stuck in the muddy driveway.

I stood on the crocheted rug for a couple of minutes holding my copy of the official papers with trembling hands. Ethan eagerly looked up from the artwork he had created on his highchair and raised his arms toward me. "Up, up!"

I lifted him out, wiped off his porridge-smeared face and hands and set him free to play. *I guess it will feel good to legally have my original name again.* Although in day to day reality it would not make any difference. Or would it? *Divorced at twenty one. A reflection of false expectations of marriage in this uptight, white bread culture? Or of my own personal failings?*

Time for the morning clean-up routine— the usual sweeping and tidying up and wiping counters and cleaning out the fridge and taking out the garbage and washing and rinsing all the dishes. To finish up I scrubbed the high chair clean, at least two or three times, until both hands were raw and swollen and far past when my eyes ran with irritated tears from the bleach and steaming water.

New Year's Day

Reluctantly, the first pale morning of 1976 opened its sleepy eyes. A purple sun on the distant horizon, barely cresting the mountains, tried its best to light the day. Looking westward as we drove through an empty Twin Forks, the January sky still cloaked the earth from the night before. No friendly moon lit the way. Pete, Ethan and I were on our way home from a celebration at Sam and sister Lizzie's place. We had brought the New Year in with a couple of joints of local homegrown, a few Kokanee and an excruciatingly long game of Monopoly, which Sam won, as usual. Unfortunately, we stayed far too late at Lizzie's and had to drive back on slippery roads in the harsh and bitter cold. The truck heater barely worked and we bundled up in old blankets to survive the drive.

And this chill was a shocking surprise; the temperature had totally flipped in the last few days shifting from warm rain, to snow and then to freezing ice pellets. Hoarfrost outlined low barren bushes, the barks of trees and edges of tall cedars. Tiny nature jewels sparkled like crystal as if caught by the frigid hand of a harsh night, then scattered playfully in all directions.

Finally, after a ten minute white-knuckle drive along slick country roads and through an empty, ghostlike town, tires growled on our driveway's packed snow and let us know we were home, shivering but safe. And what a relief to be home. *Home sweet home.*

It felt like only yesterday I had escaped from this home town, long after my adolescent meltdown, and shortly after the ending of my fiery, juvenile marriage. I had busted out of small town B.C. and explored this enormous country for a few years, hitching northward to the pristine, mosquito-ridden Yukon and eastward to Quebec, where I truly tried, but could not speak, the French I had learned in high school. I was finally called back to this mystic valley, to this fertile land, and returned a few years ago, puffy and pregnant with Ethan and with my new man, Pete, on my arm. Since we weren't camping or squatting all over the country anymore, this place had started to feel permanent. Shabby as it was, I lived in a real house instead of a barn, or a canvas tent. Or trailer. I had family here. I was back. Perhaps I was growing up a little.

My younger sister Lizzie and I had reconnected. When we were teens, the two of us got into rip-roaring scraps and even tore each other's hair out once. It was frightening to behold. For a few years we venomously hated each other. She once stole my new miniskirt and special hair brush, both of which I had bought with babysitting earnings. She lost them down by the river after getting stinkin'drunk at a roaring beach party. I looked high and low the next day and never found either of them. I have to admit, it still pisses me off when I think of it.

But time heals most everything, they say. I hope so. We were always quite different in many ways. Our dad used to rant on about how one of us was probably not his. He was the fiercely jealous type, constantly accusing Mum of messing around on him. It must be me then, who is the product of my mother's straying, as dear sis looks exactly like old dad—down to his golden locks and piercing blue eyes.

On returning from our New Year's night out, we tucked Ethan into bed and dragged the tiny electric heater in from the old shed. The orange glow warmed our hearts as well as our toes. To keep the pipes from freezing we opened the cupboard doors under the kitchen sink and allowed some hot air to flow and circulate into that icy space. It was a beater of a house, but I tried to make it homey and keep it clean anyway.

After finally hopping into bed, I cuddled up with Pete and my Narcissus and Goldmund novel. Reading under a cozy wool comforter with cool night air on my face, was my idea of heaven. Pete usually passed out long before I did. I hadn't been sleeping well and craved some company though—someone to share time with in the land of insomnia instead of simply lying there, watching those wasted minutes tick away on the old wooden clock which sat on the dresser. Tonight Pete was munching on rings of apples we had dried the past summer. Their outer skins were wrinkled, tough and brown. I tried to engage him in some friendly chit-chat about our evening out. He ignored me.

"They drink too much," he finally offered, referring to Sam and Lizzie. He scrunched his handsome face, grey eyes almost shut. Then shook his thick, shoulder-length, chestnut wavy hair. When he was serious, he looked way too intense, like someone slightly unhinged—a stoned Jim Morrison perhaps. Kind of sexy and kind of dangerous. His eyes slowly closed, lids puffy and tired.

I jumped to Lizzie's defense. "Well, she was at home and it was a party, and…"

No more was said. A quick peck on the cheek, then lights out. Shortly afterward, the snoring began.

"Damn it! It's not fucking fair!" I kicked his foot. Not violently—a tap only. He stopped snoring. But only for about two minutes.

An hour later, still wide awake, I continued thrashing around on my side of the bed. "What the hell is wrong with me? Why can't I sleep?"

No answer came from the ticking clock. No answer. No answer. No answer.

Click, clack, tic, tac, tic, tac, click click click.

Electrified

A fierce storm pulls me in all directions as I stagger through an ancient pewter landscape. I have walked this path for millennia. I am older than old. All is tiredness. Blistered feet are covered in chalky plaster of Paris, hardening with each step. A tattered, khaki trench coat covers aching bones. It has been sewn messily with sinew and patched with rabbit and feline fur, dried blood stains the edges. A fierce drying wind attempts to tear it off me. Ominously low slate clouds threaten an angry rain. Squinting, I keep trying to see the road, or even a narrow path —any direction to follow. All my muscles ache with the strain of staying upright and it becomes too much of a struggle and I finally collapse like a deflated puppet onto the barren ground. My eyes close. As I lose the connection to this reality, a soft, sure voice whispers repeatedly.

"Let go. Don't fight it. Accept it. Surrender. Surrender. Surrender."

Overhead, thunder cracks. At first it's muted and distant, but the closer it gets the louder it booms. It rips my head open. Headache of headaches. Floating above it all, I look down and see a disheveled creature lying flat on the earth, arms outstretched, legs spread. Right before the downpour starts, drenching me, a fire branch of brilliant forked lightning strikes. It hits my core. A burning current runs through, lighting up all that is me. There is no time for fear: I am electrified, electrocuted, zapped. The energy of this powerful current sears through my body. It is prickly, energizing, and deeply terrifying. I close my eyes and take a deep, extended breath.

As I return, I connect to each cell and to every drop of blood which courses through the miles and miles of my thick arteries and delicate spidery veins, like the intricate branches on a leafless tree.

Dreaming

I awoke in a calm and grateful state. My heart was warm and my muscles relaxed. The nightmare was actually a gift. I was at peace and, for the first time in a long while, slept deeply.

Later, I wrote it all down. Keeping a dream journal was a help in those days. Dreams can be intimate and revealing. Perhaps in the future those recorded dreams would be able to tell me many things about my life, about real truth, about a reason for being. For existing. I also hoped this tool might help me through all the anxious states and physical problems. God damn it, I was only twenty-one years old. As I quickly scribbled words on the pages, I remembered it was Vincent, Pete's friend from Vancouver, who had suggested keeping a journal. He was married and had two step-kids. The first time we met, we had instantly developed a strong friendship and a special connection. Or so I had thought at the time. At Christmas the year before, he had sent me a book of poetry by Rumi. Forever the psychologist, he encouraged me to seek the truth and to question. Especially to question. All things.

Whenever I thought of him, I remembered only his reflective coal-black eyes—the eyes of a wise raptor, the black of infinity. I was pulled under by a yearning I didn't understand, a need to fall into that ocean of infinity. But I also knew that I was not supposed to have such feelings for another man.

Life is so bloody complicated. Why do humans have to have all these feelings? Like desire and attraction? It's probably a biology thing - to make babies. A continuation of the species. Though why this is such a great thing is a bloody mystery. Human beings are so good at fucking up the earth, and killing each other off. So we should make more of them?

But really, wouldn't life be much easier if, in the not-too-distant future, we could go to a baby store and pick out one we liked?

The problem with this scenario is people like Pete and me would probably not qualify. We are far too poor. And there'd definitely be some form of written examination, which we'd probably also fail.

The next night after making love, Pete casually mentioned that Vincent had called. He planned to visit in the summer, probably with his wife and kids.

"Oh, that will be nice," I replied pleasantly, immediately hiding my flushed face behind a fluffy pillow.

The snowy winter dragged on, as did my gut wrenching episodes, my fatigue, my yeast infections, my inner freak outs and my endless insomnia. I began to wonder if all the aches and pains had anything to do with the birth-control pills my cranky, old doc had put me on. Sometimes I felt estranged from my body, as if part of me was floating away. Most mornings I woke feeling as if I was in someone else's skin. Of course I didn't want to get pregnant again but feeling this way was such a bloody drag. How much longer did I have to take those pills? I had read an article once that stated the hormones used to make the pills came from mare's urine! They certainly weren't natural, I had been taking them for almost two years now. A lot of the time, I didn't feel like myself, whoever that was.

Something had to be done.

And soon.

Selling Your Soul

The immense fulfilment of the friendship between those engaged in furthering the evolution of consciousness has a quality impossible to describe.

~ Pierre Teilhard de Chardin

Pete finally got laid off from the sawmill, along with a couple other guys. It wasn't unexpected. Initially, I was stoked.

And thought, *Great. It will be so fine to have Pete at home!*

The sawmill life was a deceptive trap. Some folks in town would toil away at slicing up lumber in that sawmill for their entire working lives. The money was good, but you sold your soul for the regular paycheck. Once you got hooked on the money though, you'd end up a lifer. No free time. Working for the man.

I swore I'd never fall into that trap. We continued to have discussions as to what else we could do to make a living of sorts. Maybe we could become farmers. I was a great gardener, after all. It was no big deal to grow food. Anyone could do it. How difficult could it be? Plant the seeds and watch them grow.

Earlier that year, against my better judgment, we became involved with and bought shares in The Wild Meadows Land Cooperative. Apparently it was based on the principle of collaboration: living co-operatively on a piece of land, teamwork and sharing what each of us had in skills, time, and energy. Beyond that the co-op members hadn't worked anything out. No one was sure how all of the details would sort themselves out when we physically moved to the land. I supposed we would have to keep on communicating if any serious problems arose.

Pete and I did have to invest some of our meagre savings to purchase shares though, which was a real drag. But the co-op land itself was stunningly picturesque and I prayed it would all be worth it in the end.

When we first joined we thought the majority of the folks in the group were pretty cool. Vincent and his wife Kathy were also interested and planned to check it out when visiting next summer.

Sam, Lizzie's boyfriend, my "almost" brother-in-law, mentioned he might be interested. He also worked at the B.B. Mill but swore he wouldn't be there much longer. Of course he's been saying this for a couple of years now. Sam did have a retirement plan though. He had started writing short stories of all things, on Lizzie's old manual Underwood Touchmaster 5.

"I'm hoping to become a famous author," he told me one winter afternoon as we shared a slim joint and a pot of chamomile tea.

I had read one of his pieces a few weeks before and decided it was skilfully written, except the characters seemed much too predictable: beautiful, mysterious woman meets rich, flakey playboy. Who rescues her from the bad guys, or her own personal demons or some such thing. Maybe Sam had seen too many James Bond movies.

Whatever I read in those days had to have many layers, like the music I enjoyed. I wanted to hear something new and different and became easily bored with Pete's folk albums.

The day after Pete got laid off, we bundled Ethan up and puttered into town in the rusting canary-yellow Chevy pickup to buy groceries and toilet paper at the I.G.A., our small town's only real supermarket. That's not counting the Co-op Store, which usually stocked only a minimum number of items on their dusty, rickety metal shelves. Pete and I did discuss hiking to town on the back roads which follow the marshlands and the old cemetery, but it would have been quite a trek. So even though the heater was still not cranking out the heat, we drove. Besides, it was mid-winter and way too bitter for our little one to walk, even if the weather *was* warmer than usual.

I could not live in the suburbs of any town. Suburbs gave me the creeps. I could see myself in in a tattered housecoat, white hair in foam rollers, reclining in a Barcalounger behind an enormous picture window in some old seventies' rancher, eating cheesy puffs and watching TV night after tedious night, dying a slow, painful death of boredom and meaninglessness.

So I consoled myself with the thought it wasn't really the suburbs we'd settled into; rather our neighbourhood was composed of large rambling lots with acres of unused land between older, sprawling houses and cabins. Empty fields full of red-winged blackbirds and wild grasses shared the space with a dense carpet of low purple clover, thorny blackberry patches and that wild anarchist Russian thistle, which loved to take over any unoccupied field or ditch.

Besides, our town was proudly tiny—it was one of the smallest towns in the country. There was only one traffic light and it was on the main drag. The potholes were plentiful, though. If you weren't careful, you could fall into one, and then you'd never be found!

On the drive to town Pete and I argued about how we would have to watch our pennies if we were going to make it through two months with no income. It was a long wait until the first Unemployment Insurance cheque. We would have to budget carefully. We had mortgage payments and were land co-op members, too. It all sounded good on paper, but we were land rich and grocery poor. We weren't starving, but had little extra.

After we got home, I reminded Pete I was going to an all-day Gestalt session the next day. I had heard about it from the land co-op folks and had already paid for it with our income tax return from last year. Pete thought it was a big fat waste of money, but I felt like I needed something. It would take place at a neighbour's house down the road. He said nothing after my gentle reminder, only shook his thick locks and went to bed early. Yes, of course I felt apprehensive about attending a "therapy group," but I needed something. Anything. It was worth a try.

I was plagued with constant anxiety, doubt and guilt. Anxiety about almost everything, doubt about my place in life, my role, my purpose. And lately there was the guilt, the constant guilt about my feelings for Vincent.

I thought of him a lot over the winter.

Was there anything real between us? I had sensed a strong attraction, a definite chemistry, when he visited the year before. He stopped in for a two day visit on his way to a Vipassana meditation retreat in the Kootenays. We talked for hours about all things under the sun, and then finally beneath the moon, late into the night. When he accidently touched me, I shivered. But what was real? It was all so bloody confusing. I certainly didn't want a lush, romantic fantasy or those profound, bottomless feelings to lead to a shallow, hot-pink, sexual fling.

"I'm not a shallow person," I told myself. I simply could not have a hot fling.

I could not.

Gestalt Hangover

I suffered only the sound of lone footsteps in felt-lined boots crunching along the back trail past the old graveyard and pine forest. A single street light guided me through a mini snowstorm. The flakes sparkled and shimmered against an inky sky. Only a few blocks away, across silvery lavender fields, the warm yellow lights of home led me onward.

My head was pounding, my heart was tight and all muscles were in lock down. *So much for Gestalt being so great for you!* Even remembering details of the experience hurt my swollen brain. About ten people showed up for the full day group therapy session. We sat on flat, decorative cushions on the plush red carpeted floor, and attempted to work through heavy emotional stuff. This "working through stuff" involved a lot of yelling, sniffling, crying, and pillow-beating.

"I hate you!" Jenn screamed, another young newcomer to Gestalt. She bashed the pillow with her fist then used a wooden padded bat, created and supplied for exactly this purpose, the purpose of bashing things. "Mama, why did you have to leave me? I was only a child! I needed you! I so needed you."

My overly sensitive stomach knotted within minutes. Jenn beat the pillow until she was worn out then slid down to the carpet, helpless and vulnerable, her hair a tumbled mess, her face pale and tear streaked, yet strangely relaxed. Almost immediately most of the participants crawled over and encircled her and then held her like a precious, newborn baby.

The facilitator, Fran encouraged the release of emotions, even crappy ones. "Beat the pillow! Smack it! Don't hold back!" she constantly commanded, waving her bat like a symphony conductor.

Variations of the same emotional vomiting continued through the day. The more you acted out, the more you screamed, cursed, cried, and yelled, the bigger the group hug. The support afterward was supreme, engulfing. The stuffy air hung thick with unmet needs. Participants were there to release, release, release—anything and everything.

Yet the more they released, the more anxious I felt. Muscles in my neck turned to stone and the rest slowly tightened. By the end of the night they were screaming in pain. I kept adjusting my scrawny, numb bottom on the foam pillow.

How the hell did I end up here? I silently asked myself for the fifth time when Fran, with her keen laser focus, turned to me.

"Now, Sasha," she said, flashing her gracious smile, "would you like to share some of your pain? It can be about any issue. You know you're safe here."

She was warm and motherly and there was nothing to fear. Yet all of me silently shouted, "No! No sharing! Leave me the fuck alone!"

I was the only one in the workshop who had not sat in the hot seat. But the only thing I wanted to share at that moment was a quick view of my backside as I lunged out the front door.

"Ah…No, thank you." I managed to blurt out. "There's nothing I'd actually like to share today. Perhaps another time." All red, teary eyes were on me.

"Are you sure? We're all friends here. We're all here for each other, you know," Fran said, folding her plump hands in her lap—a perfect Buddha.

We are? This I have trouble believing. You all look like bizarre strangers. How do I get out of this one?

"Sorry, Fran," I finally replied. "I actually do have a nasty headache. Will have to pass. I really do feel like shit!"

Fran smiled her condescending, all-knowing smile and finally released me with, "Hmmm. Yes. Perhaps you're actually holding on to your shit!"

The room grew silent. I smiled weakly and adjusted my sore lower back.

She finally stood up gracefully and thanked the group for having the courage to take this journey.

The therapy group wound up rather quickly. I pulled on my boots, coat, and mitts, said the expected "thank-you's" and fled. Others still hugged and chattered away as I quietly stepped over piles of smelly footwear in the entrance, trying not to trip. Icy air hit my flushed face as I closed the back door. *Only a few blocks to safety.* I took a slow, deep breath and started marching, welcoming the walk in the clean snow.

The relief at finally making it home, pulling off my boots and crawling into a hot bath after downing a few aspirins, was the highlight of that torturous day. After slapping a hot, then a frozen facecloth on my booming head, the intense anxiety started to recede and locked muscles relaxed.

Why was I unable to share my painful emotions with those people? How were they able to share while I was not?

The truth was it did not feel safe. What was I supposed to say? What if I said the wrong thing? I was looking for something more spiritual, something which included my spirit or soul as well as my mind and emotions. I wanted more clarity, not more pain. I was looking for something bigger. For meaning. For a purpose.

Damn it! Why am I so bloody uptight?

It was such a relief to know Pete didn't have to go to work on Monday. As a subdued winter sun was setting, he came and lay next to me and we made love on the couch, quietly, so we wouldn't wake Ethan from his nap. I had spent the entire day fantasizing about buttery yellow sunlight flickering through lime and sea green growth. Visions of inviting white-gold beaches beckoned.

I fell into a dreamy sleep then was startled awake by a loud noise in the kitchen. *Ice falling off the roof?*

I "saw" myself, as if for the first time, as though I were an extraterrestrial looking down on a stranger. The picture was not particularly pretty: an anxious, frizzy haired, skinny, uptight person. I pledged then and there to take things more slowly—to enjoy each moment. Much like a heavy knapsack, a rigid stiffness in my neck and shoulders hung on me all the time, dragging me down and aging me beyond my years.

I don't need to carry the weight of my world on these thin shoulders every single bloody minute, do I?

Gestalt Fran was probably right.

Perhaps I am holding on to my shit.

Perhaps I carry it around in this heavy pack. One day I may have to put it down, or it may rip open and spill out and then there'll be a wicked stench.

A stink that'll smell for miles and miles.

Dawn

I enjoyed snow shoveling but it did aggravate sore muscles. The white stuff continued to pile up.

Baby Ethan, only two, was becoming more of a chatterbox day by day. We had real conversations. And he called me by my name, Sasha. After overhearing the women in the co-op discussing this matter, I decided it was best if Ethan didn't grow up to see me only as someone in a role, solely as a mother. I wanted him to relate to women as people. It was a big deal. There were far too many men out there who didn't see women as people first. After all, it was already 1976!

As we played and shoveled in the fresh whiteness it struck me how each of those precious days was like a snowflake. Every one of those tiny, symmetrical sculptures was unique and fragile, melting quickly within the smallest fragments of time, with the slightest change in temperature or with a tiny warm breath. In the spring, those minuscule pieces melt into millions of droplets of icy water before flowing into gullies, creeks, and rivers, eventually joining all the other liquid snowflakes rushing to the ocean.

Babies and more babies continued to be born, especially to the women in the land co-operative. We were all young and fertile, I supposed. Ray and Sissy were a recent addition to the co-op. I tried to like them but was a clean freak, and unfortunately those two didn't bathe very often. According to Pete, "They're both fine. I can't smell them." Sissy said it was healthier to have some dirt on your skin. She insisted it boosted your immunity. She might have been right all along; she was as strong as a horse—and as hairy as one, too. Sissy wouldn't shave a hair on her healthy, muscular body. They lived in a tepee for a while, before throwing together their rustic cabin. The idea of living in a teepee sounded groovy, but it was a hell of a lot of work to keep it liveable. There were no walls; everything had to be put away if you wanted to have a tidy home. Sissy didn't seem to care. She liked the mess. Ray and Sissy were totally vegan, too—no dairy or anything, which I did have to admire. I had tried being vegan once for about a month but truthfully missed cheese. Personality-wise, they're polar opposites: Sissy is loud, overbearing and bossy, and Ray is wimpy, but kind. Their boy was born at home at dawn, with a midwife familiar with the Lamaze natural-birth technique.

"No hospitals for our baby!" she had proclaimed.

After their son was born, Ray and Sissy looked for a name which meant dawn. I asked Mum and being of Russian Doukobour origin, she told me the Russian word for dawn is Zarya. It sounded so exotic and I made a note to pass it on.

As time passed though, and I got to know Sissy better, I often felt the "I'm better than you" vibe. Which certainly pissed me off and didn't make for the possibility of a great friendship.

Or any friendship at all, for that matter.

Betty was the co-op's midwife. She may not have been certified, but she knew her stuff. She was grounded, calm, and confident, like an actual grownup. Betty braided her matte, lifeless hair and piled it up on top of her head neatly, much like my grandma used to, with enormous caramel tipped bobby pins sticking out. Long, flowing, baggy skirts and sheer cottony blouses made up her usual outfits. The smell of lavender soap followed her, much like a wayward spirit seeking a bodily home. She and her hubby

Mike had moved to Twin Forks from the big city of Vancouver and named their baby Zeb, short for Zebedia— just another Z name, which were so popular at the time.

Betty was around for the birth of Sissy's Zarya. She was very supportive and helped Sissy through her transition and final contractions. Surprisingly or not, those two opposites became great friends straight away.

They seemed to respect each other. You could see it in the way they looked at one another, their eyes shining and lips constantly smiling. I never totally got it.

Possibly I was way too young or too weird, or too different. I rarely felt accepted by them and was not sure why.

The Damned Trip

"What the heck?" I shrieked. "Didn't he get them fixed?"

Biting snow was hitting the windshield. And hard. Pete reached out the driver's window and tried to push the feeble wiper blade back and forth. All this effort achieved was a grinding sound from somewhere behind the vinyl dash board. We were flying down Highway 3 in a winter blizzard, trying to get to a construction site near Trail so Pete could apply for a job. We so needed Pete to get a job. The UI was close to starvation wages and would eventually run out.

"Damn, I knew we shouldn't have trusted him!" I muttered. Sure, Sam had been kind enough to lend us his old rattletrap, but he had also promised to get the wipers fixed. And he hadn't "allowed" Lizzie to come with us, insisting she stay behind and make him his hot lunch.

"My god, what a chauvinist!" I ranted on. "Can you believe it? She has to stay home all day just so he can have a bowl of Campbell's soup "warm" for him at lunch!"

I checked on Ethan, who was asleep in the back, and adjusted his blanket. "Doesn't he even know how to open a can of soup? He must know how to use a can opener! He must be capable of that! He's so self-centered. Sheesh. Well, it's her own damned fault, you know. She allows him to dominate her, so what do you expect?"

"We have more important things to worry about right now!" Pete yelled. "I'm trying to stay on the road here!"

Right! I quickly rolled down the window on my side and swept my arms across the passenger side of the windshield. The only thing either of us could see clearly were the immense snow heaps and large boulders on the side of the mountain highway. Frosty chunks of wet sleet slid down my bare arm and started to melt, wetting my coat sleeve and the sweater underneath.

"Fuck! This is not working! Let's pull over and clear it off!" My shouting woke Ethan, who started crying.

Pete managed to pull over to the side of the highway right before a logging truck, spitting gravel and sleet, roared past us, only inches from the car.

With the snow blasting down it took us hours to get to the Dam Project. Pete was hoping to get some serious work, a well-paying union job perhaps. Unfortunately, the only way to get hired was if you knew someone already working there. It was the same old shit: it's not what you know, it's who you know. Luckily Brad, a new friend, had put in a word for Pete with an engineer who worked on the dam site.

We finally reached the office site and puttered into the empty parking lot. The trailer which served as the office was covered in shiny white siding and had been plunked down right beside the alpine road. It looked strangely out of place, the only landscaping being gravel and boulders edging the muddy lot. For a few moments, the snow eased off. Pete jumped out of the car and walked up to the main entrance. He banged on the door and a stocky man came out. I assumed it was Roger, who we were told was on the hiring committee. The two shook hands as they stood outside the trailer and Roger took Pete's name and number. After chatting for only a few minutes and then waving "bye" Pete hopped back in the car and started up Sam's old beater. Wet, twisty hair strands dangled in his eyes; he looked beaten and worn out as our little family headed back down to the main highway.

"Well?" I asked cautiously.

"Roger said the company would let me know later this week." He combed the hair out of his eyes with frozen, blue fingers and stared straight ahead, trying to keep the car on the road and out of the huge potholes.

I'm not a psychic, but it didn't feel very promising.

As we started to climb a steep hill on the way home, the car crapped out. After a frantic phone call to Trail, Brad and Jenna picked us up and gave us a safe ride home—an hour's drive each way. I thanked them and God for their kindness. And later God again because I finally got my period. Pill or no pill I was a few days late and starting to worry.

Upon returning, Pete and Sam had a conference over a couple of cool ones in the pub. They decided to go and talk to the local mechanic who had supposedly put the new clutch in.

The car sat alone at the Turbo Station in Castlegar for weeks, getting covered in at least three feet of snow.

Domestic

Daddy Wes, my new stepdad, and Sam talked about going back to the Kootenays the next Saturday to pick up Sam's piece-of-shit car. Unfortunately it didn't happen as planned. No one could get away. Too busy and too much snow.

Pete and I needed to do laundry as the electrical in our old drier was toast. Our old Chevy was still not running well either so we ended up borrowing a neighbour's car.

"I'm not hanging my washing out in this frost," I told Pete. "Nothing will dry outside in this weather!"

I did not look forward to going to the old Eezy Laundromat. Ever. I truly hated sharing washing machines with all the unknown nameless and faceless—people with unspeakable messes, body fluids, and disgusting stenches on their dirty clothes. But it was a chore that had to be done and our foul-smelling garments were overflowing in the laundry baskets. And beggars can't be choosers.

It was only a five-minute drive from our house to the decaying cinder block building with perpetually steamy windows. The entire structure had once been painted chalk white inside and out. The white hadn't lasted though and now only a couple of years later, it was peeling, faded, and hoary. We managed to find a parking spot right at the front door. Inside, the patterned linoleum floor was so dilapidated in some areas patches had worn right down to the pale cement underneath. Tiny worlds of grunge and dirt festered in the corners of the room. The washers themselves smelled like something moldy had died in them.

"Oh, my god, these stink," I said, glancing at two of the cleanest looking machines.

Pete shrugged and helped me load enough washers to get a good start. Surveying my environment more carefully, I noticed pieces of filthy lint, matted hair and expired moths stuck in corners and around the baseboards. I told myself not to look too closely or it would make me gag.

Whoever cleans this building does an especially shitty job—if anyone cleans here at all.

A large, common housefly, a survivor of the harsh Canadian winter, landed gently on the windowsill. For some reason I found him fascinating. He was larger than life. After putting his front legs together, as if praying, he rubbed them quickly back and forth. Maybe he was eager for a feast. Or he was trying to start a fire. He wiped his head, methodically cleaning it. Feeling like a voyeur, I looked away.

Eventually our damp clothes spun around in the large front loaders. The steam in the room calmed me. It was actually relaxing, soothing and quite hypnotic—a poor man's sauna.

"You know, I've decided all the Gestalt stuff is not my thing." I looked over at Pete to see if he'd heard, then put my magazine down. A tattered issue of Reader's Digest from June 1972. I got up and walked over to the battered sink to wash my hands.

Pete pulled out an armload of worn towels from the first dryer, which he dumped on the room's one large wooden, rickety table, and then smirked.

"Yeah, it sounds like it's not for you!"

I glanced down the room to see how our babe was doing. *Oh, shit—Ethan!* He was bent over something, his straight brown hair hanging in his eyes. He was trying to pick up a tarnished, copper-brown penny from the tile floor. I ran over and crouched down to grab it, but he got it first.

"Gestalt seems to be totally focused on psychology, on the personality," I continued while attempting to pry the copper treasure from Ethan's hands. "But not our total selves. It's kind of limiting …"

Pete only nodded. Ethan held on tight.

"Give me that," I squawked. "Not good! No!"

Ethan screeched and mimicked me. "No, no!"

Shit. Lately, everything is a no! Where does he get this from?

I pried the penny loose and crammed it into my jeans pocket. From the back of the long room full of spinning dryers, a fresh-faced woman approached us. She smiled at Ethan.

"Hi, cutie!" she said.

An angel from the gods! Ethan stared up at her. She effortlessly squatted down to his level.

"How are you today?" she asked. "My name is Penny." She winked at me. What a coincidence! Penny on the floor and she was a shiny penny. Her cheeks were rosy and flushed. I immediately envied her healthy energy. We were probably the same age, but I felt like an old hag compared to her glowing health.

Ethan's face scrunched up as he tried to sound grown up and serious. "No!" He wrapped his tiny arms around my neck and turned his face away. But only for a moment. Shyly, he looked back and snuck a peek through those overgrown bangs, which definitely needed cutting.

"What do you mean 'no'?" Penny asked. "I have something here for you!" She glanced at me. "Can he have a Lifesaver?"

I decided it was OK, just this once.

In the end, they had a great visit. Penny picked Ethan up and carried him around. He chattered and pointed, sharing all he knew of the world.

He was so entertaining when he was in a good mood. And it was refreshing when others appreciated my child.

It didn't change my cranky mood, though. It was obvious Pete was not the least bit interested in what I thought of the Gestalt experience.

What else is new? I hastily finished folding and stacking the folded laundry into plastic mesh tubs, while he stepped out to get the car started and warmed up.

"Damn the Gestalt," I muttered. "I'll have to figure things out by myself." After some bribing (a cookie at home), I succeeded in peeling Ethan loose from his new best friend, Penny the Pretty. He waved bye-bye with his perfect plump, tiny hand, and we hurried out the door to jump into the waiting car.

Ethan fell asleep in my arms, his baby breath smelling sweet and minty from the lifesaver.

No one spoke on the short drive home.

Domestic became the theme of the week: cooking delicious bean-and-barley soup then making enough crunchy granola to fill a gallon glass jar.

Eating vegetarian was so damned easy. I never understood why people complained that it was too complicated or thought they are going to die if they missed a day without gnawing on a piece of a dead animal. In the Doukobour tradition from my mom's side, I was raised to not eat dead animals, had not eaten meat throughout my entire lifetime and was still alive. Although on some days that was debatable. Meat and all its by-products were seen as dirty food, not healthy for the body and harmful to the soul. I had read somewhere, perchance in a National Geographic magazine or some such glossy informative rag, that many people in the world did not eat a lot of meat, if any. And, apparently, most were fine. Or were versions of fine.

I did wonder, though, about my extreme fatigue. All the omnivores I knew kept pushing their thing: I needed to eat some red meat to get the iron in my blood count up. My old doc hadn't even checked my blood count. And, of course, the not knowing probably made me feel even worse. I had a lot of energy before giving birth to Ethan, after which Dr. C had inserted a birth-control device, an evil piece of twisted metal he expertly planted in my uterus—the copper coil. My body totally rejected it and I almost bled to death. After weeks of flooding and excessive bleeding, he finally removed the offending element from my tender, hemorrhaging uterus and put me on the pill. He insisted it was not healthy to get pregnant again so soon after giving birth. It was far too risky. I had to agree with him. But possibly he also thought we were too poor to have any more children. He was quite a stuffy, conservative old dude.

The pill—now this solution has its own set of problems. The two words sound menacing, like something you take that is supposed to help you but ends up killing you in the end. Kind of sci-fi ish.

"Have you taken your pill today?" A magical but toxic pill that keeps things under control. I resented putting all those weird hormones into my body on a daily basis to prevent getting pregnant. It gave me control of my own body but was a health risk, at best.

If men were the ones getting pregnant, the scientific world would have found something which worked. And didn't make you feel weird, ill or crazy.

❋ ❋ ❋

Pete and I were hanging out at the kitchen table one cozy evening, sharing a pot of mint tea and crunching on ginger snap cookies, when the haunting, screeching sounds of at least two cats scrapping, reached our ears through the drafty cracks along the door frame. The battle cries sounded like they were originating from behind our dilapidated garden shed.

I jumped up and peered out the window. "Is that Felix?"

"Yeah," Pete replied lazily. "I had to put him out. He's still shittin' on the back porch and I'm sick of cleaning it up!"

He popped a vodka cherry into his mouth—our new food thing. A nice bedtime snack.

I sat down, my back now straight as a board. "Isn't it a little chilly out there for him? Don't you care it's the middle of winter? He gets totally chewed up, scrapping with all those neighbourhood toms! And Buddy, Bear's cat is the worst!"

"Well, he'll survive I'm sure," Pete replied. "He's pretty tough. Got any better ideas, let me know. Hey, I fixed the dryer!" A tentative smile.

"Thanks. It took long enough, though!" Thinking of old Felix, I began to experience the familiar disturbing, sucking ache in the pit of my stomach. "Are you sure he'll be OK?"

"What's the fucking problem?" Pete asked. "I thought you didn't even like cats. You told me the only reason you have him around is that he keeps the mice population down!"

I winced. "Yeah, but I don't want him to get hurt! Damn, I don't know what to do! Do you actually think I don't care about Felix? Why do you say such hurtful things? Man! Do you think I'm so heartless?"

"Oh, fuck, forget it!" He stood up quickly, knocking his chair over. "I'm not into carrying on this Felix debate any longer. This is stupid."

He stomped off, leaving the open jar of bobbing, glistening cherries on the counter and the chair lying sideways on the floor.

My shoulder muscles tensed. It could be me out there in the snow and ice, with pieces of my own body getting ripped apart and gouged out with the sharp claws and teeth of a vicious, demon tomcat. There was not much which could be done when two male cats decided to go at it, though and we *had* decided not to castrate him.

How would any person like having those tender, private parts snipped off? I gradually talked myself down. *So accept it. He'll be fine. You don't actually like cats much anyway. They seem so needy, constantly wanting to be petted. And then there's the disgusting foul shit they leave buried in the garden plot and flower beds. Anyway, accept it. He'll be fine.*

I took a few deep, purposeful breaths and felt my muscles start to relax a little.

Where is all this anxiety coming from? Is it the pill?

Or is it the pot?

Or me and my damned life?

Weekends no longer crept up on me. They weren't such a big deal now. Pete wasn't working. The days all ran into each other, none being any more special than the others. Friday could be like Sunday, could be like Tuesday, almost like Monday, and on and on.

On an up note, we had started researching pyramids and their ability to preserve things placed inside them. We thought we possibly could build a pyramid in the back yard or on the empty lot across the street and store all our food in it in case anything happened, like the end of the world. Armageddon or an apocalypse of some sort had been on my mind a lot in those days. Undeniably it been predicted in many places—the Bible for example, and many new-age books of prophecy.

For a change of pace, I went to a meeting in the middle of the week with the girls from the land co-op. They were trying to organize a benefit, a fundraising dance with Pied Pumpkin. Who were a decent enough band, perhaps a bit too folksy for me, but they did get people up and dancing. The co-op definitely needed to raise some cash because there were so many legal fees involved in the purchase of the communal two hundred acres, and none of the members could, or wanted to, pay the lawyer on their own. The majority were poor, lowly hippies or back-to-the-landers.

"What should we serve?" Betty asked if only to get the business part over with. The group had been drinking rose-hip tea and chatting for an hour about diaper rash, macramé hangers, various ways to grow tomatoes, and how to knit leggings using recycled wool from old sweaters. I was getting bored and running out of domestic-goddess tips.

I knew how to do a lot of shit, but this topic really tired me. The rest of them were able to talk about muffin recipes for hours. I tried to get the focus back on track so the meeting would end sooner rather than later and I could go home, feed the boys, crawl into bed, and read a book.

"Well, how about lasagne? We can make it veggie."

My suggestion fell on deaf ears. Sissy had already decided we were going with tacos because we could do meat *or* veggie, and she threw the idea in as an answer rather than a question. Her bossy voice grated on me, but the committee nodded and agreed. Tacos it would be.

Sissy leaned over and patted my shoulder then smiled. I grimaced and ground my teeth. Hopefully, no one noticed. She kept on suggesting. "We need to have something to drink, too. How about various herbal teas and then apple juice for the children?"

The members finally decided to go with herbal teas and apple juice, with date bars for dessert. Definitely no coffee! Coffee is not healthy. Everyone knows this.

Well, everyone except me. I couldn't drink it though; my stomach was too sensitive. But I did love the bitter, earthy smell of it. The girls seemed to think it was quite evil. For some reason coffee was a real no-no with the land co-op people.

When my gut problems finally got better, I'd try drinking it again. Even a tiny amount gave me a powerful buzz, and I got so much more done.

Love and Hate

Another major dump of snow hit on Saturday night. At least four inches fell, blanketing the already white earth. The stillness outside was soothing. Pete begged to go for a midnight hike around the block, but I nixed it. Going out in winter meant serious bundling up. Then upon returning home, having to peel off the layers upon layers of warm clothing—long-johns, undershirts, etc. Almost not worth going outside, mitts and boots, hanging up coats and scarves, wiping up melted snow and mud. And then—yikes!—accidently stepping in it all and ending up with frozen feet anyway. And then having to put on dry wool socks to get warm again.

When Ethan and Pete were finally sound asleep I sat in my creaky rocker trying to read *Marital Love and Hate* by Israel Charny. It had fallen off a shelf in the library as I reached for something else. It felt like a message: "*Read This*!" So I took it home. Too many big words. My eyes kept closing and the room started to fill with the dark and gloom of mid-winter. The book was a heavy read. Perhaps a little too heavy.

How can we love and hate someone at the same time?

Sure, there were moments when I felt so irritated with Pete I practically hated him. Actually, I probably did hate him. It was usually in one of those day to day moments, when he was sitting back watching something mindless on our old, dying TV, while I still had a thousand household chores screaming at me. At exactly those moments, *I hated Pete and I hated being a housewife*. And I hated all this hate, because hate was such a strong word. And it sure didn't sound spiritual.

As I sat in the living room thinking about hating, with my book and the midnight hour closing in, I grew aware of the sawing and rattling of Pete's snoring in the bedroom. My compassion kicked in. It had been a long day. It had been a long week.

Why don't you give him a break—if only in your thoughts?

I tried and tried, but my thoughts would not rest. As soon as I stopped mentally beating Pete up, my restless mind went directly to an accident scene we had driven past at the side of the road earlier in the week. A vehicle had gone off the side of the highway, its tire tracks visibly headed off the steep bank. Broken tree limbs and torn bushes drew my eyes down to a shattered car at the bottom of the ravine. We decided to keep on driving. An ambulance and police cars had arrived at the site and a crowd had already formed in a semi-circle. We didn't know who lay in that ravine, but if we had driven down the same road a half hour earlier, we might have been in that car. *It could have been me down there. It could have been me.*

Why do I feel like this? As if someone had punched me below the rib cage. The feeling grew larger, like a deepening hole in my gut. I gently massaged it.

Why can't they make cars out of rubber or something similar? Then no one would get hurt!

I could have died. Pete and Ethan and I could have died.

Life was so damned fucking dangerous.

❋ ❋ ❋

One unusually tepid day later in January it was so hot after lunch I had to take off my coat to shovel the pathways. And before I could stop them, baby Ethan and Felix—our crazy scruffy beat up cat—began drinking water from the new puddles which appeared on the sidewalk. Lapping at melted snow.

Brad from Nelson stopped by in the evening. After Ethan was tucked in bed and the day's chores were done, Pete rolled a slim one and we all grooved out to the mellow sounds of the Incredible String Band. But when the men began rapping about meaningful guy things, like converting diesel engines, and then when they started drawing detailed blueprints on how to build a pyramid out of scrap lumber, I got restless and stepped outside for a breath of fresh air. I had wrapped a loose, bulky sweater around me and stood in yarn slippers on the wooden stoop.

Brighter-than-bright stars beckoned through wispy clouds. The massive valley mountains, like giant resting goddesses, formed a weighty silhouette against the skyline and cradled this small person. I was strangely content and at peace for a few brief moments and felt pulled upward toward the glittering, star-studded heavens. It was as if a creator had cut a million million holes in a large sheet of black felt paper and turned on a bright fluorescent bulb behind it. As I was pulled into the light, that limitless never-ending cosmos, I was also pulled downward and felt connected to the dense, snow-covered earth. Balanced and at peace.

"I must remember this moment forever", I thought.

As the years passed, those flirtatious stars, those tiny bursts of radiance, forever called me, eternally summoned me with their flickering, teasing light.

Forever calling, calling, calling from the velvety blackness of a vast deep space, an infinite numbers of light years away.

Bear's Accident

I answered the door in my archaic and tattered chenille housecoat. Our friend Brad had left at the crack of dawn, back to his job in Nelson. Pete had caught a ride with him into town to pick up groceries. He'd walk home later. He often enjoyed some time alone.

Bear stood on the landing. Our rugged, surly neighbour was a tall, stout man with hands like grizzley paws, a shiny oily face and a ruddy nose. He usually appeared greasy, as though he'd recently eaten corn on the cob and had not taken the time to wipe off the excess. His shapeless and stained khaki work pants were ragged at the bottom and he smelled like a mildewed garage. Car oil and decaying rags. This morning he had stitches on his forehead and looked like he had been in a boxing match. It was only 9:00 a.m. I could smell booze on his breath. It certainly wasn't mouthwash.

"Hey, Bear, what the hell? Is something wrong? You look awful! Where's Jane?" I glanced over his massive shoulder toward the house next door about sixty feet away. His wife was quiet and elusive, but I wondered why she was not at his side on such a day, while he was in this condition.

"Jane's fine. I'm fine. We are all fine. I survived. I made it. I made it!" He lurched back. He had buttoned his shirt messily; it was crumpled and creased, as if he had slept in it.

"Made it? What happened?" I felt a frigid draft tickle my backside and wrapped my housecoat tighter.

"Oh, shit, I went off the highway before the damned bridge. I went down, all the way to the bottom! It was quite a ride, I must say, but damned if I was going to die down there. I crawled up the rocky bank and scratched the hell out of myself. But I made it! Only a few bruises." Teetering back and forth, he stared at the purple welts on his wrists and hands. "The doc says I may have some back problems but, what the hell, I'll live."

"Oh, my God, Bear!" Feeling dizzy, I managed to grab onto the door frame. "Well, I'd invite you in for tea, but Pete's in town and I'm not dressed yet and…"

"That's OK, I'll come back tomorrow," he slurred. "Hey, have you seen my cat? Buddy hasn't been home in a few days, and I'm worried about him. He's a good guy— just likes to take out any competition, eh?" He smirked. With black eyes, a scratched face and blistered swollen nose, he looked like a circus clown who had run away from the main tent. "Have you seen him?"

"No, sorry, man, I haven't seen your cat. I'll ask Pete when he gets home. You should go home and get some rest! You look totally beat up!"

"Yeah, yeah, what else is new? OK, little lady. See you later." He turned and staggered down the driveway, headed back to his house.

"Say hi to Jane," I muttered. Then closed the door quickly. And pulled the deadbolt shut.

I couldn't sleep that night. Visions of Bear lying in a pool of his own blood at the bottom of the gorge kept floating through my consciousness. He was only our ignorant, alcoholic neighbour, but thinking of his demise gave me a taste of the bittersweet futility of life.

I'm in this body for so long and then—bam! It could all end in an instant.

Am I only a puppet? I pinch a tab of skin on my arm. *It could be plasticine.*

Is there is anything after death? It's impossible to know until we actually die, but is there another plane of existence?

Or is death the end? Does the light simply go out? And why am I so obsessed with this lately?

Slowly I left my body. It was as if an invisible force pulled at me. I saw myself sitting on the sofa. I wasn't in a body but was another being, looking down at a version of me. The experience was similar to vertigo but the force pulled me up instead of around. I was locked in helplessness and dreaded losing control. It took all of my stubborn energy to stay connected to this plane of common reality. My anxiety and terror prevented me from letting go and allowing whatever needed to happen.

Feelings of sadness and depression usually crept in after dark. As soon as the sun went down, my body ached. It was as if I were grieving. I found myself locked in the bathroom shedding messy tears. Almost every night. Nothing seemed to help. Not even a toke.

Pete never even noticed—until much later in spring.

Before February arrived, I started doing yoga postures again, this time while listening to spacey, spiritual music. I knew my quest didn't lie with Gestalt or psychology. Those methods probably help but are all about the shell, the furry hairs of the caterpillar, about the mind and memories, the psychology of a person. When I practiced yoga, when I listened to inspiring music, I connected to a glimmer of an ultimate truth. Something so abstract yet something so real. I didn't know what it was but I yearned for it with my entire being, not only with my head. There were so many things I *could* believe in. I did not want to fall into the trap of believing simply because I wanted to. I craved to believe in something actual. Something real. I wanted to know a truth which left no doubt in my mind.

Does an ultimate truth even exist? Isn't it all just a perspective?

Miracles

"I talked to Bear about his crash into the gully," said Pete as he helped with supper. He peeled wrinkled potatoes, gangly sprouts shooting out of their crusty hide. "Shit, how he survived is beyond me! It's got to be a bloody miracle!"

Peel, peel, peel.

"What a fucking bizarre world. He must have flown a hundred feet down in his old jalopy! He probably survived because he was so bloody drunk."

Scrape, scrape, scrape.

"There are huge boulders down there. It's lucky for him he wasn't totally creamed." Pete stopped peeling and showed me the white enamel bowl with the plump skinned orbs.

"This enough?"

I nodded. "Yep," and picked up an onion to peel it. "Is he still asking about his bloody cat? He seems obsessed that it's missing."

He started slicing the potatoes. "He seems to think Felix is responsible. As if our whimpy cat were so tough!"

The dull knife hit the wooden cutting board. *Whack!*

Jesus, that knife needs sharpening!

My eyes watered and burned after removing the papery-thin, crisp, yellowing skin then slicing the white meat of the stinging onion. I blinked and stepped away from the vapours. And felt like throwing up. "You know, Bear probably killed it himself, he's so damned weird! We better keep an eye on old Felix. How about we let him sleep on the porch again? I'll put down an old blanket for him."

"Yeah, OK," Pete replied and wrinkled his nose, "but I'm not cleaning up his poop."

"Fine! I'll do it. It's not like I don't do enough around here!"

Pete stopped hacking the spuds, glared at me, then threw the knife down and stormed out, leaving the potatoes half done on the counter.

"You poor, poor thing, you are so overworked!"

A sharp poke to the heart. It was another squabble, but we seemed to be having a lot of them lately. I was getting so sick of it. *What a fucking jerk!*

I leaned on the counter. After taking a few deep breaths, I crossed my cool arms and hugged myself. Glancing out the window I noticed Jane, Bear's wife, outside on her back porch, a dim light illuminating her hunched figure. She was sweeping a dusting of fluffy new snow off her steps with a worn straw broom.

The opposite of Bear, Jane had pale grey eyes and wispy, wavy hair which caught the copper in sunlight. Her skin was translucent, showing bluish veins like fading lines on a parched map. Subtle freckles dotted her thin nose and gaunt cheeks. She was thin like me but stood a bit taller when she wasn't slouched over. Her voice sounded small and reedy. She looked tired all the time. How she ever birthed a child was beyond me.

OK, it's enough. I grabbed the discarded knife and started slicing the last of the spuds. *Stop your moping. Someone has to make supper!*

The melted vegetable shortening in the cast-iron pan sizzled and spat, ready for the sliced spuds.

Pete went back to the dam project for news about a possible job. While he was gone, Ethan and I spent the day playing in the snow. Another major dump from the night before had piled up on the walkways. The shoveling turned out to be serious work. Yet it was such a pleasure to be outside in the deliciously soft, pure stuff which acted as a blanket for all winter creatures sleeping underneath—rabbits and worms and all those hibernating critters. They were the smart ones, choosing to remain safe and buried until the warmth of spring coaxed them out.

It was five thirty when Pete finally got back from his trip. He smelled of motor oil and frozen air and looked haggard and dismayed. I forgot yesterday's argument and gave him a warm hug. The van he had borrowed broke down at the Waneta Junction. What a lot of vehicle breakdowns lately! What the hell was going on?

"Roger from the dam site put in a special request for me," said Pete, "but the union shot it down."

"Shit!" I said. Not knowing how to help, I rubbed his back.

He had a hot shower and went to bed early.

I stayed up. During the daytimes, I barely kept up with housework and snow shoveling. In the evenings I worked on doodle drawings before bed, which was fun for a while, but it didn't change the empty, bored place. The tough questions gnawed their way up to the surface, their demanding, loud voices eager for a straight answer. And if they didn't get one they started chewing on my gut.

Do I need to be on some kind of medication? Should I get off the pill? Perhaps I am anemic, being vegetarian and all.

I had no answers, only problems. Only worries.

Aren't I too young to have so many problems? Who can I talk to? Who would be able to help?

No one ever came to mind.

And how did I get like this?

I finally fell asleep long after midnight and woke suddenly to a buried memory.

CLEANING DARK CORNERS

Meltdown

I walk through the silent dark kitchen and pick up a tall glass from the counter. *Need water. So parched.* As I reach toward the faucet, a loud knock at the door makes me jump. *Who could it be?* It's probably the nice neighbour I bumped into last night as we stumbled into Marc's place. I am wearing only his long cotton shirt and make sure it's buttoned up before opening the apartment door. And stop breathing as the early morning sun streams in and almost blinds me. *Damn.*

Dear Dad stands in front of me, looking shocked. And what a surprise—Lizzie, Little Sister Tattle-Tale, is right beside him! Forever tagging along, always "telling" on me! How else could dear Daddy-O have found me this early Sunday morning? He would most definitely not have a clue as to where I would be.

A grimace pulls at the corner of Lizzie's mouth. I glare at her.

"Get your stuff, you're going home! Right now!" Dad commands.

Quite the greeting—stale breath , a cocktail mix of garlicky pickles, burnt tobacco and fermenting booze. Glassy eyes scorch my face. He won`t be yelling here though. Being drunk at home is one thing. Acting out in public is another.

He glances at Marc, who has leapt out of bed and is now standing behind me, feet planted wide, arms crossed, ready to defend his new girl.

"Yeah, sure," I answer quietly, looking down. "I`ll come right out. Give me a minute."

I close the door, leaving Dad and Lizzie waiting for me on the landing. My heart is pounding so loud it makes me dizzy. I turn to Marc. He sits down on the rumpled bed situated in the middle of his small studio apartment. The room is still a mess from the night before. Clothes are scattered across the floor. Two guilty beer bottles stand on the night table.

"I'd better go. You don`t want him pounding on your door again, waking all your nice neighbours." I flush.

I only met Marc a couple of weeks ago. He was older, possibly twenty. Behind his rimless glasses I noticed kind, intelligent eyes. He had come from Newfoundland a few months earlier to work on a construction project and seemed so confident and at home in his skin.

We had first met at a grungie pool hall down the street where I hung out with a couple of new girlfriends, both of them underage. The staff never hassled us. Some days we looked older than the twenty year olds. Lots of black eyeliner, mascara, white matte lipstick, and cheap perfume dabbed behind the ears and knees. We always tried to look older. We wanted older boyfriends. Guys our age were too damned dull and more like little brothers. The popular crowd was also too boring. Besides, other than in art and drama class, I never actually fit in. And I never tried to. Or so I told myself.

So what did I want? I wasn't sure. I wanted something different from what all the grownups had. And I was so bloody sick of having to be the good girl, constantly having to help with housework and babysitting and being a second mom to my spoiled little sister, Lizzie. I wanted liberation from expectations. I had been taught to think for myself. But the world I saw, with kids still starving in Africa and wars all over the planet, looked pretty fucked up. I certainly didn't want a stifling mortgage, working at jobs I hated, living inside boxes, working in boxes and driving around in big boxes with wheels.

I definitely didn't want to end up like my mother—nice, nice on the outside but a lonely and troubled hypocrite underneath. People pleasing hypocrites. All of them. I had come to the conclusion most adults were frauds—telling me to be a certain way, yet acting another. Saying one thing and doing another.

I finally left Mum and Twin Forks with Lizzie in tow, because Mum needed a "break" and moved to the West Coast with Dad and his new family. We both thought it would be fun. It wasn't. After a few solitary months, I had made only a couple of city friends, mostly the tough greaser chicks from the neighbourhood. And Dad's drinking problem was a lot worse than I remembered.

When Marc finally asked me out on an official date, I was ecstatic.

He picked me up on Saturday and we walked in drizzle to the corner bus stop and jumped on one heading west.

In downtown Vancouver, we cruised tacky sidewalks covered with bits of old gum, snot bundles, vomit and who knows what else. Massive department stores selling all kinds of crap, neon lights flashing green, then red, red, red,red. Damp ocean air trapped the smells of the city: salty Chinese food, rancid deep-fried oils, stale nicotine and festering hidden mildew. Sour alcohol reeked from the makeshift beds of lonely, homeless people seeking shelter in doorways and in mossy, gloomy alleyways only partially hidden from view.

Time does fly when you're having fun though, and the next thing I knew, it was after 6:00 p.m. *Shit, I was supposed to be home by five o'clock!*

"I've got to find a pay phone!" I glanced down the street.

Marc spied one at the end of the block then pulled a few dimes out of his Levi's pocket. I stepped inside the booth and gingerly dropped the change into the pay-phone slot.

"Can I please stay out for a few more hours?" I pleaded, my best good-girl voice. "We so want to see *The Yellow Submarine*. It's on at a theatre right down the street and..."

"No. Come home right now! Did you forget? You're supposed to babysit!" Dad spits, his drunken voice hoarse and gritty.

"But why? Lizzie can babysit!"

He always said Lizzie was too young. She was his favourite. And he only wanted to go to the pub. His home away from home. It was Saturday night, after all. He'd stumble home in the early hours, ready for a fight or dying to wake up the entire household because for him, the party never ended. I didn't mind babysitting my half-brother once in a while but jeez! Lizzie *could* actually babysit. She was turning thirteen.

Fuck it. Enough being the good girl!

I slammed the phone down and pulled a newly acquired pack of Player's out of my purse. With a flick and a burst of flame, I was back in the mood.

Whatever is in this shit, it sure helps.

Marc searched my eyes as I came out of the phone booth. "How did it go?"

"It's fine. He's being difficult. What a jerk! I don't care. Let's go!" I was ready to party on. The rest of the night was a blur. We caught the last bus to his cool pad around midnight.

But last night was so long ago. I slowly get dressed. My hands tremble. As I step over for a hug from Mark, I notice the blood stains on the sheets. Now turning rusty brown.

"My blood—I guess it`s official. I'm no longer a virgin."

He looks away.

"Who the hell cares, anyway?" I ask, not expecting an answer. "It's all a bunch of stupid, uptight religious crap."

I shuffle back into the bathroom and look in the mirror. I don't appear any different, only a little frightened. I *am* a bit disgusted with myself. Dark circles surround sad eyes. At the pit of my stomach something swims and swims, is lost.

Whose eyes are those anyway? They don't look familiar. I grab a damp washcloth and return to the crime scene to try and scrub the stains out. The mess spreads. I scrub some more, but it only gets worse.

"Leave it," Marc says. He grabs my hand then lets it go.

It's only a few steps to the front door and out to face the music. Dad and sis still stand on the landing. He's puffing away at a relit old brown stogie.

"Meet me at the place, tonight at six?" Mark whispers.

I nod. My hair smells like urine.

The drive home with my tormentors drags on through dreary streets. At nine o'clock on a Sunday morning, a lot of stores are closed and most lights are still out. From the back seat, I glare at the back of Dad's and Lizzie's heads, throwing invisible hate daggers, tearing big chunks out of their hairy mops.

After the front door is closed, the rest of the household vanishes like birds at a feeder scattering at the sight of a large hawk. I try to make it to my room but Dad grabs my arm and starts yelling. I pull away, but he manages to throw me over his knees.

"What the hell do you think you're doing? Running around like a little tramp exactly like your mother! And sleeping with some dope head! This is something your mother should have done long ago!" He whacks me across my behind.

"Yeah, I guess we were all so fucking spoiled!" I scream, trapped under his hairy arms. I clamp down with my teeth through his cotton pants and bite his leg. He immediately lets go, and I struggle free and run to my bedroom, slamming the wooden door so violently the window rattles on the far wall.

I lock it. My ass stings. Tears stream down my cheeks. My mouth tastes vile and dry. I holler through the barricade, my voice raspy and screeching.

"Damn you, I am so done here! I'm leaving this fucking dump!"

"Good! I've pretty much had enough of you! It's time you went back to your mother's! You either behave or you go back!"

Something glass-like hits the kitchen sink and shatters. I hear his steel-toed work boots stomping out the back door and down the concrete stairs.

"Great! I can't wait to leave! I hate it here. It's a fucking hell hole."

I feel like breaking something, my fists have turned white. I'm suddenly exhausted and collapse on the floor, sobbing.

❋ ❋ ❋

We meet in the park. Marc and I stand on wet grass, between piles of sodden black earth in a corner of our local sanctuary. Puddles of murky rain reflect thick clouds. Chain-link wire mesh surrounds the tennis court in the background. A day's stubble accents his concerned eyes. His face appears even more ruggedly handsome. The sky hangs heavy, a dark mantle.

"Oh Sash, I'm so sorry it all came down like this," He somehow manages to say all the right things. "I like you a lot, you know. I wasn't looking for any trouble with a chick's dad—I mean you're not just a chick, but …" He looks past me to the busy highway beyond. Transport trucks and lines of speeding cars imitate distant ocean waves as they fly down the freeway, throwing up gloomy swells, whoosh, whoosh.

"Yeah, man, I know. No problem." I try to keep my cool, but today it's a problem. It's actually a big problem. "So when is your company heading up to Calgary? Maybe I can …"

"I'm sorry," he whispers softly into my tangled hair. "I can't take you. You know I want to. But there's no telling where I'll have to go after the job is finished. I'm permanently on the road. I only stay put for a few months at a time. It won't work! I can't."

Of course he can't take me. I'm a foolish child, not even finished school yet and he is so free and grown up and has a real job.

"Are you sure? You know I can go anywhere. I can quit school. It would be so easy. It's all a bunch of bullshit anyway! I could waitress?"

He shakes his tousled head. "No, I'm sorry. It won't work."

I take a deep breath. "Yeah, OK. I guess if I can't go with you then I'll probably head back to the old fucking mill town. Back to the middle of nowhere."

The sun has already set. An icy wind cuts into my neck and shoulders.

We kiss, the rock on my chest grows heavier.

"We'll keep in touch," he says. "I'll write you." He smiles. But his eyes are too serious. A squeeze of a cool hand, he lets go.

"So long, Marc, peace out," I whisper, flashing the sign as he trudges off. I turn toward the main roadway, hugging my white vinyl raincoat tightly. It's covered in smoggy drizzle and the bone chilling, never-ending, west coast rain. My damp, grimy runners plow forward through swampy puddles as tiny ripples spread outward in perfect, ever-widening circles.

The Brownie

"Come on, it's the weekend. We have to do some celebrating or something different for a change!" I smiled at Pete and presented a fat, dark brownie on a decorative glass plate. "Please, Pete. I don't want to get stoned all by my lonesome self."

Eve trying to share her apple? But my Adam was having none of it.

"Please?" I tried again.

"No, sorry. I don't feel like it tonight. I want to play my banjo and read. You go ahead."

He tried to smile, but I caught a downward turn of the mouth—his quiet disapproval.

"Okay, fine. Well, have fun then. More for me!"

I left him with his precious banjo, walked into the kitchen, and chomped down on the yummy, chocolaty mess. I then headed off to the bathroom to hide until it kicked in. A deep comforting bath was what I needed. Within twenty minutes or so, my world started to change. Time as I knew it—elusive time—sloooowwwed down. All my senses heightened. The room and all objects in it glowed with a warm light, appeared sharper, brighter and more outrageously beautiful.

Why couldn't I live in this place forever? The water which was pouring out of the bathtub spout was a miracle: *magical colours and glistening wetness, here for me, so I may bathe and rejuvenate. What a divine, perfectly wondrous thing! Oh, water, all humankind would not be here if not for you. It is true. Water is life.*

An enormous housefly with shimmering wings landed on a beam of light which outlined a diamond-shape on the white plaster bathroom wall. Had he somehow followed me from the laundromat? Perchance he had caught a ride within the warm, folded clothing in the baskets. His dinosaur-like eyes, ancient and multifaceted, clicked symmetrically as he checked out his surroundings. Those spacey orbs followed me as I wrung out the washcloth. I was being watched. After admiring his lustrous wings and intricate joints I blew gently on him. He rubbed his front paws together and wiped his scaly face. *What a lucky fly, getting to bathe in my steam.* As if hearing my thoughts he suddenly cringed and made his getaway, flying off to the windowsill on the opposite side of the room.

I did enjoy a long soak in the deep tub and started to hope Pete might join me. But I heard nothing. Not a peep or a whisper. He didn't enter or open the door to my sanctuary. He didn't even come in to pee. It had been a good hour. Now this was not like him. I slipped into a clean flannel nightie and tip-toed out to the living room to try and seduce him. I had to admit I missed him. I missed his body against mine, the taste of his salt and the warmth and passion of his skin on mine.

"Pete?"

He was sitting on the floor in the living room, strumming his old Gibson. I felt like an intruder.

"Yeah?"

He didn't look up.

Slowly I walked in and sat down beside him.

He sighed—much too deeply.

"What's wrong?" I asked, my voice high pitched and squeaky.

"Nothing's wrong, man. I just need some space." He patted my knee lightly and went back to his strumming.

"Space?" I felt slapped. "Yeah, OK. I could use some space, too!"

Tears started before I'd left the room. We had been spending a lot of time together since he had been laid off; possibly too much time together.

Still, right then I felt totally rejected. I needed help. Help of any kind. And immediately.

Retrieving the Kahlil book from the pocket of my apron, I flipped open a page at random and soaked up each word. It helped. I managed to chill out, then made a cup of tea and went to bed early, on my own. I ignored Pete completely, leaving him to his twanging and plucking.

"...Life is older than all things living, and when we weep Life smiles upon the day and is free, even when we drag our chains."

~K. Gibran

Spring Fever

Balmy weather blessed us with its warmth those last days of January. Pete insisted that he had spring fever. In January. Our little family enjoyed a long, leisurely walk up to the edge of the cemetery and to the older, crumbling gravestones where mammoth ponderosa pines watched over the sleeping dead. Brittle snow patches in the tallow fields on both sides of the red dirt road reflected the sun so brightly it burned my sensitive eyes.

Ethan walked all the way in his little snow boots, leaving toddler tracks behind. Earlier he had climbed onto a kitchen chair and stood at the table, playing with a dishrag and pretending to be making bread with it. He took a corner, folded it inwards, laid it flat then pounded on it with his cute little fists—exactly as I did when preparing bread dough.

Now why can't I enjoy baking bread that much?

The phone jangled right after I tucked him in for his nap. Our line—two short, one long.

"Hi Sasha. It's me. How are you?" Vincent's deep voice sent an immediate quiver up my spine.

"Hey, Vince, what a surprise! I'm good. How are you?"

No answer. I searched awkwardly for the right words to get the conversation going. "So, is it raining there?"

"I'm fine and the weather is fine, Sasha," he replied. "I may be coming up for a short visit. A friend from here is driving to the Kootenays and I can catch a ride next Wednesday. You guys busy? I could crash on the couch." He cleared his throat. "You know Kathy and I are interested in the land co-op, right? I definitely want to check it out."

"Yeah, that'll be cool." I paused. "There's lots of room. I mean, not *lots* of room. We have pretty basic digs as you know. But the sofa is available."

I heard a light laugh on the end of the line. "I'll let Pete know. He's in town with Sam, getting spark plugs for the truck."

"Well, say hi for me. Are you still keeping up with the journal writing?"

"Yeah, yeah. Well, to be honest, sometimes I miss a day here or there."

After we finished chatting, I hung up slowly. My heart hammered inside my head as I leaned against the kitchen wall to steady myself. I had to sit down.

Why does he have this effect on me? Grow up, girl!

Actually, I had completely stopped writing in my diary. Too busy. Or so I told myself. Not important busyness but the usual domestic crap.

Try as I might, even distracting myself with tedious boring housework, I could not shake his vibe. Vincent's pull was like a calling from a distant land. A land where warm, ripe figs and dates and olives grew plentifully and siestas in the heat of the day were the norm. Sometimes I could feel a breeze on my hair and silken garments against my legs in this golden land where sheer drapes floated and danced, uplifted by plumes of sandalwood incense. And where tall, arched windows framed indigo starry skies.

How can I handle his visit? Will he notice my obvious attraction, my flushed face and excitement, or will he notice my shrouded guilt instead?

When Pete returned from town, I mentioned to him Vincent might be catching a ride out on Wednesday. He said, "Super cool!" and seemed genuinely pleased that his old friend was coming for another visit.

Pete's warm response only deepened my self-reproach and growing guilt.

As it turned out, Vincent did not visit for quite a long time. He kept saying he was heading over but would cancel at the last minute. I should have shut him down and purged him from my mind and my heart.

I should have. But I didn't. I didn't purge him from anything.

His absence only deepened my desire.

I accidently met a new person in the local library a few days later. And, as we all know, there are no accidents.

Larry was in the homesteading section. It was quite sparse, but it had a few good rags, like *Mother Earth News* and *Mother Jones*. We both reached for the same mag at the same time and the conversation started. Surprisingly, Larry used to work with Pete at the mill in Mid Town. He and his wife, Jo-Anne, ran a small farm and had a jersey cow who produced a lot of milk. He mentioned they had a surplus at the time which they would be willing to sell.

Whole milk, straight from the cow! This could be what we're all lacking.

I followed Larry out to their place on the edge of town to meet Jo-Anne and purchase the first jar of the fresh, good stuff. As we turned onto Dusty Road, I realized their home, a new trailer, surrounded by raspberry bushes and young apricot trees, sat on familiar land. I had a forever dream of living on Shady Hill. It overlooked the entire valley. Perfect setting, safe yet sunny, tucked into the mountainside. I had talked about it one day when Karl and I first got together, but we ended up renting a tiny place right in town. He had laughed and said, "Dream on, girl." Sometimes dreams end up being simply dreams.

While sharing a pot of tea, I admired Jo-Anne's elegant curtains, embroidered with yellow and purple pansies. Sunbeams reflected off white appliances in her clean, spare kitchen. The yeasty, grassy smell of fresh cow's milk overpowered the small space.

We all enjoyed good conversation and I felt so welcome and at home.

Before heading back to town, Larry carefully placed a jar of white gold on the floor of the old Chevy. The drive back down the sharply winding mountain road proved a challenge. My hands shook all the way, yet I managed to keep an eye on that jar. I carefully and gratefully stashed the prize in the old fridge like a secret treasure, like the best food of the gods.

No one suspected at the time unpasteurized milk could possibly make anyone sick. And whether or not it made us sick, we would never know.

It was the tastiest, freshest milk we ever had.

I started to feel better right away. This lasted a few days.

Visitors and Doctors

Spider, a cousin of Pete's, stopped by unexpectedly. After we twisted his rubber arm he agreed to join us for a simple supper of soup and bread. He had remained unsettled for years, crashing with friends and sometimes camping on his own in remote areas. A pure idealist with a heart of gold, he once set up a "free store" off Thunderbird Lane. When people were done with their old furniture or used clothing, they would simply drop it off. Folks in need could pick up what *they* needed. It worked for a few months, but most tended to drop off a lot of their broken-down belongings and worthless junk instead of taking it to the town dump. After Spider left on one of his lengthy road trips to the four corners, Arizona or Utah perhaps, the free-store shack was taken over by hungry field mice, rats, and fierce, masked raccoons. The makeshift roof eventually caved in and fungus, wild grasses and moss grew over the discarded possessions, reclaiming them all back to the welcoming earth.

Despite having a big heart, Spider was high strung and had trouble living in the world. He was unable to settle anywhere and experienced severe panic attacks and sometimes had trouble separating reality from make-believe. I tried to help and had previously suggested he read *Autobiography of a Yogi* to help him get a little more grounded and to get a clearer picture of himself. It seemed to have worked. He appeared to be doing especially well. He was meditating regularly. The difference was obvious: he laughed more easily and appeared so much calmer. I envied his transformation and discipline.

As he was leaving, he mentioned he might be moving to Calgary later in the year. I was disappointed. Even though we rarely saw him, we would both miss him.

As I tidied up later in the evening, a beam of dusty light streamed through the window and landed on my shoulder, like the caring and tender touch of a gentle spirit.

A surprise visit from my sister the next day caught me in the middle of defrosting the old fridge in anticipation of Vincent's spring visit. The spring visit that never happened. The entire house smelled like castile soap, white vinegar and lemon, a few of my favourite natural cleaners. I hastily opened the back door after throwing the filthy rag into the soap bucket. The burden in Lizzie's heavy eyes was obvious. Her five year old boy, Jared, stood next to her, tightly grasping his mom's hand. Both looked tapped.

I welcomed them in for tea and they removed endless coats and boots. Jared ran into the living room to help Ethan dismantle a wooden block house.

"Catnip this time, good for the nerves." I suggested, putting water on to boil and filling a teapot. "So what's going on? You looked totally bummed!"

"Oh, shit, Sam wants to move to Vancouver," Lizzie moaned. "I think he's getting laid off at the mill. Or quitting soon. Jeez! I don't want to move to bloody Vancouver! What the hell am I going to do there?"

She could be right. At least she had some work in Twin Forks, housekeeping at the Blue River Motel. It didn't pay much, but it sure helped with the rent. She loudly sipped her tea and twisted her scruffy over-bleached blonde hair, tugging on its strands. As a child she used to twist her clothing. As the older sister, I had to slap her hand when we were in public or within minutes anyone in the room would be able to see her underpants as she twisted and turned the edge of her skirt all the way up to her waist. Then she'd chew on the end. The adults would laugh. I was always embarrassed.

"Wow," I said, trying to offer some support while scooping more unpasteurized honey into my tea. "You *are* in a tight spot. If Sam moves to Vancouver, you'll have to get a roommate right away or find a cheaper place!"

"I know, damn it! It's not for sure. I'm so fucking sick of moving." She tapped her spoon on the side of her cup—another nervous habit.

"Is he still writing his stories? It's not going to put food on the table! What is he thinking?"

Liz and I shared a joint of home grown leaf she had managed to "borrow" from Sam, did some man bashing and reminisced about old times. Nothing seemed so serious after a while.

But after she left, I was totally drained.

How can this be normal? Perhaps I need to meditate more.

Meditation did usually seem to help a little. Mostly, I sat perfectly still for as long as possible and concentrated on my breath. According to most major belief systems, all answers lay within. So I needed to slow down, stop focusing on the outside world quite so much. And just go within.

I decided a short nap before dinner was the best plan.

Weather became another obsession. I recorded it in my journal daily. I started to wonder if it could be a reflection of my moods or a metaphor for how my day was going to turn out.

Perhaps I had been a navigator or explorer in another life. If you believe in this sort of thing.

Lately it was frigid, cloudy, dark and overcast. A good time to rest.

Perhaps a daily nap was not such a bad idea.

Poor Pete was in a world of fever and pain for two days straight. It sounded like it might be an abscessed wisdom tooth, but it was next to impossible to see a real dentist in that hick town. He took a few aspirins before bed in the hope of the pain subsiding. The next day, he had to go back over the mountains with Sam and Lizzie to pick up Sam's old car, which was still sitting in the same spot after the last breakdown weeks before. I'm surprised it wasn't stolen or sold. But it was a junk car, so who would want it anyway?

While I made supper, Jared and Ethan, those two rascals, took all of Pete's socks out of his dresser drawer and chucked them into the bathtub where I was soaking kitchen towels with a little bleach.

It took many washes before I could get the chlorine smell out.

Those two were double the trouble.

I felt totally relieved when Lizzie and Sam finally returned and picked Jared up, long after the sun had set.

Smoldering

After a few weeks of cool reprieve, a smoldering yeast infection, which had been driving me crazy intermittently for the last couple of months, returned with a vengeance. The old doc had put me on antibiotics-penicillin and also Mycostatin, a vaginal cream. It seemed to help at first but was now totally useless. In fact, things below were getting much worse.

What the hell? Why do I get this? I tried to get some relief from the ferocious itching by soaking in a baking soda bath. It helped about 10 percent.

Hannah, a member of the land co-op, came over for a few minutes and recommended douching with myrrh and goldenseal. By then I was willing to try anything. The stuff the doc gave me was totally useless and might even have been making things worse. I wanted to tear my hair out.

"I would rather have to deal with Pete's toothache. It's probably easier to cope with pain than this freaking itching. This is the worst kind of torture!" I muttered to myself while punching down the rising bread and forming the loaves to put in pans. I slapped those loaves harder than usual. Smack! Smack! Smack!

Hannah had also suggested cutting back on the sugar, as it was a supposed trigger for yeast. The birth control pills could also aggravate those kinds of things.

I'll have to make some changes!

We also talked about being vegetarian and Hannah suggested I try multivitamins with iron in case my weakness and dizziness were due to anemia.

I had asked my doc about the possibility of anemia in my last check-up, but he only frowned and kept filling in his medical forms, his pen scratching on the page, totally ignoring my question.

❊ ❊ ❊

To top it all off, Pied Pumpkin, the band booked by the co-op to play for our fundraiser cancelled without warning. Most were damned disappointed, but I secretly rejoiced because I'd be having my period that night. Periods were such a hassle in those days. Sometimes I felt like I was bleeding to death. Having to change pad after soaked pad.

More blood letting: Karl, my ex stopped by for the fifty bucks. My portion of the divorce fee! It was scheduled to take place this spring. He initiated those legal proceedings yet somehow had convinced me to share the costs.

Sometimes I'm such a wimp. I could have said, "No, I'm not going to help you pay for your divorce. If you want to get married again that is your business, and you'll have to cough up the cash!"

I wasn't going to feel any better after the legal proceedings were over. Simply paperwork. I felt no bonds with Karl and hadn't for years. The law was so damned silly. Whose law was it anyway? It was men's law, written by men. People would stay together if they wanted to, not because a piece of paper said they could or could not. And in this case, Karl had emphasized that "someone" had to say they had committed adultery.

Oh, well. I wasn't the first, and I wouldn't be the last, I suppose. We were separated when I met Pete, so technically it would be perjury, but who cares about all that now? Certainly not me. That gave me some measure of comfort.

It was the cheapest, fastest way to get this over with. Someone had to be wrong in order to get that stupid marriage dissolved.

I managed to get to the health store and bought a few bags of herbs. I tried the myrrh-and-goldenseal douche and it worked. The itching stopped. A small miracle! I was so relieved I cried.

Dring-dring—dri-i-ing! I raced inside to reach the phone before the ringing stopped. "Hello?" breathless.

"Yes, 'ello. Is Sasha there?" The syrupy British accent could only belong to my doc. It was about time he returned my call. I had left a short message with his perky receptionist days before when Hannah's herbal treatment stopped working after just a few days. My vaginal tissues were worse than ever— swollen and itchy.

I finally had him on the phone. "I'm sorry to bother you again, but the treatment you prescribed has not been working. I'm actually feeling much worse."

"These things can take some time, my dear," he said, irritation in his affected voice. "Have a hot, relaxing bath, try some Epsom salts, blah, blah, blah, and if it's not better in two weeks make an appointment and come in and see me again."

"Two weeks? But, I don't know if I can …"

"We'll see you soon, my dear," he said curtly. And hung up.

I held the receiver in my hand, feeling like bashing it against the wall. I was so sick of his condescending attitude. He was such an upper class, stuffy old bloke and took himself so seriously, calling women "dear," "darling," or "sweetheart."

An aunt once told me if a man calls you dear, darling or sweetheart all the time he either hates women or doesn't remember your name.

He doesn't give a damn about my minor problems! He is a doctor and so important and so fucking busy!

I screamed silently into my hand and bit my palm. Then grabbed the dishtowel and forcefully smacked it against the chair three or four times. A small measure of relief.

It was time to switch doctors. I booked an appointment with the only other doc in town, Dr. K. A few weeks back Pete and I had shared some good raps with him over beers in the pub. He was young, smart, approachable and mellow.

He also smoked pot. So he was a little more modern. Not a dinosaur from another generation.

He could be a little more compassionate.

At least we had something in common.

Nasty and the Mice

Everyone had serious mice infestations. Those little suckers bred like crazy—perhaps because the unusually warm winter meant they weren't getting frozen out. Our dear Felix was still nowhere to be found and seemed to have vanished into thin air overnight. We borrowed Nasty, Lizzie's cat, to help us get a handle on the increasing invasion.

Being the great mouser that he was, Nasty caught one the next night. I heard a high-pitched squeal and knew it was the little bugger's end. It tore at my heart. Even though the mouse tribe was getting out of hand, I felt only sadness for the demise of those poor little rodents.

But we could not take it anymore. I often heard them scurrying around on the countertops in the middle of the night, leaving their Sen-Sen droppings. It became a health issue. Along with constantly scouring the counters with water and bleach, I had also started storing a lot of our dried goods in jars. Even with all the extra care, they still managed to get into our bulk rolled oats. I had to dump the entire box into the compost. They had chewed right through the heavy-duty cardboard with sharp little razor teeth. They were teeny but feisty and determined as hell.

While wiping down the counters, I imagined having a new super power, the ability to chew my way through those day-to-day problems and the heavy, restricting boxes of my negative and pessimistic thoughts.

On garbage day, I left the black plastic bag on the roadside and went back inside.

We composted a lot but there was still an extra bit of crap that was a pain to deal with. "Do you smell something horrible when you go outside?" I asked Pete.

He was finishing the dishes and looked over at me with soap bubbles on his hands.

"Ahhh. No."

"Well, it does stink. I'm going to have a look around when it stops snowing."

"Be my guest, it's probably someone's garbage."

Ethan ran over and climbed onto his favourite vinyl, beat-up chair to help with the dishes. Typically, Pete and Ethan made a mess, and I would end up having to clean it up, which sucked. On the other hand, it was great to see the two of them sharing chores. Once in a while, Pete tried to be a good role model for Ethan. Hopefully, my boy would learn that men also needed to clean and cook and deal with all those boring domestic duties.

After crouching down and petting Nasty, I shook off a handful of his shedding white hair then kicked him outside to make sure he didn't do his business somewhere in the house. He could clean up the outside now that he was done with the domestic mice. He was a good cat and hadn't freaked out about not being in his own home. We had given him a little pad of butter when he first arrived, which was supposed to ensure he wouldn't stray. This was an old Russian wives' tale I had learned from Mum: *When a new pet comes to your home, make sure to give him a little butter and he will stick around forever.*

❋ ❋ ❋

B.B. Sawmill, Twin Forks branch, called and asked Pete if he wanted work. Yes! *This is going to be so much better for Pete than driving to the other mill, a half hour away, especially when the roads are icy and slippery in the winter. Right on!*

We were ecstatic. Even Pete was starting to worry about how much more penny pinching we could actually do. A penny only went so far, after all.

He would start the next Monday. I was so damned relieved I actually slept through the entire night for the first time in a long while. I hadn't realized how anxious the penny pinching and lack of money had made me.

So that could explain the insomnia—at least in part.

It had been a long and sleepless winter.

The Gift

Sam and Lizzie fought a lot that spring. So one weekend, I got Mum to babysit Ethan for a day and Pete and I drove Lizzie and her boy over to Kelowna so she could spend a few days with Dad and his brand-new wife, Pat. She was the third one now. Or was it the fourth? Both Sam and Lizzie needed a break from each other. How does the old saying go? *How can I miss you if you don't go away?*

It was a breath-taking drive over the mountain pass. Early February was not close to spring, but we could see it coming: a hint of ground, a few bare patches of terrain and mottled olive spots on the hillsides. The snow had started melting underneath masses of greying, pebbly piles which had been pushed to the side of the road by monster plows. Baby waterfalls glistened off steep rock faces. The occasional beam of sunlight reflected back, hitting me directly in the eye.

We were greeted by our newest stepmom, a tall, strong-limbed woman with, thick white wavy hair and a welcoming smile. She immediately reached out for Jared, who slumped into her arms, still not totally awake from his nap on the road. We marched into the entrance and removed our outer gear and hung them on the coat tree by the door.

"Your father should be home shortly," said Pat. "He's just finishing his shift at the store." She meant Family Hardware. He was already the manager of the Electrical Department a few short months after they had settled in.

Pat tucked Jared in for a nap then joined Lizzie, Pete, and me at the kitchen table where she had put out a selection of cheese and crackers and snacks along with a pot of Orange Pekoe tea.

I finally asked about Dad. Lizzie and I had not seen him in a couple of years. He had stopped briefly at Twin Forks to say hello after Ethan was born and surprisingly had acted like a "normal" person in the few minutes he had managed to fit us into his busy schedule.

He wasn't drinking anymore, but he still had issues and had become a workaholic. Never enough time to visit with Lizzie or me. It wasn't that different. He wasn't ever available. He wasn't really there for us.

"So, how is he these days?" I asked, reaching for a slice of pickled beet to put on a rye cracker. "Is he still going to AA meetings?"

The other two stopped their munching and glared at me as if I had broken one of the Ten Commandments.

I was feeling a touch anxious about how Dad and I would get on once he entered his new home. My stomach did whirls and flips, and the dark, sticky tentacles of a headache reached for the back of my neck.

Pat graciously offered me a plate of sliced chicken. I shook my head.

"Are you still a vegetarian, Sasha?" she asked. "Oh, I'm sorry, of course you are! Lizzie?"

Lizzie wasn't quite as fussy. She jabbed a few slices of white meat with her fork and threw them on her plate.

After an uncomfortably long pause, while Pat topped up the snacks on the serving plates, she finally answered. "Yes, your father has been doing exceptionally well since he stopped the drinking. He goes to meetings every day and has a great sponsor—an older man who lives in the neighbourhood."

Lizzie had her opinion on the matter. "Well, good for him! But damn, was he ever drinking too much? I mean he's still working, right? He could still drive! How much is too much? Did he get pulled over in a DUI, or what?" she poked repeatedly at another slice of cheddar cheese. "I sure could use a beer right about now. It's been a hell of a week!"

"Oh God, Liz, take a break, why don't you!" I whispered loudly.

Pat smiled wryly. "Oh no, we don't have any alcohol in the house these days. You'll have to go downtown if you want any booze.

"Yeah, I know, I know," said Lizzie, slicing her chicken. Her hair, unwashed and stringy, hung in her eyes. Kohl eyeliner was smudged on her eyelids and magenta lipstick was smeared giving her a ghoulish appearance. "I read all about it in some pamphlet at our stupid library."

Pete stifled a snicker, the rest of us ignored him. Then he jumped, as if kicked. Lizzie glared at him with her penetrating stare. I squinted at him, trying to get his attention. He avoided my questioning gaze, preferring to load his plate with more food. A rattling noise at the entrance caught our attention. We turned as Dad walked in, a grocery bag full of snacks and chips in his arms.

Pat walked over and took it from him. "Thanks," she whispered. "They're all here."

I detected a touch of fear in her voice and suddenly felt like an intruder in my father's home with his new happy family. My heart started to race and I glanced toward the balcony door at the far end of the hallway. The closest escape exit if I needed to run.

"Hey, hello guys," Dad said. "Glad you made it!"

He looked like the same old dad, only not so bloated and not smelling of booze and stale cigarettes. He appeared tidy and shaven and somehow fresh. His hair was still golden, but greying at the temples. Intense blue eyes shone clear and fierce.

We spent the next half hour chatting about the weather and the early snow melt, about Sam and Lizzie's tiffs and their deepening divide and about Dad's new job. The entire time my stomach felt like it was knotting. This was an entirely different person. Or was it? *Who the hell was this person?*

He stood up and headed for the bedroom, saying he had to change from his work clothes and leaving us to finish our tea and figure out what to do next.

Lizzie, who had methodically chewed on her now torn and bloody fingernails the entire time, blurted out, “He quit smoking too, right?” She glanced apprehensively down the hallway then spoke in a hoarse undertone to Pat. “I do need a smoke! Damn, it’s been a couple of hours. Is there anywhere I can have a smoke?”

Pat folded her arms across her chest. “Well, if you must, you can go out to the back balcony and puff away.”

She grabbed an empty black olive can sitting on the counter, its jagged silver edges sharp and dangerous and handed it to Lizzie, who took it, looking perplexed.

“Use this for the butt,” said Pat. “And don’t start a fire!”

“OK,” said Lizzie. “Thanks. I guess.” She grabbed her purse from the floor and began to rise to make her exit at the exact instant when Dad returned from the bedroom holding two wrapped presents. One was a foot square and wrapped neatly with a pink bow on top. The other was wrapped loosely with white tissue paper.

He brought them over and cautiously placed them on the table. “I forgot to send these at Christmas. We were moving and things got super busy. But these are for you. One for you, Elizabeth, and one for you, Sasha!”

He placed the large one with the bow in front of Lizzie and the small, ratty looking one in front of me.

“Wow, thanks, Dad,” said Lizzie. “I’m sorry I didn’t send you anything!”

She ripped it open, not bothering to save the expensive paper for another time. In seconds, after throwing out handfuls of shredded newspaper from the box, she dug out a hefty, sparkly crystal ashtray, its rim smooth and its bowl embedded with star patterns. "Ha, Ha!" she laughed. "Thanks, Dad. Exactly what I needed!"

She bounced up and gave him a hug. Both of them radiated joy like they were part of a secret cult—the smoker's cult. *Only he was not supposed to be smoking anymore! And it was bad for her! She should just fucking quit!*

Without thinking it through I let them know how stupid this was. "How beautiful, but wouldn't it be better for Lizzie if she quit? Isn't this encouraging her to keep smoking?" The words flew out, soared, crumbled and crashed against the festive atmosphere.

Dad turned to me with laser-sharp eyes. Zap! A familiar hole opens in my gut.

"Well, Sasha," he said, "at this point, Lizzie is still smoking and it really isn't any of your business, is it? She will quit when she's good and ready!" He looked at his favourite daughter. "Right, Lizzie?"

Lizzie held her ashtray tightly in her lap, head down. "Yeah, sure. I will," she said. "I plan to, anyway." A quick, secretive smile.

Dad's expression changed immediately. "See there. Everything is fine! Now let's see what you have."

I was boiling mad. "What I have? Does it matter what I have? You don't give a damn about what I have! It's never going to be as good as what Lizzie has! Because you know what? She has always been your favourite! From day one. I only get the leftovers, like this present. I don't want your fucking damn present!"

And with that I stood up, threw my gift on the floor like a toddler in a tantrum, and headed out to the balcony. I ran down the short hallway, stepped outside onto the frosty landing, and slammed the glass door shut. It rattled loudly.

A chickadee flew briskly out of an enormous blue spruce next to the deck, landed on the clothesline and began to chatter. "Chickadee-dee-dee." I stood shivering, trying to settle the waves of hurt and old anger.

"Hi, chickadee. You are so damn lucky to be a bird. You don't have to deal with all these fucking people!" Chickadee blinked at me with his tiny reflective black eye, flapped his wings and flew off.

I stood there shivering for a good two minutes before the door opened. Dad stepped out. He held my coat and boots. I thought he might throw them into the back yard, but he carefully passed them to me. I took them and quickly put them on. I didn't want to die out there. *Woman found frozen on back balcony*. Not good.

"It's too cold out here," he said. "Why don't you come back inside?" His arm reached out and he tried to put it around my shoulders. I pulled away.

"Yeah, well, who the hell cares, anyway?" It wasn't rational, but perhaps my brain was frozen. Or my heart. Something was frozen.

"I care, Sasha," he said. "I care."

He seemed to mean it. The hardness in my chest started to melt. A teeny bit. Was it my heart warming? Maybe it was, because I now had boots and a coat on. But something was definitely shifting, was changing.

He went on. "I know I have been a crappy father, and I haven't always been there, and I'm sorry. You know I'm sorry. For the past."

Before I could say the right thing, Lizzie showed up. She stepped outside gingerly, carrying torn tissue and an object in her hand. Inside the messy bundle lay a framed photograph. Lizzie handed it to me and I stared at it. It was a pewter framed black and white photograph of Dad and me when I was only three or four. He was holding a cute toddler in his strong arms as we both smiled at the camera. The glass was broken, but the picture was not damaged. A long time ago, I had asked for a copy of this photograph, and here it was. He hadn't forgotten.

"Lizzie is not my favourite," he said. "She is more like me, this is true, but I love you both. You are different from each other, that's all."

Lizzie spoke up. "You're the one who got all the attention in school, you know. Because you were so fucking smart—and cool! So I had to have my own gig! I couldn't be exactly like you." She pointed at me with her sharp finger.

Me, cool? Where does she get this crap from?

"Yeah sure, Lizzie, but you got away with murder. You stole my stuff—my clothes, money, and hairbrushes and shit. Mum and Daddy would say, 'Oh, don't make a scene! She's having a hard time. She'll grow out of it!' Having a hard time, my ass, you were a fucking little crybaby!"

"A crybaby!" Lizzie shot back. "Man, are you ever mean! Where did you get that from?" Her thick, blonde hair stood on end.

Dad stepped in. "OK. Enough now! It's all in the past. It's time to move on. Let's apologize, and we can all try to do better in the future!"

Seemed like a good enough plan. For now. I was tired of this fight. After Dad and Lizzie shared their toxic stinky cigarette, we shared awkward hugs and headed back inside where Pat was playing cards with Jared, who was now wide awake. Pete was washing the dishes with a smug look on his face.

What the hell is going on with Pete now?

He ignored me for the rest of the visit, playing with Jared and talking to Dad all evening about the problems with Ford trucks, or some such thing. The entire household crashed early.

The next morning at daybreak we headed home. Pete and I barely spoke the entire way, each preferring to mull over yesterday's events in our own minds.

Almost a perfect visit.

Lost and Found

After returning from the Okanagan, I had another look around the mucky yard for Felix. Strangely, Old Nasty had also disappeared before we left on the trip. We searched for him high and low before taking off, but he was nowhere to be seen. A couple of inches of melting snow still patched the ground, and I followed my nose. And then I found him. We usually stored a bunch of old lumber behind the storage shed: 2x4s, plywood, and scraps for odd jobs.

"You never know when you might need a few boards," my grandpa always said.

I carefully lifted up a piece of grey, weathered plywood, and there he was: Old Felix, frozen and covered in gravel and sawdust. Parts of him were already rotting and decomposing. I gagged and ran to the house and dragged Pete out to see. He put on his leather work gloves and helped me put the half frozen corpse into a plastic garbage bag. We left him in the shed until we could figure out what to do with him. It looked like someone had smashed his head in. It was all flat and misshapen. Who the hell would do that? Who the hell would do such a thing?

Oh, my God, are we living next to a killer? I went straight into panic mode.

Our crazy neighbour, Bear hadn't been around for weeks and Jane never looked in our direction anymore when she was outside. *Damn!*

I told myself to get a grip and to remember that each person is presumed innocent until proven guilty. Even Bear. But it didn't help. I was freaked right out. And Nasty was still nowhere to be found. What the hell was going on?

In the evening, after Ethan was asleep, we wrapped Felix in his smelly, moth-eaten porch blanket, dropped him into an old potato sack and deposited his slowly decomposing remains into the garbage can. What else do you do with a dead cat in the middle of winter? The ground was still too frozen to bury him, poor dude. We held hands and said a little goodbye and a blessing to send him on his way.

"Dear Felix, thank you for being part of our family these few years. We hope your new world is friendly and warm and there are a lot of treats for you. Thanks for catching all those mice. We'll miss you. Happy trails, dear friend."

Poor bugger. I played out many versions in my head as to what did him in. The mystery hung in the air like a heavy cloak. I wondered whether I should have let him stay in the house the night he vanished. Poor old Felix. I decided it was not my fault, though. I would not blame myself. Would not.

We continued to look for Nasty a few more weeks and then little by little forgot about our other little furry helper. We forgot he had also seemingly vanished into thin air.

Larry and Marsha, the milk people, accepted our invitation for tea and came by for a short visit. They finally admitted it: they were Jehovah's Witnesses—exactly as I had thought. I hated to define them this way, but it was at the back of my mind. My fear was they'd try to convert me.

When will they bring out the leaflets with the heavenly realms painted on the covers? Jesus in a flowing robe, his hair long and wavy, standing on a hillside with lambs and lions frolicking together, beams of light pouring down through fluffy clouds and out of the middle of his palms? And didn't they need a quota of converts in order to get into heaven? I was afraid to ask.

Their children were adorable and I did enjoy Larry and Marsha's company. They were extremely civilized, compassionate and practical even though they were blindly religious. Their youngest daughter was only nine months old. Ethan was amazed to see someone younger than himself. He would walk up to her and peer into her little face like he couldn't quite believe she was real. He'd repeatedly poke her plump leg with his finger. This made her cry, but it was hilarious at the time.

Another entire day was wasted on getting through one of my major headaches and by the end of it I was totally worn out. To top it off Pete and I had to attend a big land co-operative meeting which took place at Gary's house; a charming, large post-and-beam home overlooking the river. The meeting was also a potluck so each of the co-op members brought something great—well, usually great—to eat.

I had to keep asking, "Is it vegetarian?" as I poked at various offerings in casserole dishes, large platters and enormous serving bowls.

Quite often I got "the look" and then the sarcasm. "No, but it's got meat from a deer I hunted myself last year. You should try it! It's delicious!"

Or, "Yes, it's veggie, with a bit of tuna."

The salads were pretty safe but one never knew. Once, I discovered a mouthful of non- chewable crunchy bits so turned away from the group and spat them out into a paper napkin. I didn't really want to know what it was. It didn't taste like food to me.

When the group was on their lemon pie and rosehip tea, Gary and Hannah dropped the bomb. They had been dating for only a short while, a few months or so, but had talked about moving in together and were considering putting one of their shares up for sale. Neither of them was certain, but they wanted to give the co-op a heads up. This news was a shocker, to say the least!

The entire room was silent for a good two minutes, except for the sound of folks scraping the last of the pie off their plates and stacking their dishes together. Everyone looked downward.

Damn!

Following a lot of back and forth chitter chatter and folks asking personal questions, Gary and Hannah agreed they would try to wait until the Wild Meadows Co-op had rustled up some new members before selling Hannah's shares. Everyone agreed to have another meeting soon to sort out the details and come up with ideas on how to recruit new people.

Those meetings crushed me. I didn't contribute much and let others ramble on. Perhaps I was a little too young to express what I was actually thinking. Most of the members of the co-op were people in their thirties and forties. Not ancient, but well- seasoned. I also didn't find it easy to contribute to conversations in any group when there were so many participants.

Those who talk don't know and those who know don't talk? Mum's voice. I usually preferred to hash things out in my head first.

I usually saved my special thoughts for sincerely special people.

People who seemed to actually care about what I thought and what I felt.

People like Hannah and Gary, from the Co-op. Sometimes Pete.

And people like Vincent, of course.

❋ ❋ ❋

Life got busy again with Pete back at work. I swung right into the good little housewife routine. I even made a pot of Mum's Russian borscht—full of veggies and butter and salt and cream. So tasty it was addictive. In the olden days, back in the early commune days, the Doukhobour folks would fry the onions and tomatoes before adding it all to the soup pot. But with the new time saving recipe a person could cook it all in one pot. And it was so much healthier because it wasn't fried.

"Too much fried food can kill you!" the older Doukhobor ladies swore. And then muttered their mantra, "Toil and a peaceful life, toil and a peaceful life."

The best borscht was made with stewed tomatoes you canned yourself after growing and harvesting them in your own garden. This was also true for the carrots, beets, onions, and especially the dill. Cheap potatoes could be found everywhere in Twin Forks; in fact, in late summer hundreds of them escaped the harvester that pulled them off the deep brown loamy fields. They could be picked up for free in the early fall, right off the ground, before the frost hit and then thrown into a sack to be taken home and peeled, steamed, mashed and eaten. With butter, of course.

Doukhobour Vegetarian Non-fry Borscht

Ingredients:

1 ½ qts. (or 2 cans, 28 oz. each) stewed tomatoes, mashed or blended

1 large grated carrot, or 2 medium

3 medium/small peeled beets: 1 grated fine, 2 cut in halves

5 to 6 quarts of boiling water

½ large yellow onion, peeled, and diced fine

2 to 4 tbsp. salt

8 medium potatoes (Russet or similar), 4 of which will be cut into quarters, the rest diced

½ large head of sweet, green summer cabbage, shredded fine, crossways, against the grain

1 small green pepper, cored and finely diced

¼ cup finely diced fresh celery and leaves

4 tbsp. dill leaves, dried or fresh

½ lb. of salted butter

½ to 1 cup of regular fresh cream

1. In a large, 20-quart soup pot, simmer the stewed tomatoes with the grated carrot and beets for about 10 min.
2. Stir and add enough boiling water to fill the pot two-thirds full. Add the diced onions, beet chunks and 2 tbsp. salt. Turn up heat to a rolling boil. Add boiling water, as needed.
3. Add the 4 potatoes, all cut into quarters. Stir and let boil.

4. When the potato chunks are soft and cooked through, remove them with a slotted spoon, mash well with a bit of butter (4 tbsp.), 1/8 c. of cream, a dash of salt, set aside.
5. Add the diced potatoes to the boiling pot of veggies then add the shredded cabbage, mashed potatoes, onions, green pepper, and celery. Stir well, turn down the heat, and let it all simmer until cooked. May take 15 min. Do a taste test. Nothing should be crunchy.
6. With a slotted spoon, remove the beets, if desired; if you leave them in the pot, the borscht will be darker and sweeter.
7. Stir and add the butter and cream. More cream Will make it white, less Will make it orange. Sprinkle the dill on top of the hot soup. Cover with the lid and let sit for 10 min.
8. Stir and serve hot!

Serves a small army (12) of borscht lovers, or a family of three for a few days.

After it cools, it can be refrigerated for days or frozen in plastic containers or jars (leave at least a 1-inch space at the top if they're glass jars).

Great with a dab of Co-Op sour cream, a slice of fresh homemade bread, cheddar cheese, and a sprinkle of cayenne and/or or black pepper.

Out of Body

My physical ailments continued, undefinable but still debilitating at times. By nightfall I often ended up with a massive headache and a sore stomach. Some days I also vomited. It was a relief to get my period, as my symptoms abated after that.

I continued to experience a version of an out-of-body experience. It usually started with deep feelings of sadness and loss. Some parts of me became numb and tingly. A heavy, wool-like darkness washed over my mind and I felt the impermanence of all things physical. It was real but difficult to explain to anyone. Least of all to Pete.

One night I saw the possibility of the ending of all things.

All people eventually die. Does anything last? What is the ultimate reality?

I would eventually fall asleep and only remember these experiences in the harsh light of the morning.

THE SHADOW SIDE

Sleep Addiction

Pete and I spent more and more of our days angry and frustrated with each other. On the days he wasn't working he usually slept in. And was sometimes so lethargic when he did finally get up, he had no energy to do anything. Then he'd get angry at me for complaining about his lack of help and would withdraw even further. It was a vicious cycle. The best thing for me to do was to try and understand his weakness for sleep. I had trouble simply accepting it. It seemed to be his addiction.

Just because he doesn't have to work at the mill on his days off, it doesn't mean he can do nothing, does it?

He would crawl out of bed around noon, smoke a joint after breakfast, and hang around reading and practicing guitar riffs. Sometimes he'd plunk away on his old banjo, usually out of tune. When did I get a day off? And if I did, I sure wouldn't waste it on sleep.

Maybe it was time to undertake a new house project. After talking about it for weeks, I finally bought some wall paint for the kitchen. *Good-bye yucky, greying flesh tone! Hello, nice taupe tone with white trim.* As long as I kept busy fixing the house, I had some purpose other than simply being a housewife or a mother.

I also planned on sewing some yellow, gauzy curtains for the kitchen windows. It would all look so much cleaner and fresher. Spring was coming. Vincent was coming. Someday soon, I hoped.

On Sunday morning, I brought Pete a large mug of tea, shook him gently, asked him nicely and even encouraged Ethan to jump on him. Trying to rouse Pete from his narcosis, his unconsciousness, his deep sleep, whether he had partaken of the herb the night before or not, was like trying to rouse a hibernating chunk of granite—dense, heavy and immovable.

"Come on Pete, let's get a move on," I begged. "I've made buckwheat pancakes, your favourite! There's still one left for you. We have to get over there. I promised we'd be there for brunch!"

"Yeah, OK, in a minute." He covered his head with the pillow and turned away.

"We don't get to see Dyeda and Baba very often," I pleaded. "Please, they're getting on, and she made your favourite veggie tarts: pyrahi with sauerkraut and the bean ones too!" I shook the blanket.

He groaned. "I'm way too tired, why don't you guys go? You could bring me some back—for later." He sank down and disappeared under the covers.

I stood there trying to understand. This seemed to be a habit—to sleep in when he didn't want to do something. Avoidance mechanism. But he usually loved visiting my grandparents. The Doukhobour food was a special treat. I was surprised he couldn't rouse himself.

"OK, fine. Damn you, Pete! Ethan and I will go on our own. You better be up when I get home, though! And please take the compost out when you finally crawl out of your womb! It's overflowing!"

I trudged out of the bedroom after shooing Ethan out and slammed the door behind me. I heard a low grunt then, "Yeah, sure."

Ethan and I had a lovely brunch with Baba and Dyeda. They tried to teach him some Russian words, such as sookonka (dishcloth), khleb, (bread) and chazka (cup). My grandma's kitchen was shipshape as usual. She ran it like a sergeant in the army. All the vegetarian food was tasty and fresh and cooked to perfection. As usual, before we left, she wrapped a bundle of Pete's favourite vegetable tarts in a white flour-sack dishtowel and then carefully filled a small cardboard box with goodies, including her specialty, a small jar of beet relish (vinaigrette).

"For da husband," she said, smiling widely. She gave us a hug and ordered Dyeda to walk the care package out to the truck with us. He deposited it carefully on the passenger side for our short drive home. I noticed his enlarged girth and gave him a timid hug. He looked a little like Santa.

"Baba feeds me too much!" he said, and rubbed the watermelon belly protruding from his center. We both laughed about this. He waved as I backed out of the driveway.

I thought about the dangers of my grandpa's belly. Baba made the best food, but Dyeda had recently recovered from a stroke. Wouldn't it have been safer to back off on all the salt, heavy butter, and cream dishes? But what the heck, he was getting on in years and he loved her food.

So perhaps the things we love can ultimately kill us. Loving something may not be reason enough to continue on, unless you are prepared to let other things go too. Like your health?

Turning into the driveway I noticed the lights were not on in the house. It was already three in the afternoon. It had been noon when Ethan and I left. I carried my parcel to the back door and then Ethan and I stumbled in, almost tripping over Pete's boots. The bedroom door was still shut.

Goddamn it, Pete! Enough is enough!

"Pete! Get the fuck up!"

I marched into the bedroom after hearing rustling sounds behind the bedroom door. I flipped on the overhead light and glared at the useless lump of flesh.

"Jesus, you didn't even take out the damn compost or sweep up! It's going to be time to go to bed in a couple of hours. Man, you need to get some help with this bloody sleep addiction! I may as well live by myself if we can't even share an occasional Sunday afternoon! What are you? A vampire?"

He started to sit up and then mumbled, "Settle down—fuck off and leave me alone! What's the big deal? It's none of your damn business!"

He picked up his rumpled jeans from the floor and started pulling them on. "So, did you bring me some of your grandma's treats?"

"Treats? Did I bring you treats? Yeah, I brought you some treats!"

I walked over to the package of fresh tarts and relish I had placed on the table in the kitchen, grabbed them and picked up the compost bucket from the counter. It was cumbersome but I managed to slip on rubber boots, open the back door, and walk across the sloppy garden. In one swift move I poured the entire rotting mess from the bucket onto the pile by the apple tree. I pulled out the still warm, fragrant tarts from their wrapping, ripped each of them in half, and tossed them onto the pile. The white dishtowel fell to the ground in a puddle shape. I opened the jar of magenta beet relish and poured the colourful mix over the mound. Diced green pickles, grated lime-green Granny-Smith apples, and sliced white onions highlighted the mix. So much texture. Almost like an oil painting. I threw the small jar and dirty dishtowel into the now-empty compost bucket and stormed back to the house, my boots making sucking sounds through the wet soil and leaving deep imprints.

Pete stood in the doorway holding Ethan, my dear boy, who was now sniffling and wide-eyed.

"Oh, baby," I said. "I'm so sorry. Sasha is not mad at you. It's okay. Don't cry."

Ethan reached out his arms and I carried him back inside, leaving Pete on the doorstep, arms crossed tightly over his chest.

At nightfall Pete went out on his own without saying a word. He left me alone in our bed while I pretended to sleep. I listened to Ethan's deep breathing. Pete quietly and slowly got dressed and tiptoed to the kitchen and locked the door behind him as he stepped outside. Click clack.

I heard his footsteps at the front of the house crunching on the roadway but refused to get up and stop him. I didn't even sneak a peek out the window. I let him go. Perhaps he needed a long walk.

Over the next few days, gangs of frisky ravens flocked to the special treats in the delicious dessert pile—fresh compost left for them by those silly humans. Ethan watched them from his stool under the kitchen window as they ripped apart and swallowed chunks of tender, rotting morsels, finishing off their meal with large mouthfuls of deep-red beets, which stained their beaks like lipstick.

Over the next week or so, Pete was a little softer, and we got along a bit better, but he still spent a lot of time sleeping.

Nothing I ever did seemed to change that.

Not until much, much later.

Just Be Here Now

While preparing a late supper, I decided life was pretty much a play. Like on a stage. Except the stage was the earth and all life played out on the earth. The rest could simply be props and my take on those experiences were the audience. Was I the lead actor, the writer, the director, and the audience?

And then there are those pesky emotions. Are emotions real or true? And what about love? Is love only an emotion or can it endure time and physical destruction?

I had recently read *Be Here Now* by Ram Dass and was trying to follow his philosophy but found it wasn't enough. It wasn't enough. Pete suggested my feelings could be a yearning for a God.

Did others have feelings like this? Yearnings for something more—something deeper, something true. And for a purpose.

Some days I thought seriously of joining a monastery. It had to be the right one though. I wasn't a Christian, after all. Nothing against Jesus, he was one of the first real activists after all and a cool dude to boot. It's simply the fact most Christians I met were hypocrites. For example: how could someone believe in the commandments like "thou shalt not kill" and still believe in war? Invading other countries and killing innocent civilians? Nope, did not jive!

Earlier, as I got out of the truck at JoAnne's place, the gallon jar I had brought for the milk rolled out and smashed in pieces on their concrete driveway. It took forever to sweep it up, and there were still hundreds of tiny shards left in cracks in the pavement, impossible to remove.

Night Terrors and Day Dreams

"Hey, will you get that? Please?"

The phone continued, dring, dring! I was busy making sandwiches. Ethan was screaming in the other room. Meanwhile Pete sat at the table, finishing a crossword puzzle from the local newspaper.

"And could you please take out the garbage before you leave for work?"

He stood up. "Oh, my God—don't have a heart attack or something. And don't worry, I'll be out of here in no time! I can't leave fast enough!"

Pete picked up the phone and answered politely. It was infuriating right then. I wiped my hands on my apron, picked up my screaming kid, and gave him a hug. Ethan had been teething lately and was flushed and cranky as hell.

Pete's face lit up. "Hi, Vince. Yeah, I'm good, man. How are things with you?"

I headed for the bathroom and removed a couple of baby Aspirin from the medicine cabinet then tiptoed over and tried to listen in without Pete noticing.

"Shhh. Shhh," I repeated, rocking Ethan in my arms.

He loved the sweet Aspirin and started to settle down right away. I wet a clean washcloth, sneaked back into the kitchen and threw it into the freezer for him to chew on later. Pete sauntered into the living room, dragging the phone cord behind him. I only caught bits of conversation and felt stupid following him around. Like I was spying.

Finally Pete plunked the receiver onto the cradle. I sat Ethan down on a rug in the living room and he immediately became immersed in a book, pointing out animals and muttering their names and inventing his colourful stories. I picked up the lunch kit full of healthy food I had prepared and held it out to Pete, a peace offering. "So?"

"So," Pete said, "they may be coming out in a few weeks."

"Who?" I asked, playing innocent.

"Vincent and Kathy! Who else?" His eyes drilled into me suspiciously.

"I'm so sorry," I apologized. "I get so damn bitchy when you have to work the night shift! I don't know why it is. It's like I feel trapped here when you leave. And every day there is so much to do before you go. I have to make your lunch and ..." I didn't tell him about my recent night terrors or the noises I had been hearing. He might not understand.

"Hey, don't do anything on my account. I can make my own damn lunch!"

Ha, what a lie. He hates making his own lunch!

"I know," I said, crossing the floor and tentatively reaching out for a hug. He'd be gone in a few minutes, and I'd be left alone. Except for Ethan, and he was only a child and couldn't rescue me from the dangerous, invisible demons which lurked outside.

Pete patted my back lightly then grabbed his green plaid jacket off the hook. Ethan got a quick kiss and then my man was off. I watched the truck drive away. Why was I so freaked out? The last couple of weeks I had been experiencing intense flashes of terror and dread at night, like there was something lurking or hiding outside the back door.

As the crimson, fading tails of truck lights disappeared into the night it was as if I was dropped into a deep dark hole — an emptiness nothing could fill.

And then I thought of the smile and the warm black eyes.

Nothing, except for Vincent.

❋ ❋ ❋

I bolted upright and pulled my covers tight. Strange rustling, scratching noises woke me from a light sleep. Someone or something was out there. Crunching and growling sounds, like footsteps, followed the scratchey noises.

Pete was still on his graveyard shift. I was totally alone. Ethan, sound asleep in his crib never woke to the bizarre sounds.

Much like a trapped hare or weak mouse, I was done for. An unspecified something was out there, trying to feed off me. A disturbing sensation overpowered me, like an emotional sucking, a gummy pulling. But no way was I going outside to check it out.

I tiptoed to the kitchen and silently yelled, "Fuck Off!" with all the strength and force of my mind. I was commanding it to leave. "Leave, damn you!" I had to fight it or it would eat me alive. There was no choice.

And if I did not fight it, would I go crazy? I was afraid to discuss this with just anyone. They might have thought I was losing it.

After grabbing a large kitchen knife, I returned to bed, and lay wide awake holding it with clenched fists, my hands turning white, until 3:00 a.m., when the invisible being finally retreated. It was like a vise loosened and I was free to breathe again.

I recalled an incident as a teenager, before nodding off. I still lived with Mum and family at the ranch and often woke in the night to the sound of heavy footsteps walking along the side of the house—only on the side where my bedroom was. Back and forth. Crunch, crunch, crunch—like a man in heavy boots. No one else ever heard it except for my cousin, Marty, who had lived in that house before we did and heard the same frightening sound. And only when he was alone.

My mom ended up talking to old Dr. C. who recommended a herbal tonic. It tasted vile and bitter and made me gag. It didn't make a bit of difference.

And now, I worried at night when I had to sleep alone in our tiny house. What if one night when I wasn't vigilant enough, what if one night an evil force lurking outside would somehow sneak in and hurt me and Ethan? Or possibly steal my soul?

Or mess with it somehow.

❁ ❁ ❁

The next day I decided to stop taking the pill. I threw them all into the garbage can. Enough was enough! My yeast infection had returned and I was so damned tired of having those out-of-body experiences. I was sure they were happening because of the strong hormones. Perhaps this was why I perpetually felt so anxious and went through these horrid night terrors. Whether the hormones came from pregnant mares' urine or not, it was all too freaky. I was so done!

I was also definitely done with old Dr. C. We totally lived in different realities and on different levels. We simply vibrated at different frequencies. I decided to try someone else.

Cool Dr. K, the new doc, told me I needed to make an appointment and get fitted for a diaphragm, which was kind of weird. Every woman was different, apparently and there were different sizes of cervixes. This was totally mind blowing. Who knew?

At the very least, I was taking a small but a real action and felt relieved. I bit of weight had been lifted from these bony shoulders.

❁ ❁ ❁

Occasionally I babysat for Leslie, a new friend from England. Leslie had a richness of facial wrinkles for her age. The spider lines and gouges spread around her eyes and grooved deep around her mouth, much like a contour map. She did smoke a lot of rollies and drank a lot of strong coffee in the daytime and far too much wine at night. This could have explained it. She was thirty-five, which was kinda old, but not that old.

Her little girl May was delightful and Ethan enjoyed her company so it all worked out. Why would anyone want to move to Twin Forks though, a small town in the middle of nowhere? From England of all places? Wasn't England quite exotic and full of old civilizations and history? Knights and swords, lords and ladies dancing. King Arthur and Shakespeare and all the culture. And The Beatles of course. Perhaps that was a different time. Stacey explained that she was sick of all the old "traditions" and customs in England.

"It's so bloody stifling. I can't breathe when I'm over there." She loved the laid-back vibes in this area.

Speaking of laid back vibes, one day we all took a trip out to Giles, a small village where a lot of hippies and draft-dodgers from the States had moved. A loose kind of commune had sprung up at the edge of town. The tiny village had become a magical, non-conformist haven of non-stop partying in the summer; folks partaking of the herb, strumming beat- up guitars and sharing home-made wine, playing volleyball and swimming in the deep jade waters of the river. And most walked around in the nude. After initially arriving at the beach to relax and enjoy a swim, I worried about how I must appear to others. I felt shy and embarrassed, but after some time luxuriating in the sun, playing water Frisbee and chatting with a family on their blanket next to us, I realized no one really gave a damn. No one stared or made insulting comments. We all had our bumps, warts and imperfections. It was so damned silly to have to conceal and clothe our bodies, especially when it was so hot outside.

I guess most people were raised with all the religious, uptight stuff about our bodies being sinful and having to permanently be covered! But, man, if you believe in any kind of a god, that is how he or she made us, isn't it? So why can't we simply accept that we are all perfect? Exactly as we are.

Well, perhaps some people *look* a little more perfect than others.

That evening, I sat outside and directly faced the exceptionally warm sun. The scene in front of me appeared in pieces like photographs printed on the back of my eyes. Like images from a movie—scenes captured in time and existing only because someone was observing them, that someone being me. Lately, I was also seeing energy patterns, swirls around living things such as the apple trees or vibrations off Ethan playing on the dirt road. They appeared as fuzzy halos or pale rainbows.

Is this a gift? Am I ill? Or am I losing my mind?

I didn't know, but usually feared the latter.

I tried to get up early most days, before Ethan, and do some yoga and meditate. But it rarely seemed to happen. Perhaps I lacked the discipline. And since stopping the pill, my body felt strange in a different way. My new body could be trying to merge with the old body, minus the hormones. I read somewhere we create new cells all the time; old cells die and new ones are constantly created. Then why do people stay sick and die from their illnesses?

So there must be a presence connected to our physical bodies that stays ill. Even if the body heals.

Perhaps an emotional or spiritual body.

Another mystery.

* * *

The last few months when Pete and I made love, I felt like I wasn't participating completely. There was no obvious physical reason. My yeast infections had cleared up and I even had a glass of wine first to loosen up, but I was watching what was going on from afar and analyzing it instead of losing myself in the experience. Possibly that's just how sex was supposed to be.

I had been wondering whether sex could be more of a spiritual experience than simply a physical release.

A deep, intimate connection, perhaps? Was sex for love or was it for pleasure? Maybe you had to be with exactly the right person for that.

We're not just animals, after all. Or are we?

Other than it being enjoyable, what was the whole point of sex if you were not trying to get pregnant and make babies?

Just a Housewife

"What do you mean you're just a housewife?" Pete called from the other room. "And so what if you are? Everyone has to do something!"

I was sweeping up the mud-spattered kitchen floor; the more I swept, the more the mud streaked. I threw the broom down with a whack and stomped into the living room where Pete was stretched out on the couch, finishing an article in a magazine.

"I'm so fucking tired of my role here, Pete!" My voice grew louder and now I was screeching. I untied my apron and threw it on the floor. Kahlil's precious words spilled out of the pocket and lay scattered on the floor. "I don't know how, but somehow I've ended up being this busy housewife and mother. Taking care of all your needs, Ethan's needs, keeping the house clean and cooking! And in the summer I end up having to do all the gardening and yard work and canning and on and on. Some days all I do is move objects from one part of this reality to another. I don't mind pulling my weight, but if this is all there is to life, I can't take it!"

Pete rose and stood staring at me, his eyes bulging, ready to flee.

"All I do is wash, wash, wash, wipe, clean, clean, clean, pick up toys, wash toys, wipe, wipe, wipe, sweep, mop, dust, wash, wash, wash, put things away, stack, fold, scrub, sort, wash, wash, wash, peel, chop, boil, fry, on and on and on..."

"Oh, my God, are you friggin' losing it?" Pete raised his eyes to the ceiling. "Fuck!" he muttered.

My voice grew shrill and loud but I couldn't stop. "I'm so afraid of becoming a dumpy, boring, conventional housewife who ends up physically and emotionally neglected by her husband. And by life! I never want to end up like those middle-aged women I see at the IGA, pushing their grocery carts full of crappy food, only thinking about what to make for dinner. They all look asleep. Their eyes are dead. You know what I'm talking about! Pete?"

Pete shrugged and shuffled back and forth. He was going to bolt at any second.

"Those poor old bags. They've traded their dreams and freedom for a sense of security. A wedding band and a roof over their heads. The bills paid. They've given up. I can see it." I gazed out the darkened window far across barren fields. "They've given up their dreams of a life full of exploration and adventure. And mystery. Where is the mystery? Now they're safe, but they're bloody bored out of their minds. I'll slash my wrists before I end up like that!"

He continued pacing, waiting for a break.

"Sorry, man!" I whined, suddenly realizing how horrible I must sound. "I don't know what's going on with me. Everything feels so irrelevant lately. Anything I do feels so bloody trivial. Anyone can do my 'job'!" Like would it actually matter if I disappeared?" I collapsed onto the living room floor and lay there, gazing up at the ceiling, tracing brown water stains on the textured tiles with tired eyes.

"Maybe it's from stopping the pill. My real hormones must be affecting my mental state. I don't know. I'm completely sick of everything."

"Sick of everything?" Pete repeated.

I kept staring at the stained tiles. "Yes, everything. And don't look so surprised. I'm sick of being here, stuck in Deadsville, sick of trying to be a good mother and make a nice home. Being a good little housewife doesn't make me happy. It's boring and meaningless. It's not what I want. I feel like I've taken the wrong path! And now it's too late. I have all these responsibilities. Shit." A deep, bottomless groan escaped my chapped lips. "I want more. I don't know what it is exactly, but there has to be more."

Pete slowly rubbed his tired eyes. "I have a roaring headache. I can't help you today. Sorry, I can't talk anymore. Can we take a break from all of *your* problems for a change?"

Barely hearing his voice, I whispered, "I need to do something creative. Something that will make a difference. Something satisfying."

"Well go ahead and do it then!" He crossed the carpet to the bedroom and slammed the door.

My tears released and flowed like spring run-off, soaking pinched cheeks.

I stayed on the floor for a couple of hours. After pulling a wool blanket over my chilled body, I fell into a meditative, dream-like state, a billowy place somewhere between being totally asleep and the drifting off place. Much like falling off a cliff in slow motion. I could hear the fridge motor grinding away in the next room, muted and far away, as if I had cotton stuffed in my ears. The sound of a car's tires on the distant roadway struck a deep chord and my heart flickered like a humming bird's while trying to break free, its tiny wings beating against cage walls.

Why do I feel so alone lately? I know many people here but don't feel connected to most of them. Pete understands me, sometimes. But I have to explain things over and over, and it's so bloody tiresome.

I nodded off and woke only when he got up to use the toilet in the middle of the night and tiptoed past. The floor squeaked as he padded by.

* * *

Silly arguments flared up all week. The next spat was about finding time for making love. We agreed to a night rendezvous in bed after all chores were done. As I was finishing in the kitchen, he came by to let me know time was running out.

"I'm getting tired. If we don't get started soon, it won't be any good," Pete said. He was leaning in the doorway, picking at a hangnail, bored and sleepy, at home with himself, slouching comfortably in his patched long johns and tattered, fuzzy slippers.

I lost it.

"Is this some kind of chore to get finished with so you can go to sleep?" Furiously, I threw the dishrag in the sink. It had started to smell cheesy and needed a good wash.

Pete cringed. "No, I didn't mean it like that!"

"Why do I even bother anyway? God, sometimes you are so fucking unromantic!"

And then the sparks flew.

"*I'm* unromantic?! You never approach me! Why do I have to be the one to make the first move? And when you do approach me, it feels like I have to service you or something. Where's the romance for *me*?"

"Service me? Is that how it is for you? You mean like the Maytag Repair Man?"

I fled into my favourite sanctuary. "Forget it, then. I don't need you. It's not worth it! Damn you, Pete!" I slammed the bathroom door and bolted it shut.

After a few minutes of utter silence, Pete tapped gently.

"I'm sorry, Sasha. I didn't mean all those things. I was mad. Please let me in. Sasha?"

I sobbed quietly, sitting on the frozen toilet. I finally unlatched the squeaky door and fell into his arms.

"I'm sorry, too," I said. " I can be such a bitch, I know. Forgive me?"

He looked surprised then led me to the bedroom, holding my icy hand lightly and carefully as if I were a small child.

"Let's go to bed, Sash," he murmured. "We're both just really, really tired."

Not Getting It

It was obvious there was something amiss in my partnership with Pete. Whenever I got to have a few brief moments of quiet when nothing was happening, the deathly silence and emptiness cast a cool gloominess, chilling me.

It hit me like a ton of bricks while preparing fried potatoes for dinner. I had meticulously peeled and sliced four large spuds into a ceramic mixing bowl, then spooned out Crisco into the fry pan, setting the heat to medium. I had thrown in a few tablespoons of butter for good measure. As soon as I threw those white, raw bits of potato flesh into the shiny black cast-iron pan, the hot mess started up. Spitting and splattering as soon as they hit the pan, repeating, over and over, "Spitter, spatter, spitter. What, why? What, why?"

I stirred and flipped them with the spatula then salted and covered them with the speckled enamel lid.

It gave me a few moments to stand and observe those talking spuds.

God, what the hell am I doing here, anyway? Why am I in Twin Forks? Why am I with Pete? And whose voice is in my head? A much wiser voice, but also a shit disturber from another place.

I lifted the lid off the frying pan to stir the spuds again and was still contemplating the meaning of the universe as a hot splatter jumped out and burnt a pea-sized circle on the top of my hand.

"Ouch! Damn it, this is no time to be dreaming, you silly girl!" I yelled to no one in particular.

Even after fifteen minutes under a stream of icy tap water, the tiny wound throbbed all night with excess heat and searing pain.

Fried spuds were no longer on our dinner menu.

❊ ❊ ❊

A few days later, Mike and his wife Betty, the midwife from the land co-op, were over for tea. I had nearly fully recovered from my recent meltdown. The four of us sat around rapping about the importance of having something to do in life that is creative or at least an expression of oneself. I tried to express how frustrating it was not to have something meaningful and creative to work on.

"I know what you mean," Betty said. "If I don't get any knitting or crocheting done in my day, it drives me crazy. I can't be only a maid, or whatever. However, someone has to take care of the little ones. The men have to work, after all. Someone has to pay the bills. For now, anyway." She smiled and adjusted a bobby pin in her hair, then pulled a loose thread in her clean but patched denim skirt.

"But you're a midwife; it's not full time, but I know you love your work. What would you like to do if you had more free time?" I asked.

She looked puzzled. "Actually, I don't know how the heck you have any time left over at the end of the day to worry about all this. With your gardening, the cooking, cleaning, and looking after Ethan and Pete?"

"I know! It's like a full time job!" I replied.

She still looked perplexed.

Pete and Mike started fidgeting, tapping their fingers on the kitchen table and adjusting the thin pillow pads on their chairs. They decided to leave their jasmine tea and headed outside to check on something. They mentioned truck problems, but I knew it was a bunch of BS. *Probably going for a toke.*

Betty didn't partake of the herb and got ticked off when Mike smoked in front of her. So off went the men. As they made their escape, Pete kept his eyes lowered, not looking at either of us. He shut the door quietly on his way out. I only felt envy.

When Betty got up to tend to her babe in the next room, I continued trying to express my discontent and confusion, making comments about the frustrations of the housewife role. She completely ignored me. I could hear her cooing and babbling as I stood in the kitchen, preparing a fresh pot of herb tea. I crumbled leaves of dried mint from last year's garden and dropped them into the glazed brown teapot with the chip on the spout. So, I had tried to share my feelings, but it hadn't made a bit of difference.

Betty didn't get me at all.

I yearned to be outside with the men, having fun and chatting. Joking around and talking about real things. Instead here I was, still stuck in the house, still trying to be a good little hostess and pretending to be interested in tedious, domestic things.

As the weeks flew by, I continued to feel extremely tired, disinterested and fatigued. Nothing seemed to satisfy me. *What is it I want?*

I loved books and had long been searching in them for answers, but the answers weren't there. Their wisdom and advice sounded good on first readings. But only a few days later I was back in the same place.

Nothing sticks, or not anything I can feel. Or see.

Pete and I survived another tedious co-op meeting. I usually prayed they would end early. This time the prickly energy was thick and you could cut the tension with a butter knife. No serious meltdowns went down and all were civil and polite, but there was a difference. Now that Hannah and

Gary were officially a couple, the co-op needed to find another person, or pair, to buy into the deal. And find them fast.

One or two more suckers...oops, what am I thinking? These are all very nice people I'll be sharing a hundred acres with, out in the middle of nowhere.

While we sat in a large circle, and listened to everyone's concerns about how to recruit more members so we could pay the next mortgage, and how many folks could get out to the land to do some fencing the next weekend, and all of the surveying problems, and who will please take the minutes, I snuck away to the bathroom and hid there as long as possible. Hopefully no one could read my mind, but in my opinion, the entire co-op thing seemed to be crumbling.

Of course I felt like a traitor. Curiously, part of me hoped it would crumble. One especially serious issue I hadn't considered when joining the co-op continued to nag. I was afraid to bring it up. Wouldn't bad feelings erupt when the hunters in the group killed those cute little prairie dogs and wide-eyed deer for meat right in front of the vegetarians? I for one, would definitely feel sad and resentful having to watch some innocent critters being slaughtered for food when we were surrounded by veggies, grains, roots, fruit, nuts and seeds. There was so much to eat, what was the reason for having to kill, to terminate a life early? Habit? Belief you would end up unhealthy, grow sick and die? The taste?

I've had trouble thinking about these gruesome killings, never mind seeing them happen in front of my face. This issue of what is okay to eat was always troublesome.

I felt like I belonged to a strange and unusual cult. The cult of non-meat eaters.

Working It Out

Pete and I finished putting up the ceiling tiles in the new addition. The small room was to be for Ethan, our new-old baby who was nearly three. It had taken a couple of years to purchase the long list of expensive building supplies. All of those 2x4s, plywood and drywall, flooring and paint cost us a few pennies. How had lumber become so expensive? We were surrounded by thousands of miles of trees.

But we needed more room; it had become way too claustrophobic in our tiny house with only the living room and kitchen to hang out in.

On any given day toys covered most of the floor. One morning I nearly twisted my ankle after stepping on a miniature car. It was on the edge of a large field of colourful Lego building blocks and I was hurrying, as usual, to turn down the bean-and-barley soup simmering on the stove. One minute I was trucking along, my feet on solid ground, and the next minute my right foot stepped on a rigid object, slid for about three feet and gave out from under me. I fell backwards and landed with a thump on my bottom. It was sore for a couple of days but luckily the ankle survived. Not the little toy roadster though. It was totally smashed. Sadly, it was Ethan's favourite.

Surprisingly, I totally enjoyed putting up the ceiling tiles: picking them out of the cardboard box on the floor, climbing the aluminium ladder one step at a time, and popping them into place. One by one, row by row, the entire ceiling got done. I could neither hurry nor worry about how it would look when finished. It was good to slow down for a change and actually be in present time, moving my arms and hands to place the tiles in their perfectly allotted home.

Climbing up and down the ladder was a good workout, too. Pete, of all people, the one who rarely broke into a sweat, mentioned that perspiring was healthy.

"It cleans out your toxins," he insisted.

I imagined sweaty secretions, like tiny rivers, carrying away all the nasty poisons from hidden caverns in my body where they lurked, creating ill health and chaos. I imagined those cleansing rivers bringing dangerous toxins to the surface of my skin.

And finally I envisioned washing them all away in a cool, clear bath.

The physical work had been good for me. The next day, I was able to hold my busy mind in the present moment for longer periods of time. Perhaps I was beginning to spend more time in the here and now. Every single moment could be fulfilling, no matter what I was doing.

In the evening I got to put my feet up and sit in the rocker and read *Truth Journal.* It was free and arrived once a month in the mail. In this issue, Roy Eugene Davis talked about how negative thinking was a waste of energy.

Of course it is. Right on, brother.

I had been working on trying to stop the old groove of negative thinking. All the complaining in my head was a waste of time. But how to stop it? Almost impossible. It was an addiction. I tried to observe those thoughts when they came up, and not to react to them. What I was thinking seemed to make a small difference. Labelling it positive or negative didn't seem to help either. The key was noticing the thought, but not getting upset or judging it but, simply accepting it as "negative thinking" or seeing it as just my thoughts. Paying attention to how I reacted to my thoughts seemed the most important thing. How much of my thoughts are true or "real" anyway? I knew my fears were flaming a train of negativity.

Just notice. And notice what you notice. It sounded so damned simple. But it was so painful and so tedious. My ability to focus was messed up.

After the last big co-op meeting Pete and I had a serious rap. Each of us had done some deep thinking and were both feeling anxious about whether we could cut it with some of the folks. Pete was also concerned about the meat-eating thing—not specifically about people eating the flesh of dead critters but more about the killing of animals on the land. Either way there were going to be hard feelings.

Although we didn't have to be part of the killing, we would have to witness it. If these hunters were going to be casual neighbours a ways down the road it would be different, but this was going to be a closed community, like a family. We would be living only about one hundred feet apart.

It had come up before. The hunters and meat eaters felt they should be able to "harvest" whatever was there. I had stayed silent. How I hated the word. Harvest. As though creatures were agriculture, planted there on purpose by invisible farmers, like potatoes or carrots that needed to be dug out of the ground and stored in the root cellar. I believed these animals were live, sentient beings, much like humans, with a life and emotions and a will and families of their own.

They feel pain and fear as much as we do! And what if one of the hunters was not a good shot with the rifle or bow and arrow, and accidentally shot someone?

As time went by it was painfully obvious I would have to be the one to bring up this prickly issue. No one else would touch it with a ten-foot pole. My stomach stayed permanently knotted. It was a showdown I dreaded even more than most.

❋ ❋ ❋

Vincent called right after 11:30 on a night when Pete was working late. I was still troubled about the co-op and it was great to hear his voice.

"What's happening?" he asked. "You sound kind of bummed out."

"Oh, I'm fine, I guess," I replied. "Was thinking about the land co-op. You know about the meat-eating thing?"

"Oh, for sure. It would be a difficult one to get used to. I could probably handle it, but I know how sensitive you are." His voice got quieter.

"Yeah, I wish I wasn't, but watching a Bambi get shot in front of me might be a deal breaker. I don't know what we're going to do. Hannah and Gary may be leaving, so we're looking for two more people…or a couple." I stopped breathing. "Are you and Kathy still interested?"

"Oh man, of course we are. But it would mean leaving this area. I love the ocean. I'd miss it. My contract ends this spring, so we'll see. We'll try and make it out there soon— meet the group and all. Being on call is the shits, and they keep changing my hours." Vincent worked at a group home for addicts and the mentally ill.

"Yeah, OK. Sounds great, give me a little notice when you guys know."

I heard a rattling noise in the background.

"Yeah, for sure," he said. "Well, I should go. Kathy made her famous noodle casserole and I had to work late, so she's warming it for me now. Take care, my good friend. We'll talk soon. Love you."

"Ah, yeah, of course, you'd better go. Say hi to Kathy."

"'Bye," he said. He put the phone down gently. I heard the sound of a click then a lonely hum on a dead line. I held the plastic earpiece in my trembling hand.

My heart was in my mouth, and my mind was spinning. He had said "Love you," but he called me his good friend. So I'm a good friend who he loves? It didn't feel like a good friend kind of conversation. His voice was too warm, his words too understanding.

It's like he gets me.

But then his voice turned suddenly distant and he had to go. Then there was Kathy.

And there would forever be Kathy.

What the hell is the matter with me? I slammed the receiver down and headed into the living room to find something, anything mindless to watch on TV.

Valentine's Day

Saturday evening started out casually enough at our house, sharing a few beers with Sam and Lizzie. But only half an hour in, we got into some pretty weird conversations. Sam had been contemplating the idea of a group marriage thing. I never would have guessed. One never knew what the heck he was thinking or what wheels were turning behind those emerald green eyes. Sam was usually relatively calm and down to earth.

What do they say about still waters running deep?

Pete was as stunned as I. "Well, what would be the point of that?" he asked. "I think having a relationship with one person is quite enough, thank you, and sometimes so bloody exhausting—why would I want to?"

He caught me glaring at him. "I mean…"

I let it go.

"Well, it's not like you'd go and pick someone up," Sam said. "It would have to be someone you cared about." He ran his fingers through his slightly receding brown hair. A bit of grey already showed in his fuzzy, Elvis sideburns.

"I don't know." I started clearing up the russet brown beer bottles. "It seems a little too crazy. You'd truly have to have your shit together. You couldn't be jealous or petty or anything." I thought of Vince then shook it off as I stashed the bottles in a cardboard box beside the stove. They clattered and crashed.

"Yeah, I know, I didn't mean you or anything," Sam said. "But it might be possible—with the right person."

"Seems like too much fuckin' work for me," Lizzie said, and dug into her worn, black leather purse for another smoke. Her thick, blunt bangs hung in her eyes, hiding the deepening furrows in her forehead.

Sam stood up and grabbed his corduroy jacket. "Damn," he said, "How about we forget all this crazy talk and go to the bar and have a few beer!"

Twenty minutes later we had landed a babysitter and were out the door. Three hours and six beers later, I was feeling no pain. And no jealousy either. Until Lizzie, drunker than usual, pulled Pete out of his chair and dragged him onto the dance floor.

So he can dance after all.

My old, but not necessarily trusted friend, the green monster, hiding under surface layers of murky denial, poked me sharply in the heart.

Still, the place was hopping and the rhythm-and-blues band was decent, so it was a nice break from the regular routine. I enjoyed myself once the beer did its work and didn't feel quite so high strung or neurotic after a couple of cool ones. I couldn't imagine drinking a lot on a regular basis, though. The hangovers were too painful for those of us with sensitive nerves.

About an hour before closing when I was having the most fun, Pete sat down and proceeded to get into a big political discussion with the bartender Mitch, about the present federal tax system.

"It seems to favor the wealthy getting wealthier on the backs of the poor working stiffs." He blustered.

I kept trying to get his attention so we could share a dance, but Pete only said, "Yeah, in a minute," and kept ranting on.

I sulked and sat guzzling my beer, all the while pretending everything was fine, trying to block the cheerful, loud chattering going on around me. I picked at the markings on the tabletop with my fingernails—messages left for loved (or now unloved) ones. "GS loves AL" and so on. Encased in hearts and arrows. *Shit! And it's Valentine's Day!*

"Damn you, Pete, I may as well go home!" I stood up and was starting to put on my winter coat when a strong arm grabbed me.

"Hey, where are you off to? There's still a set left!"

I turned to face Sam who was flushed and warm from dancing. His eyes were glassy and reflected the lights of the low stage. "Take off your coat and dance a few with me," he asked. "Please?"

He removed the coat from my hands and led me gently to the rectangular dance floor, now tacky with dried booze, melted snow and road salt.

"Where's Liz?" I asked. "Aren't you two going to need a ride home?" I had looked around earlier and couldn't see her. It it wasn't long before I forgot about Pete and Lizzie and all my aching problems. I grooved out to the music, sliding and twisting to the slick rhythms, letting my body enjoy the beat, letting it run through and energize me.

Sam grinned the entire time, his attention focused on me. He saw me. Feeling his stare felt good for a short while, but after a couple of songs, I began to feel a little naked, a little weird, being the recipient of all that intense focus. Perhaps I'd sit out the next one.

As the song ended, he took two steps over and gave me a warm hug. Shit, it was too warm. It felt clammy, not clean, and I pulled back.

I spied Lizzie. Was it Lizzie? Yes, it was. She was locked in an embrace which looked a little too intimate. She was wrapped around a skinny man, rubbing her plump thigh up and down his leg. Who the hell *was* the guy? Well…that was *my* guy. That guy was damned Pete!

The rest of the night was spent in a long, dragged-out fight as Pete tried to convince me they were only horsing around, playing, trying to make Sam and me jealous.

Well, they sure did a good job of it! It wasn't April Fool's Day, after all! It was Valentine's Day! The bastard.

Lizzie laughed and told me to lighten the fuck up. I had always wanted to lighten up, but those kinds of antics were not going to help.

Sam said nothing, except, "It's going to be OK." And patted me gently on the back.

I was so bloody mad at Pete I slept on the lumpy, fold-out couch all night and woke up with severe neck pain and a headache.

Valentine's Day would never be the same for me. It had lost its sweet, syrupy, fluffy hearts-and-flowers spirit after that disturbing night.

I never realized before how jealous I could be—or how painful jealousy could be. And over Pete and Lizzie of all people!

Fitting

While waiting in the doctor's office, I began thinking about how I could make some of my own money. I could start my own business or perhaps do more babysitting, or do something, anything, to make some cash.

How about silk-screening erotic pictures on bed sheets? How about on very expensive, good quality silk or cotton. It could be the new "in" thing!

My own true hormones must be kicking in again and getting back to normal.

After waiting an extra forty minutes in the waiting room, I finally got into the doc's office and was fitted for a contraceptive diaphragm. The diaphragm was definitely an awkward little piece of soft rubber to be shoving up my delicate parts. It looked like a miniature flying saucer! How was I supposed to take this seriously? But hey, it was supposed to work and, like most contraceptives, it apparently worked if you used it.

My new regular doctor had an emergency to attend to, and I was seen by a substitute who was outrageously good looking and had a dazzling smile. He was gentle yet so sure of himself. His hands were large, beautiful, strong and confident. And he smelled divine—a clean, alluring scent. Kind of like Old Spice. But new, not old.

Was I bad, or was I Bad?

He was also totally compassionate and seemed sincerely concerned about my low iron levels. He recommended making another appointment to discuss this with my new doctor. "Of course, I said."

And forgot about it right away.

As I drove home from the clinic, the sunlight reflected off the car ahead of me, and I had a flash: the land co-op had only one real agreement and it was the land. It wasn't as if a group of people with similar values, needs or goals got together and decided to share a piece of land in a cooperative way. It wasn't even a group of close friends. It was only a group of individuals looking to live on a big piece of glorious wilderness. We all imagined how groovy it would be to live in a sharing, co-operative space, but no one actually knew what it meant. There was no real guidebook. Now that it was trying to come together, it didn't seem to be working. It wasn't at all like I expected. I wasn't even sure I liked most of the people involved.

Maybe I just don't like most people.

Finally, at the annual land co-op meeting, after discussing and debating how best to find new partners for the group, I got my courage up and raised my concerns about the killing of animals on the land.

Slowly I raised my trembling arm. But I was determined—it was now or never.

"I hate to bring this up today. I don't want to bum anyone out, but it's been nagging at me and I have to speak."

All faces turned to me. I felt like throwing up.

"Well, I was thinking…what would happen if one of the hunters shot a deer in front of our house—it would be quite upsetting and traumatic for me, never mind Ethan or any other kids we had…I mean, could we have some ground rules? How about no hunting on the property. Or? I don't know. Any suggestions?"

Everyone looked stunned. No one expected this from "quiet little Sasha," who never spoke up about anything. The group spent an entire hour debating the pros and cons, most agreeing folks should be allowed to "harvest" what comes onto the property. They decided to table it until the next meeting when it became obvious this was a hot topic.

Before the meeting broke up, Betty, of all people, reacted with a lot of hostility, letting us know this was not a problem for her. She was a fellow vegetarian yet glared at me as she spat out her words.

"We all have to be tolerant of others if we expect to live on a piece of land together!"

Surprisingly, Matt and Elaine, the hunters, who actually did live off the land—trapping, hunting, and fishing—and permanently walked around in buckskin and moccasins, were the most understanding and compassionate. They came over after the meeting ended and gave me a warm hug.

"I know it's a drag," said Elaine, "but we do have to talk about all this shit."

Later as I was helping tidy up, I walked into the kitchen and overheard Betty and Sissy hissing about something, their snaky heads down. When I entered, they quickly glanced over at me and then pretended to be washing and drying the stacks of dirty dishes.

Come on, you don't have to pretend nothing is wrong.

You don't have to ignore me, either.

Old Friend

March crept in like the lion it was, roaring with heavy rains for weeks and weeks. Most of the snow disappeared off the roads and the days stayed lighter, longer.

Pete was still on graveyard shift. We both hated it. He went to work at night and came home early in the morning when I was getting up, groggy and not conversational. I never rested properly and usually got an erratic night's sleep. After a long shift, Pete was irritable too and even though he could crash anywhere, it must have totally screwed with his internal clock.

I ran into an old friend from Junior High School in the dairy section of the I.G.A. Lynette was reaching for a pint of cream. We used to be the fringe intellectuals and rejected the popular girls with all their trivial concerns about runs in their stockings and the latest hairdos. We were extremely opinionated and wrote for the school newspaper. Of course this had all changed when I moved to the coast and had my major teenage meltdown. She had moved away to Kamloops, so we lost touch after Grade 9.

Lynette set the pint of cream into her grocery cart. We hugged briefly. "Last I heard you were hitchhiking all over the country!" she laughed. Her smile could still light up anyone's brooding heart.

"I was on a wild journey for a while, that's for damn sure. Finally I hitched up with Pete, and now we're settled down and have a boy who's almost three! Pete works at the mill. And you? Have you moved back to town?"

"No, just here for the weekend. I'm finishing up my law degree, so I have to get back to my studies at UBC. In Vancouver! It's so much bloody work, my brain hurts!" Lynette sighed and touched her temples.

We both laughed.

I immediately felt a twinge of envy. *Shit. That is what I should be doing. Or something like that.*

"Well, let's try and get together before you head back." I said, finding a pen and a scrap of paper in my purse. "Here's my phone number. Make sure and call me. It'll be great to catch up!"

Lynette seemed eager to reconnect and we parted, joking about how the ability to make a good pot of borscht was actually the most important thing to accomplish in one's lifetime.

I listened for the ring of the phone all afternoon and tidied up the house, hoping Lynette would call. The phone never rang all weekend. By Sunday evening it was obvious that my old friend was not going to call. I thought of her often, but we never reconnected or saw each other again.

The next night, eager for more information about how to get rid of anxiety and negative thinking, I attended a promo meeting at the library for a Silva Mind Control workshop, a self-help therapeutic technique designed by a dude called José Silva. It was supposed to use guided imagery to rewire negative grooves in one's brain. It all sounded interesting but way too expensive at $195.

I drove home in a blue funk after trying to figure out how to come up with so much cash. I didn't even bother to ask Pete if we could afford it.

❋ ❋ ❋

On Saturday night we headed out to see Pied Pumpkin at the Legion. They finally made it to Twin Forks. A lot of the co-op folks showed up. Most shared a joint or two in the gravel parking lot, which was surrounded by half a dozen great maples, their tiny, tentative red buds still waiting for more spring warmth. Tall, stately fir trees stood on either side of the hall like ageing custodians guarding the fort. The pale yellow lamplight of a spring moon hung casually above the distant mountains. All of us bathed in its glow before heading in to share cheap, green beer on tap and sit around circular tables covered with stained red-checkered tablecloths.

I made sure to sit by the door. The smoke from stogies and cigarettes was far too strong, constantly catching in my throat. A choking haze filled the entire room.

One of the roadies opened a door at the back along with a couple of the large-screened windows and shouted: "If you get chilled, get up and dance!"

And we were ready for it. The high-energy fiddle and guitar music took folks out of their everyday bullshit. For a few hours, the entire room had fun.

Sam came by after his shift at the mill and sat with us for about half an hour. He asked me to dance and of course I said yes. Pete sat at a back table and watched, his eyes shining black in the dim lights of the dark room.

The Indigos

If you can tell me what is death, then I will tell you what is life.

In a field I have watched an acorn, a thing so still and seemingly useless. And in the spring I have seen that acorn take roots and rise, the beginning of an oak tree, toward the sun.

- Kahlil Gibran

Another weekend came and went. Time was slipping casually through my fingers. I was growing old much too quickly.

I was going to turn 22.

One night I had a dream about dying. In it, I had only three months to live and went from moments of deep despair to highly illuminating episodes with a group of unusual looking children. All had milky indigo- blue eyes and silver white hair. They held hands and ran and giggled and played in radiant wildflower fields. At the end of the dream, I was not afraid or sad and accepted the fact of dying, which was revealed to me by one of the children. Without moving her mouth, without words she said, "It's going to be OK. Nothing ever really goes away, it just changes."

Upon awakening, I realized everyone was going to die a physical death at some point and there was no need to freak out about it.

Why am I so anxious all the time then? Perhaps I'm more afraid of truly living than I am of dying.

I listed all of my fears in my journal:

> *Afraid of the future, afraid of not succeeding, afraid of failure and terrified of rejection and abandonment. Perhaps more afraid of my own bright light, if I ever found it. Of being noticed, of standing out, of actually being seen.*

What if I don't measure up? And what if no one loves me in the end?
What if I get left behind? What if I have to spend my life alone?

Living is so bloody complicated.
Dying is a much easier concept to live with.

Laid Off

"Are you kidding?" I screamed. "That's great! Let's celebrate!"

Pete returned home early with good news. He was getting laid off. Again. Of course I was glad he was getting a respite from the brutal work. But not glad for the lack of cash. *This may become a problem.* I pushed down that specific worry. For now, anyway.

Lizzie had stopped by for tea, and I put the kettle on to freshen the pot.

"Yeah," Pete said. "Hopefully, I have enough weeks to get UI. It'll sure be a nice break from the old slave chain!" He dropped his lunch kit on the counter. "I'm going to wash up and crash. I'm beat."

He headed for the bathroom, glancing at Lizzie for a brief second. "Hi ya, Lizzie. See you next time."

"I wish *I* could get on pogie for a few months. Shit." Lizzie droned, "But I don't get enough bloody hours at the hotel." She lit another cigarette.

I turned my chair sideways to avoid breathing in the chemical-laden fumes.

"It's been on my mind lately, I really want to get a job to help out. It would be great to get out of the house. Since quitting the pill I've been having all these weird symptoms. And my period was a week late this month! I thought for a minute I was actually pregnant; damn, that would have been fun, eh?" I imagined myself with another toddler to chase after. "I don't even feel hungry lately. I don't know what the heck is going on. I usually feel OK in the daytime but by evening feel like crap!"

"Oh, jeez," Lizzie said, waving her hand at me. "Have a beer and another toke! It works for me!" Her laugh, deep and husky, echoed off the walls and appliances. If we did happen to have a puff, the two of us would be laughing our heads off for the entire morning.

Pete finally came out of the bathroom and shuffled across the kitchen floor and glared at us. “What’s so damned funny?”

Lizzie winked at him. “Don’t worry, Pete. We’re not talking about you, big boy. Go to bed! I’m visiting with my sister.”

The joking and laughter continued long after Pete had passed out in our bed.

Initially, I used to love it when Pete was laid off. The pressure was off for all those domestic duties I had grown to hate more and more. How did women manage to raise more than one child at a time? I had only one, but it was becoming clearer to me I wasn’t cut out to be a typical housewife.

When Ethan had to stay inside during those short spring days, he would get cabin fever and would end up antsy and cranky. He’d frequently pull at his jacket from the hook by the doorway and pleadingly repeat, “Outside? Outside? Outside?”

I got where he was at.

Outside in March was definitely where it was at.

We got outside the next weekend. All the melting snow had formed little brackish lakes. Ethan and I put on rubber boots, found a couple of sticks from behind the garden shed, and spent hours digging away and creating little canals to help the water drain off the driveway. It was a hell of a lot of fun.

I felt like a kid again, and in the evening ate a filling supper and slept soundly through the entire night.

It was such a welcome break from the heaviness and sleepless carbon black nights of winter.

How precious the small joys, how deeply they are missed when gone.

Mice and Men

It wasn't long before the blasted mice returned. We ended up entirely overrun by them. Their shit appeared on the counters every single morning. It was disgusting. I made sure to wipe everything down before going to bed, but their little presents always appeared before dawn.

We heard them in the walls at night, scurrying about, scraping, scratching, and scampering through the dark tunnels they had created, reproducing batches of tiny pink rodents in their messy nests. They got into my oats again. Being obsessive about filth, I again threw out the entire box.

They eat anything that isn't in glass or concrete.

I hated to exterminate them, but it was time to get some real mousetraps, not those useless live ones. Our mice were far too smart for those humane traps. We had tried them earlier in the year and they were a failure as well as a waste of time. We hated to slaughter the little buggers but had no choice. And it wasn't healthy—we had a toddler in the house.

Damn it! Now we would have to listen to those traps in the middle of the night: Snap! Snap! Snap!

Someone had to clean those traps, too. I couldn't do it. Old Pete would have to be The Man: remove the mouse corpses, throw the little mangled bodies into paper bags, and carry them outside to the garbage can.

I did start to wonder though—how slaughtering the nuisance mice was any different from my problem with the folks in the co-op wanting to kill deer, squirrels, rabbits, and other varmints for their food? Different reasons, but it was still killing. *Killing is killing, isn't it? Shit.*

Sometimes I feel like such a fucking hypocrite, I thought, while filling the wooden, spring-loaded guillotines with small chunks of cheddar cheese and dried morsels of peanut butter.

* * *

Toward the end of March Mother Nature teased us, as she does every year, with the promise of summer, with the smell of wet loam and mysterious blends of eastern zephyrs scented with the freshness of melting snow. Hordes of blackbirds, starlings, ravens and large crows started hanging out around the gnarly apple tree and the fermenting compost pile. Fat, leathery worms which had survived the harsh temperatures of winter and been saved by the underworld heat and safety of rotting compost, were now pulled out and gobbled up by those hungry birds.

Ethan was amazed by all our feathered friends and liked to stand on his wooden chair by the kitchen window to watch their fearless antics as their azure ebony feathers gleamed in the sunshine.

One morning he said, "There is a cat!" ten times in a row.

I looked out to where he was pointing. He had spied Bear's cat walking on the fence. Aha! So Buddy, Bear's scrappy old tom, had returned from whence he had disappeared.

Since Felix bit the dust and Nasty disappeared, I rarely saw Bear and Jane and their boy outside. They seemed to have holed up in their house for the winter. A murky gloom permeated their entire back yard. The sad weeping willow tree cast dark, flickering phantoms across their back door. Their roller shade was usually down and frayed curtains drawn.

Still, summer was coming. I could feel it in my bones. My appetite had returned and for some strange reason I was feeling calm and emotionally normal.

Whatever that was.

Brad and Jenna

Brad and Jenna stopped by on their way back from the coast and ended up joining us for an early dinner.

"I do miss this valley, you know," Brad mumbled as he slathered more butter on the grainy rye bread fresh out of the oven and still warm to the touch. "I definitely miss the climate. It's pretty grey and damp in Nelson in the winter. Gets a little dreary some days."

I was surprised. "Yeah? That would suck. But isn't it a much more hip place—with more modern thinking? And they certainly have a neat downtown scene! Lots of cool, artsy new shops and fresh ideas. And more interesting people, eh?"

Brad brushed the hair back off of his forehead. "Well, yeah, this is true. More far out, I guess." He looked mystified. "It's almost too far out, too funky lately. Lots of ungrounded folks living for today. Deadheads, peace freaks, enviros, draft dodgers. I know this is happening most places, even here in Twin Forks, but there it's really exploded. It's freaky."

Pete looked up from his bowl of soup. "And that's a bad thing...how?"

"Well, like I said. Some folks are a little too spacey and unfocused. Unbathed, hippie folk with their dogs and teepees moving into the area, arguing with the loggers and rednecks about how many trees should be cut!" He laughed. "Don't get me wrong. I'm anti-establishment for most things, but I certainly don't see myself as a hippie. A lot of these freaks appear to be lost. Or confused."

I gagged and nearly choked on my bread. Because Pete and I were quite certainly hippies. And lately I was pretty confused.

Brad carried on. "But hey, speaking of spacey, how is the co-op doing? When are you guys moving out to the land?"

We knew Brad was not a big fan of the Wild Meadows Land Co-op. He thought Pete and I were wasting our time and money. He'd told us this many times. He also heard recently about Gary and Hannah moving in together and that the co-op was on shaky ground.

Pete looked at me across the table. "Not great, to be honest," he said. "There are some problems to be solved, for sure."

Jenna put down her soup spoon and dabbed her immaculate mouth with my linen-hemp dinner napkin. A special gift from my Russian great aunt. Hemp napkins from the old country.

"Well, neither of us is surprised," Jenna said, after a deep sigh. "They're all a little..."

Brad cut her off gracefully, his perfectly arched eyebrows raised. "Immature? They're all a little immature! And irresponsible. All of them, except for Hannah and Gary. I totally understand your reservations about the whole thing. We were tempted to sign up when it first got started, but after I met a few of the members..." He shook his neatly trimmed head, "Ah...no. No."

"Well, it's good to hear this from someone else," I said. "I know something is not quite right. But I'm not sure exactly what it is." I exhaled, feeling more relieved.

So I'm not the only one.

Brad looked over at me, frowned and continued. "When it comes down to the real work, no one is going to pull their load! Lots of people with stars in their eyes. And this is all fine to have a vision or to be idealistic, but you have to have your feet planted on the ground, man! Who is going to do the heavy lifting?" He lifted an imaginary something. "You can't all simply move out to the middle of nowhere in the woods and set up a shack!"

He scraped his bowl with the soup spoon. “All of you are going to have to find a way to survive and live out there, which is a hell of a lot of work. You can only log so many trees. And no one will have power for a few years, either. Unless you buy a generator—and they're expensive.” He wiped his fingers on the napkin and started waving them around. “A lot of those young dudes and chicks are city folks who don't have a clue what it means to live off the main grid. What's going to happen when they run out of firewood in the middle of winter? Who's going to hike out and cut down and buck a larch tree with three feet of snow on the ground? How many of them can even operate a chain saw? Or build a shelter? Only a few of those folks even know how to garden.”

He shook his head. “Are they going to be driving the thirty miles into town whenever someone needs a bar of soap? Who is going to do all that needs doing?”

Jenna nodded along in agreement. She was from New York, now lived in a nice apartment, and liked her creature comforts.

Brad finished his soup and patted his lips. The rest of us had let him carry the conversation and hadn't said a word as we wiped up the soup in our bowls with crusts of bread.

Brad ended his rant. “Remember last spring when I lent tools to Ray? Well, I may as well have thrown them away!” He piled his silverware into his bowl and threw his napkin on the pile. “When he finally returned my cross-cut saw and crowbar, they were rusted, and the saw was so damn dull, I threw it out! Damn! And besides, some of those funky dudes are not easy to get along with!”

He grinned at me, as if he knew what I was thinking, “And you may have noticed some personality problems there. No offense to anyone, but there are a few putzes and doofuses in that bunch." He sat back in his chair, smiled and patted his stomach. "Thanks Sasha, great meal!"

They all nodded in agreement. I thought of Sissy. *A little too bossy for me. Usually in my face and trying to lead the meetings and have her way.*

Later, over homemade apple sauce and freshly made yogurt, Brad insisted he meant no harm to anyone specifically in the co-op. He hadn't hit it off with everyone in the group. Except for us and Gary and Hannah, he didn't connect. Everyone got it.

After they left, my stomach ache returned and my head started to pound.

"Why the hell is it every time we talk about the co-op, I end up with a stomach ache? Are we doing the right thing here? I don't know anymore."

"I don't know either," Pete said. "Maybe you're right. We don't have to move out there. We could simply stay here in our little shanty. It's not so bad, is it?"

We called it a night and hit the hay.

I smoked a lot of homegrown in the spring. It was one thing that did agree with me. It slowed down time and usually enabled me to enjoy whatever it was I was doing, even if it was simply washing the dishes.

For about a week in mid-April I rode a wave of gratitude and felt positive and glad to be alive for a change. A welcome respite The preceding dreary weeks had been a struggle; it took all my effort to come up with even two or three things daily to be grateful for.

I was finishing *The Crack in the Cosmic Egg*, which basically said that we create our own reality and that if we believe certain things strongly enough, they will become real to us.

It all sounded good, but I wasn't sure how true it was.

And besides, how could you prove that?

Dinner at Hannah's

"Where is he?" she asked, open, childlike face aglow, eyebrows arched. Hannah and Gary were two of my favourite people and had invited Pete and me to dinner. She also had a little crush on our Ethan and loved to spend time with him at co-op meetings, teasing and chasing him around while he screeched and laughed.

"Soooo very sorry," I apologized. "I left him with Mum tonight!" And hung my head in mock shame.

I could have brought him. But damn, I needed a night off.

My neck muscles started tightening and I stretched my head slowly to the side to ease the discomfort.

Hanya Banyana, as she was called, enjoyed children's company as much as anyone else's. Sometimes she dressed and even talked as if she were five, wearing psychedelic pink sweaters, white folded ankle socks, and sateen ribbons in her hair. Being short and tiny added to the effect.

Throwing her thick, cocoa brown, waist-length braids behind her, she gestured with her arms towards the foyer. "Well, then enter you two, you'll just have to do!" she said, and rolled her eyes theatrically.

Gary poured each of us a grey ceramic goblet of homemade cherry wine and we spent the rest of the evening eating homemade veggie pizza and fresh salads loaded with shredded cabbage, toasted sunflower seeds and fresh bean sprouts.

After the main meal we spread out on the Persian rug in the living room and shared a joint. I drooled over Hannah's Kermanshah Tree-of-Life carpet, an antique from the 19th Century. Hannah had such good taste. I briefly envied her luxurious surroundings. Soft cushions and bean-bag chairs created a cozy atmosphere around the low, round mahogany coffee table. Enormous hexagon beeswax candles flickered in the corners of the plant-filled room.

"Another one?" Gary asked, already rolling another dubie. We were finishing the home-made apple crisp with vanilla ice cream—my dessert offering. I desperately wanted to lick the pale blue earthenware bowl, but held back, working on appearing mature. And cool.

When the discussion turned to work-related matters, I tuned out. I had nothing to contribute, seeing myself on a par with a scullery maid. Cinderella would be the best I could hope for. As Pete droned on about his mill job, whining about the shift work, the rednecks he had to work with, how physically demanding the work was, the low pay and about how glad he was to be recently laid off, boredom dragged my eyelids down, and I had to shake myself awake after ten minutes.

Hannah spoke up. "I'm so sad for you, Pete. I hope you find something better soon. But I have to confess, I must be so damned lucky, because I, for one, love, love, love my work!"

I sat up. "Well Hannah, I'm so happy for you. You are such a free spirit and you have a teaching job you love that pays all your bills! It must be great! But you know… don't you feel at all trapped? Aren't you the least bit worried about doing the old nine-to-five for your entire life? You know—punching the clock, day in, day out, year after year, then retiring when you're too old or too crippled to enjoy those last days?"

Pete frowned. Hannah looked puzzled. Gary stopped cleaning the seeds from his stash.

But I couldn't stop. "And then ultimately, when you're a senior and it's your time to enjoy life, most of us will probably drop dead of a heart attack or a stroke, or cancer or some debilitating illness. At best you'll end up alone in an old-age home that smells like Lysol and urine and probably die in your sleep! Alone!"

Suddenly the room filled with a stunned, awkward silence. Perhaps I had drunk too much wine. I did feel a little dizzy.

"Sorry," I whispered.

Hannah bailed me out, "Well, no. I don't worry about all of that. About my whole life? Who knows what I'll be doing or where I'll be in thirty years? Or forty years? Never mind about retiring. I never want to retire. I swear I'll forever be doing something I love. And as far as paid work, well, it's a choice I made. I finished high school and then said to myself, 'Self, what would you not mind doing for possibly ten, twenty years?' So I went to college, got my degree, and here I am today!"

She winked at me and smiled. *Of course. Such a simple answer.*

Easy for her to say, but college costs money and I barely graduated, so it would have been a stretch. And back then, I was so pissed at everyone and everything, no way would I have been able to sit in a classroom and cram more information into my little brain.

Hannah hung her head then glanced at Gary. He gave her a serious look.

"Speaking of life choices," she continued, "we haven't actually told anyone yet, but I have to share this, it's driving me mad." She cleared her throat. And hung her head. "Ah, well… I recently found out I may never be able to… to have children. *Ever.* God knows we're trying, but I'm so worried. I love children, but it may already be too late. I may already be too old—and I'm only thirty six!" Her face turned crimson and she stared at me with sorrow in her eyes. "Now you, Sasha—you have no reason to complain. You have such a gift; you have a beautiful healthy son. You have Ethan! You're so bloody lucky!"

Tears welled up in her warm, brown eyes. "Oh, man!" She inhaled, let out a deep belly sigh, and carried on. "Whew! It's all right. I'm fine. I'm fine."

She shook out her hands as if getting rid of something. Gary gently touched her shoulder and then sat back, holding a fat rollie. She carried on, "No more work or business talk now! Well, except for one thing—some real news."

She sat totally still, her legs crossed, her spine straight, a perfect yogini. She then raised her hand and put finger to pursed lips. "Well, it's kind of a secret." She paused for effect. "I am leaving the co-op. I know we told everyone at the meeting we would wait for a new set of people to buy my shares, but I can't wait. I need the money for all the doctor visits to the coast, and all that. And I don't think it's a good mix of people. I may never see all my shares paid back, but it's the right thing for me at this time." More stunned silence. "Now Gary, he may have other plans ..."

Gary looked down pensively, thick eyebrows outlining his eyes, chestnut mop of curly hair tangled and messy. He spoke slowly and carefully.

"I'll hang in for a while and see what happens. After the last meeting, I'm not sure. I'm seriously thinking about leaving, though. When I first joined the group, I had this silly fantasy about building a summer cabin on the land. It's not a money issue for me. As a CA, I'll have no trouble paying the mortgage and then building a small house, but I may not be able to get along with everyone. I'm not referring to anyone in particular, but some of those people are whacked!"

We all laughed in agreement.

He tapped on his ceramic wine glass with his clean fingernails. "So many different values and lifestyles. I did want to be part of something, though. A community perhaps. It's so damned disappointing. I did want it all to work!"

A minute of dead silence hung in the stuffy air. Pete cut through the strings of pessimistic, heavy thoughts that floated like cartoon balloon bubbles above our heads.

"Whew!" he exclaimed. "Man! I do have to say I'm not actually surprised. We have our doubts, too."

Gary offered him the joint. Pete accepted it and pulled on the rolled herb. Heady smoke again filled the room.

Hannah jumped up and opened a window to let in some fresh air. "After the last meeting I can see the whole thing is not going to be a lot of fun." She unfastened her thick braids and started to comb out her shiny hair. "It's nothing to do with you guys. You all made a good point at the last meeting about killing animals on the land—how dreadful it would be. I totally understand. It would break my heart, too!"

My throat felt parched and dry from all the weed, and I reached for my wine. *Be careful. Not too much.* "Oh man, I do feel quite stupid. I wonder now if I should have brought up the whole killing animals thing. And yeah, how the hell are people going to feel when one of those idiots shoots a beautiful deer in front of our children? And they'd have to gut it and skin it right there. Can you imagine the smell? And the flies?"

All heads nodded head in agreement.

"I think we both know in our hearts what we're going to do, but we'll have to give it some time," I said.

Pete looked up at me with questioning eyes.

Digesting

The morning after Hannah's dinner I awoke with another major headache. *Fuck!* I had drunk a little too much wine. Whenever I thought of Hannah not being able to have children, I felt like vomiting and dry heaved over the toilet bowl. It felt exactly like morning sickness.

Late afternoon, I ran into Hannah and had a chance to apologize before it ate me up completely and before it affected our growing friendship. I wanted to stay friends and was afraid that all my chattering about meaningless work and an early death had been a trigger for Hannah's confession about her infertility. If I hadn't brought up all those subjects about life choices, Hannah wouldn't have been reminded of all her troubles.

I felt responsible.

She was coming out of the post office, sorting through and shuffling various-sized envelopes and a glossy magazine. I was heading in to check the mail and opened the heavy glass door for her.

"Hello," she said. Her eyes looked a little puffy and circled with dark shadows but otherwise she appeared to be her chipper self.

"Hey, how are you?" I asked, a little less than chipper. "I hope we didn't stay too late last night. You must be so exhausted!"

I jingled the keys in my jacket pocket—a nervous habit. Somehow the tinkley noise and feel of cool metal on my fingers were a nice distraction from my anxiety. Which could hit at anytime, anywhere.

"Oh, no!" she replied. "Gary and I usually stay up late. I'm so used to it! It was wonderful to have you guys over. Maybe we can all drive out to the land sometime and hike around." With a quick smile, she turned to go.

I remembered the confession of her barren womb and felt a wave of sorrow. "Oh, Hannah, before you go, I want to say how sorry I am. You know, the fact you may not be able to have kids."

She swayed backward a little. "Oh, that!" She laughed a tiny nervous laugh. "Well, it's not for certain, but if that's the way it is, then that's the way it is. I have a lot of children in my life, so not to worry. But it's not your fault, so don't apologize. Don't be sorry."

Then a harsher tone. "I have been noticing lately though, how most of the women around here are constantly apologizing for things that are not their fault. Are they honestly sorry, or are they passive aggressive? You're a treasure, Sash, but you have to grow some teeth! Life is not for the super meek." She frowned and started waving her finger. "I don't believe the old Bible saying, "the meek shall inherit the earth". Perhaps that means small animals and insects. Perhaps it means native or aboriginal peoples. That makes sense. Perchance the kind people shall inherit the earth. I don't know you very well, but it appears to me..." She stopped her tirade and waved her hand in the air as if trying to capture a word.

"Yes ...?"

She picked up her thought. "...that perhaps you may have a small co-dependency problem, and perhaps you could use some support and feedback." She paused for a few beats then plunged in again. "I recently heard about a group starting up in the Legion. They have free weekly meetings. It's all about empowerment. A twelve-step group called C.O.D.A., I think." She spelled out the letters. "It stands for Co-dependants Anonymous. It might help you to become more at peace with yourself. If you ever want to try it, I'll go with you." She glanced at her watch. "And so now, dear Sash, I must run. I'm late for my tai chi class. It was so good to see you. Let's stay in touch!"

She gave me a quick hug and ran off; a brisk wind rushed in as the glass door slammed shut. I raised my hand to wave. Too late.

So much information. Overwhelming.

Is she right? Do I need to grow some teeth? Perhaps I used to have short, soft baby teeth and now that I'm grown up, I need sharp, shiny white adult teeth to bite, chew, and digest all life has to offer.

As I opened the metal box on the far side of the small, stuffy room in the post office, I imagined piercing fangs, sharp and biting. Empty—no mail today. I headed back out to the truck. An unhealthy looking raven, scraggly and starving, flew directly over me and dumped a big wad of raven shit on the driver's side of the windshield.

Damn! Talk about digesting.

After sorting through a pile of junk mail and rusting screws, I found a small, oil-soaked cotton rag behind the seat and started wiping off the shit, but it streaked, making the mess worse. There was nothing else to do but to carry on and pretend it wasn't a big deal.

Somehow I managed to drive home, peering through yellow-grey smears the entire way, trying to stay on my side of the road.

Hannah inspired me to be more disciplined and healthy, and I started doing yoga again. It was amazingly beneficial even after only a few days. My joints felt more lubricated and didn't creak all the time when I moved. They felt more co-operative. But I couldn't get rid of my pot belly no matter what. I decided it was simply the way I was built: lightly freckled and skinny with a little watermelon belly.

Why do we have to look like movie stars, anyway? I'll never look like one, so why bother trying. Who wants to spend an hour each day putting on makeup and doing your hair perfectly just to get the admiration of some horny dudes? I have better things to do.

Besides, when I wear makeup, I look like a hooker.

Perhaps that's the point.

And what did I hear on the local radio today? Tammy Wynette's song: "Sometimes It's Hard to Be a Woman."

Oh, Tammy, now you're stuck in my head.

Meditating also helped somewhat, too. But it wasn't easy to sit in one spot for forty minutes and focus on my mantra. Sometimes I nodded off for a minute or so. Other times, I felt free of my body if only for a few seconds. My aches and pains receded into an ocean hum a billion miles away. The hum some heard but no one ever talked about.

My pessimistic thinking and my old negative habits always had a way of creeping back in though, like grasping vines, twisting the life out of me and bringing me back down to earth with a solid crash.

How To Live on Pennies

Pete picked up our first UI cheque from the post office and we were shocked to see the amount. We would be receiving only $400 a month! This was cutting it pretty close. How could anyone live on this pittance?

But there was some good news too: we were allowed to make an extra $100 before anything was deducted from our monthly cheque. Pete could get some extra work at the local packing house, loading bags of onions or potatoes onto trucks. It was rough dirty work, but at least it wasn't full time.

I hoped I could get a few days a week there, too. They're regularly looking for warm bodies who agree to work for next to nothing—typically older, uneducated women—to cull the potatoes and weed the onion fields.

It was tedious, mindless, backbreaking labour. Still, we were going to have to pay the bills somehow.

A little job might give me a nice break from the Mommy-housewifey thing, I thought, while looking up the number to call.

I didn't even consider waitressing. I tried it once before and was terrible at giving the correct change after serving people their disgusting food: bland, boiled veggies, burnt-carcass burgers, and butchered animal parts with stale fries. And there was always the looming pressure of having to feed all those hungry people while smiling and being nice to them—no matter what. And to clean up after them and their children, who sneezed and coughed and picked their noses and spat up on tables and on the filthy floor. *Almost as bad as being a housewife. I guess someone has to do it though.*

Just not me.

Small Town Plagues

I set the table with small, turquoise glass fruit bowls and removed the soiled plates. Pete and I had invited Mike for dinner because Betty had gone to the states to visit a sick friend. We felt sorry for him. Mike had to be a bachelor for the entire time—possibly two weeks—and he wasn't a good cook, usually burning or undercooking his meals, so we both swallowed our dislike for Betty and invited him over.

I had thrown together a meal of cottage cheese squares, salad, and had fried up a quart jar of canned yellow beans with butter and garlic. Mike brought his boy over too. This worked out well; the little ones spent the entire evening building fortresses in the living room out of boxes and old sheets.

"So, how are you two feeling about the co-op lately?" Mike asked, as he poked a piece of canned pear with his fork and popped it into his mouth. Sugar juice dripped down his long straw-coloured beard. It appeared there was no getting out of the dreaded co-op conversation.

Pete spoke first. "I wondered how long it would take before we'd get into this!"

I jumped in. "Well, to be honest, Mike, it's all feeling a little shaky. We want it to work out, but..." Betty and Sissy had become the best of friends. And I didn't trust either of them. I solved this dilemma by turning the question back on Krishna. "So what do *you* think?"

"I don't know, man," he replied. "Some folks are saying the group is too big, that it would be more cohesive with fewer people." He set down his fork and drank his fruit salad juice as if the bowl were a cup.

"Oh, yeah?" Pete was getting cranky. "Who is saying that?"

Mike flushed. "Well, I can't specifically remember exactly who said what, but there's talk."

"So 'they' would like a smaller group," Pete retorted. "And who would 'they' like to see leave the group?"

"I'm not sure," Mike replied. "I haven't talked to the entire group but... anyway, we aren't cashing in our chips yet." He smiled, trying to smooth out ruffled feathers.

But Pete did not smile and certainly did not want his ruffled feathers smoothed.

I felt the tension in my back and neck, and my headache was returning. So much for a nice, social dinner. We had planned to end the evening with one of my favourite games: blackjack, using pennies or macaroni bits instead of poker chips.

But Mike obviously could not take the friction and left early, saying he had chores to take care of. Pete and I both knew it was a lie. He wanted to get the hell away from us and from having to discuss the co-op and all its damned problems and failings.

While shopping downtown, we ran into Sissy and Ray. The four of us stood in front of Nellie's Vitamins and chatted about the co-op. Ray and Sis actually told us they were not into keeping it going as it was. They wanted to form a new co-op with only Mike and Betty.

So. It is true after all!

At home, we fought about the bloody co-op again. Pete, the bastard, sided with Sissy. He seemed to think it was a normal thing for two sets of friends to want to form a co-op on their own. All I saw were Sissy's evil intentions. Not only had she decided the co-op was folding, but she was right there for the spoils. How many people was she talking to in the background, trying to get things riled up?

How could he take Sissy's side, like he couldn't even see how two-faced she was! What was wrong with him, anyway?

❋ ❋ ❋

The entire town ended up with a nasty flu. Some called it the small town brown plague. I could barely move for twenty four hours, stayed in bed most of a day and had even less than my usual appetite. Pete bought me some canned tomato soup and Saltine crackers. It was such a blessing. He could actually be so kind at times. Once in a while I actually noticed how much of my bullshit he put up with; my criticisms and complaining, my nagging, my anxiety, all my fears and worries.

Ethan got over it all in one day. I cut out all milk products and gave him only juice or sugar water, every few hours. He had started out with vomiting and runny diarrhea.

How people work in hospitals and medical professions was beyond me. I could never be a nurse. The smell of vomit makes *me* vomit, even if it is my darling baby boy.

While recovering from the flu, Pete and I ended up watching the first half of a television movie, *Helter Skelter,* based on the Charles Manson case. It was about the investigation of the horrific Tate-LaBianca mass murders orchestrated by the pseudo-hippie cult leader, Charles Manson. Why did they call him a hippie? He was not a fucking hippie—definitely a fake hippie! A real hippie would not be into murder and carnage. *A hippie believes in love and peace. Everyone knows this.*

The movie itself was extremely disturbing.

I kept asking, "Why? Why? Why?" Manson was obviously psychotic and dangerous. Is it possible each of us is capable of such horror? He did seem to have some kind of power over others though, especially his crazy female followers. It was as if he had hypnotized them. Those women appeared as nuts as he was.

How many people personally affect me this way? Having some power over me—and not to my benefit? Aren't we all spirits or souls trapped in dense bodies? It's too bad his soul ended up in such a broken and twisted vessel. *Or was his soul already broken and twisted before ending up in that body?*

We watched the conclusion the next night, against my better judgment. It was absolutely depressing.

Ironically, it was the first day in a week and a half that my body felt close to normal.

Before bed, I sat outside to clear my head and came up with a conclusion of sorts about truth and the purpose of life. There is no universal truth. We're here to live our destiny and follow our path, which isn't always clear. There is probably a God of some kind. We have the free will to choose whether he or she exists. Or doesn't. Both could be truths.

And what if there is not just one truth; what if there are multiple parallel truths, like parallel universes?

Is there life after death?

Or is there is NO THING?

The Nothing with the capital N.

If there is Nothing, then I wouldn't know it, and if there is something, I would continue on.

I decided it would not matter, in the end.

By the end of April our lazy sun had woken from its winter slumber. It streamed in through the gauzy buttercup yellow curtains I had sewn and hung in the kitchen. The rich warm colour sent me to old India or Morocco perhaps, countries and times far, far away.

While punching down bread dough I heard a timid knock at the back door. I glanced out the small kitchen window and gasped.

It had been months since we'd last seen Jane from next door. She appeared bone weary, and her skin was dull and pasty. She stood holding her son Bobby's hand. He was older than Ethan, probably four or five, and large for a toddler. He usually acted more like he was two, though.

"Hi, Jane, long time no see." I opened the door with a dishtowel to avoid getting dough on the doorknob.

She nodded and stared down at her boots. "It's such a nice day, and Bobby keeps begging to play with Ethan," she said. "I'll keep an eye on them, if you're too busy." She wore a threadbare peach sweater and faded brown synthetic pants, the kind with permanent seams down the front.

"Oh, Okay. Great," I replied, reaching deeply for a cheerful tone. "I would join you guys but need to get the bread in pans. Come on in, and I'll get Ethan's jacket on."

I stepped aside to let her enter.

"Thanks, but we'll wait out here in the sunshine," Jane said. "Send him out when he's ready." And smiled dimly.

Ethan peered around my ankle-length granny skirt and shook his head up and down eagerly. His eyes sparkled as he started pulling his jacket down from the coat hooks behind the door.

Bobby grinned from ear to ear and stuck his pudgy thumb in his mouth, drooling and giggling. He tugged fiercely on his mother's hand and acted like he was going to run away. She nearly fell.

He must weigh more than she does.

Instead of reining him in though, she merely stifled a tiny laugh and squeezed his hand tighter.

I felt a little disoriented but was not sure why. "OK," I said. "He'll be out in a sec. I'll come out later." Ethan started getting dressed. He was raring to go.

Within minutes the boys were tearing around the gravel and the soft mud in the driveway. Bobby was much huskier and larger, but he had fewer vocal skills. He sprinted back and forth, flailing his arms and body around like a floppy doll or cartoon character. Ethan ran after him down the road. But when they stopped to chat, Bobby looked somewhat perplexed. They managed to communicate eventually, pointing and babbling before feeling the urge to run again. Like two colts who needed the joy of play and movement.

I pummeled and pounded the taut, yeasty dough into oval shapes, then slapped and patted them before planting them into metal rectangular tins greased with Crisco. I poked them with a sharp fork to allow air bubbles to escape. Lastly, I put the oven on. They would have to rise again before baking. At supper time, I'd slice a loaf while it was still warm from the oven and slather the slices with butter and later, honey. I could already taste it. Sunshine and warm weather was a great appetite booster.

In the evening, I noticed light sunburn on Ethan's young cheeks.

That's not a good thing. Sunburn in April!

What's happening in the heavens these days?

Judging

"Yeah," I said.

The frowning judge's chilling, watery eyes scorched into my breastbone. Worn, grey metal eye glasses sat at the end of a long, beak nose and even from yards away in my witness box I could see the grey matted hairs and drying snot stuck in his flaring nostrils. *Yuck.* My empty stomach did a quick flip.

"You must answer the question 'yes' or 'no', young lady," he said.

Damn! Just another stuffy, old codger!

"Yes," I replied crisply.

"Yes, what? Did you, or did you not commit adultery?"

I scanned the room for a friendly face and saw Karl, my ex, nodding gently, his eyes large and eager, waiting for me to give the correct answer. Pete sat next to him and looked distracted, methodically picking lint off his old newer trousers, like he was in his own world. The three of us had driven out in the old Chevy to the court house in Kelowna to get this marriage thing dissolved. I had to formally take the stand and even swear on the Bible. *How bloody weird. Just to get divorced?*

"Yes, I did commit adultery," I said. I felt faint and took a deep breath.

"Will the young lady please take the gum out of her mouth?"

Promptly a court aide dressed in a suit appeared and walked over to hand me a white, creased tissue he had pulled out of a Kleenex box picked up from God knows where.

I slowly pulled the wad of Juicy Fruit out of my dry mouth and placed it gently into the tissue, then folded it over many times.

The aide took the offensive offering by the corners and tossed it into a green metal trash can. Thunk. The judge's pen tap, tap, tapped on his commanding oak desk. My skin was boiling. My heart pounded so loudly I was positive everyone else could hear it. Sweat trickled down my back. I couldn't wait to get the hell out of there.

"The young lady must answer the question, yes or no. Without the gum, please!"

I have already answered the fucking question.

It took another few seconds to calm myself down.

"The question, sir? I thought I had already answered it." I smiled cautiously and tugged on a red button hanging loosely from my sweater.

Perhaps he is simply an unhappy old person, trapped in this horrid role. Cross-examining young ex-virgins who must say they have committed adultery to get a stupid little piece of paper which states 'Now you are free! Not married anymore!'

"If you want to waste the court's time and play games, I can make sure you are here a lot longer than a few minutes!" Spit flew from his tight, parched lips. "Don't waste the court's time and don't waste my time. Answer the question! Did you or did you not commit adultery?"

I sat up straight. And so, as Karl and I had agreed upon, I lied. It was a small but necessary lie. "Yes, I did. I did commit adultery. Sir. Your honour."

I bowed my head. *Whew—that should do it.*

"Good!" the judge snapped. "The young lady may now step down. Your decree shall come by mail. Sign the necessary papers and check with the court reporter on your way out!"

He started to climb down from his cathedral chair and turned to me. He caught my gaze. Lizard, watery eyes misted over. "And have a safe journey home, my dear, a safe journey home."

I nodded at his retreating balding head and quickly made my way back to my official ex-hubby and Pete, who both looked extremely relieved.

My laughter escaped before I had a chance to stifle it. It echoed loudly through the large, hollow room, off the heavy wooden doors and ornately paneled walls.

I practically ran out of that room. Pete and Karl hustled and tried to keep up but I was not slowing down. After checking with the sleepy court reporter we all headed to the closest pub for a cool one to celebrate.

For sure, this was the most free I had felt in a long time. A tiny part, a smidgen of me, hidden behind all those fears was free. I had moved a tiny boulder. Not a monster boulder, but perhaps the road forward had one less obstruction, one less log jam.

I pondered this and more, as the three of us celebrated the legal end of my long forgotten, short, intense marriage to Karl, with a draft beer, a grilled cheese sandwich and fries slathered in ketchup.

A Cool Change

Some things never change. I had to keep calling my new doctor. It seemed like in my world doctors were all pretty much the same: control junkies. After three weeks of hacking and feeling exhausted, I decided I was never going to kick this flu thing.

After finally getting in for an appointment, Dr. N. gave me a prescription: powerful antibiotics for a raging sore throat and chest congestion. They were supposed to kill the nasty bacteria in the respiratory system. He said he didn't know about my fatigue, but suggested I eat some red meat to increase my iron levels. I laughed. "Yeah sure, I'll think about it."

Some days I felt one hundred years old, waking in the mornings with all my joints aching.

This can't be right, feeling this old, at my age.

I agonized over whether to take the antibiotics or not. Everyone knew they were bad for you.

"Eats lots of homemade yogurt," Hannah suggested "It will help. Antibiotics are super powerful and destroy the bad and good critters in your digestive tract. The yogurt has the good bacteria for your gut."

While packing for our yearly trip to the coast to visit Pete's Aunt Sally, I started to think about how great it would be, after the co-op broke up, to buy a couple of acres out of town and have a few goats and a dog.

I wasn't sure about chickens and recently hadn't been into eating eggs. It was kind of gross to crack open the brown shell and see the translucent white, twisted umbilical cord and sometimes a developing fetus, staring back at you. Those chicken pieces went straight into the compost.

So maybe no chickens. But they're so clucky, cheerful, and cute. Perhaps a couple of Rhode Island Reds, or Plymouth Rocks. Or even white Leghorns, although their bums always look dirty because their feathers are so white. We could sell the eggs. And composted chicken-manure tea is a great fertilizer for tomato plants.

Pete was trying to finish building a tiny portable greenhouse before we left. We'd eventually have to move our weed plants to a location in the wild though. They were such healthy, vigorous plants and would take over in no time.

"We should be able to grow what we want in our own yard! The law is so bloody stupid. Come on, it's only a plant! A medicinal plant that's been used for thousands of years!" Pete fumed as he stapled the heavy plastic onto the board frame.

While packing, my stomach did flips whenever I thought of Vincent, who we also planned to visit. This fluttering sensation in my heart was so distracting. It was as if a special gate made of weathered mother-of-pearl and twisted arbutus stood at this entrance. A splendid, multi-coloured butterfly would flutter in and its fragile wings would beat against the tender walls of this heart. After only a few moments the creature would escape. I would immediately shut the gate. Bam. This gate could not stay open. Something mean could enter and scorch those lush, tender vines. So I shut the gate often. And would then feel nothing. Absolutely nothing. For hours. And hours.

I was so excited to be getting away though, and kept reminding myself to breathe deeply. My frayed nerves were fried and Pete and I fought all the time. I needed a fresh view—a new perspective. A trip to visit Aunt Sally and then Vince and Kathy would be great.

Or so I had thought at the time.

The Trickster Masquerades as Lover

Felix, our missing feline, sits on a flagstone which rests next to a pebble-strewn pathway. He looks comfortable, peaceful and healthy. His thick coat is dishevelled and wild. A pouty kitty mouth smiles at me, turning up at the corners. Chamomile yellow eyes glisten, damp at the corners.

As I slowly approach he morphs into a hag like, white-haired woman, bent and twisted, with the arctic and intense sapphire eyes of a wolf. She then mutates into a glittering snake with diamond patterns and spirals from another realm, patterns that shape shift and glow. Her forked tongue flicks out. A warning or an invitation? I tremble.

As soon as she spies me, I am caught in a stare that pries deep; she holds me with a gaze that bores into my soul. A sharp stabbing starts up behind my right eye. She speaks. I am mesmerized and can only stand rigid, helpless and frozen. Her voice envelops sounds from another time and dimension, a revereb which penetrates fiber and bone.

"Beware, my dear. Beware of the trickster, the magician, the shaman, the one who will masquerade as a lover. You know he could be anyone." She shakes her enormous, shiny head. A waterfall of shimmery scales spray off her. Disco lights. "A new friend of any age or persuasion, the young man who stocks the shelves in the grocery store, an aging plumber with a beer belly, a sensitive artist, a slick lawyer, a street musician, a tree planter. His sensual energy locks into your cells. It is useless to refuse. You could be eighty, you could be thirty, perhaps a young maiden, not yet deflowered. But when this lover comes a calling, you cannot say no. You must follow. Even if it nearly kills you. For he will destroy your life as you know it. And then leave you. Completely free, but alone. Yes, so very alone."

She hangs her enormous head and sheds crystalline tear drops then slinks gracefully into an upright cobra pose. "But my dear he will also leave you with a knowing. A gift you will never lose. A precious gift which must become part of your essence. You'll be left knowing what it means to be completely loved by an earth being, if only for a brief time. Or so you will tell yourself."

Her features revert to those of the old woman. "You can fight it, you can deny it, but all the forces in Universe conspire to bring the two of you together. This force, like the opposite ends of a powerful magnet, is as formidable as the blizzards of winter, as primal as the mating call of all earthly ones. And yet woefully, as all-consuming as a prairie fire, leaving only ashes and cinders behind."

The snake-hag curls into a coiled spiral and smiles. "So beware, my dear friend, for after this demon lover comes a calling, you will not recognize yourself. And if you don't want this or are afraid of change, then you better run like hell if you catch even a whiff of him in your circle. For after all is done, and you are broken, and he is gone, you will be permanently changed."

As she quickly evaporates right in front of me, I hear the laughter of a storybook wicked witch, deep and rich and honest. The kind that sends jagged, thorny quivers up a spine.

I awoke. My covers were on the floor.

But I was not cold, not cold a bit.

In fact I was fiery hot and sweating, as if I had a fever.

Vincent and Kathy

When we got to Vancouver we dumped all our stuff at Aunt Sally's and headed over to Vince and Kathy's.

Vincent answered the door and invited us in. He looked a little ruffled, but was the same man of my recent daydreams: not traditionally handsome, but charismatic, with deep-set, licorice-black eyes and thick, straight raven hair with purplish highlights. He still wore it tied back with a leather strip, which suited his high cheekbones and aboriginal features. Pete had once mentioned that his friend was of Irish Italian descent, but Vince swore his grandmother was First Nations. He would not say which nation though. I could never pin him down. A little weird. But I didn't care.

Goosebumps covered my arms and I felt a sense of coming home as he hugged me.

Kathy flew in from the fragrant kitchen to welcome us. She was strikingly beautiful with clear, wide-set green eyes and long, shining blonde hair. *My god, she could be a Barbie-doll model.* I felt like a mouse around her—a little grey mouse with a small, squeaky voice.

The men and children hung out in the living room. The twin girls, Carson and Carole, hung out with Ethan and started on a game of Chinese Checkers right away while Vincent set up the chess board. I could hear them all discussing our trip until music from the albums on the turntable drowned out their chatting and joking.

I helped Kathy set the table in the bright kitchen and filled her in about the trip down.

"Oh, man, it was so bloody tiring. We drove all night. I feel like crap today, have this flu thing in my chest, too. But I finally got in to see the doc before we left and am finished the antibiotics and am starting to..."

"Antibiotics?" Kathy growled. "Are you kidding? You should not take those, my girl! Drugstore medicine is crap! It'll kill you. Have you tried goldenseal or echinacea? Both are especially good! Remind me to give you some before you go." She expertly flipped and stirred steaming veggies in a large wok. "Are you guys staying at Aunt Sally's? She's such a dear. We saw her at the farm market the other day. She is looking a lot older though. Even with her little dog to keep her company, it must be excruciating to be alone for so long." She threw some Braggs soya sauce into the mix. An orange blue gas flame sputtered as she turned off the burner. "Maybe she just needs to find herself another man!"

She laughed throatily and flung her hair back over her shoulder. I quietly smiled back.

Throughout the entire strained evening Vincent remained casual and distant. He made many curt, snide comments about anything I ventured to share. I couldn't say anything right. He acted like a different person from when he had visited in Twin Forks the year before. We had a real connection then—talking for hours and hours about philosophy, religion and recent world events.

But on this day, at his house, he acted like we'd never shared anything.

Who the heck is this guy? I wondered, as we all ate supper. And pretended to enjoy it.

Kathy was her usual sassy self. She didn't seem to notice the bickering between us, or chose to ignore it. I feared she could be quite superficial at times. I wasn't sure there was a lot of substance there.

On this visit it also became obvious how much of a tyrant Vincent could be: irritable and needlessly heavy-handed with Kathy's girls. If they screwed up, he yelled at them and sometimes smacked their little hands with whatever was handy, like a spoon or a pencil. Their wide, blue eyes would tear up and they'd withdraw into themselves or run away. Vince's discipline felt too patriarchal and abusive. It made me cringe.

The next afternoon I walked into the kitchen and had to witness this first hand. Carole had stolen an extra cookie out of the cookie jar. Vincent had seen her take it and commanded her to "Stop!" He smacked his young step-daughter forcefully on her hand with a metal spoon. Whack. She dropped the cookie immediately. Crumbs lay scattered all over the kitchen floor.

"Don't hit her with a spoon! It's only a cookie, for God's sake."

"Now, Miss Sasha," Vince replied, his voice tight, strained. "Do not be telling me how to raise my girls! You do it your way and I'll do it mine."

What the hell? This was not the gentle, philosophical voice I thought I knew.

"I won't raise my girls to think stealing is OK!" As he walked away, he forcefully threw the spoon into the kitchen sink. It clattered and the sound flew out to the edges of the room. My teeth immediately ached.

Carole glanced up at me, a tear in the corner of her eye. She ran off to her room, sucking on her scarlet hand.

I tried to understand. Vincent was supposedly a psychologist, after all. *He should know about the correct way to raise children. Shouldn't he?* I certainly didn't know. It was all so damned confusing.

Raising kids sure is difficult. You want them to listen, but they are their own persons. Aren't they?

This is what Kahlil Gibran says anyway: 'Your children are not your children; they are the sons and daughters of life longing for itself!'

Even with his spiritual questing and fine words, Vincent regularly had to be in control. He acted forceful with Kathy, too. She was pretty spunky but on one of our last visits to their house before we headed home, she answered the door. Her eyes were bloodshot and swollen.

"It's hay fever," she explained, when I asked if she was all right.

But even through the lingering aroma of sweet grass and incense, I felt the heaviness of tears in their house. That evening, I confronted Vincent. "How is everything with you and Kath?"

He shrugged. "Fine. And you and Pete?"

Before I could answer he stomped off to the bathroom. I heard the water running for his evening bath. A nightly ritual of some sort.

It became obvious I didn't know Vincent at all. At times I still felt like putting my arms around him or being alone with him to talk for a while. But too often he was distant and irritable. There had not been any real communication between us. By the end of the visit it was as if I had lost a good friend. I missed who I thought he was.

The last chance Vincent and I had to connect was during a walk in Stanley Park the day before we left. Kathy volunteered to babysit Ethan so I didn't have to worry about anything or anybody.

Pete, Vincent and I shared small talk and then hiked along the walkway for a good hour. We finally ended up chilling on a rocky point overlooking the wild spring ocean. After sharing a joint we retreated, each into our own world.

While sitting I fell into a dreamlike peace. Something opened up. A sienna beam from the setting sun hit me right in the face, like a spotlight. Although my skinny bottom went numb from sitting in the lotus pose on the firm, inflexible boulders, I was in heaven for a few seconds.

Right now the world is mine. Not mine to own or possess, but mine to experience, to love. No effort. No stress. I don't desire anything. I don't need anything.

For those precious moments, there was nothing to strive for. This sense of freedom was all I'd ever wanted, along with the feeling that all is perfect and divine.

But those moments always pass, it seems. Across the mounds and crevasses of rock and moss, I felt Vincent's stare. And opened my eyes to catch him looking into me. It was thrilling. For a split second, I felt seen and not mousey at all. I was all he ever wanted. I saw it in his eyes.

Pete dozed on a concave rock below us. He saw nothing. My hair fluttered gently in the cool breeze and my skin began to tingle.

But longing turned to confusion in Vincent's searching eyes and he looked away to an image making its way through the gathering cumulus clouds.

Bald Eagle, king of the coastal skies, dove down and seized a glowing salmon from an inky ocean pool. A miracle to see, its sharp talons held onto this poor wretched fish which fought for its life, thrashing and flipping about. The eagle held tightly onto his prize and quickly flew off, disappearing behind three ancient cedars.

Pete stirred and carefully sat up, looked around and pulled on his wrinkled denim jacket. I avoided his questioning glance. A salty cool gust whipped through my heart. It was way past time to go. I looked over to where Vincent was sitting.

But Vincent was already gone, walking down the trail back to the parking lot, his heavy footsteps crunching on loose gravel, the silhouette of his wide hunched shoulders deepening my confusion and my hunger.

Someday

A fading rainbow peeked cautiously through the misty clouds covering the fertile valley bottom. The spring downpour was finally letting up. Pete and I had driven all night and were in the home stretch.

It'll feel good to unload our all our crap and to crash. To sleep for hours and hours. To lose myself in dreams and reverie.

We picked up a couple of hitchhikers outside of Osoyoos, right before the steep winding hill. We had borrowed Brad's van for the trip and the two weathered drifters managed to make themselves comfortable in the small space on the floor. Even though vibrantly young and healthy, their craggy skin was lined prematurely and they smelled of stale rollies and unwashed pits. Wrinkled, crusty eyes shyly took in what would be their bed for the next couple of hours. Grimy and scratched up hands offered us a basket of blueberries first. Neither of them seemed to care they weren't clean or perfectly dressed men. Both were friendly and kept us awake with tales of picking fruit in the orchards and hitching all over Canada.

After they shared their great road stories and nodded out, I felt a twinge of envy. I missed the wayward gypsy life. I missed the adventure of being on the road, of not knowing what each new day would bring—new vistas, new people and experiences. The constant rhythm of the windshield wipers eventually soothed my yearnings though and lulled me to a light sleep. Whisch, whisch, whisch.

After dropping the grateful drifters at The Province cafe, we turned off the main highway and hit the short stretch for home. I awoke, shook numb legs and struggled to sit up. Vincent's words repeated in my head. "I am going to try and make it down for the May long weekend. How does that sound?"

He sheepishly tried to reach out, giving us small gifts: a few joints for the road, sandwiches Kathy had packed up for a lunch break. Pete gave him a warm hug and assured him all was well.

"Of course, any time," he said and slapped his friend on the shoulder. "We'll be gardening and working on the house."

I had avoided hugging him goodbye, pretending I needed to use the washroom before hitting the road. I stayed cool and detached and decided to let go of all the expectations I didn't even know I had.

After returning from our trip, bedraggled and burnt out, we were obliged to attend a heavy land co-op meeting.

It dragged on for three intense hours. Many ended up in tears. The co-op was in its death throes. Before adjourning the majority voted to sell the land and cash out. Only Mike and Betty thought the co-op could still survive.

They're such optimists. What's wrong with them? And what about starting a co-op with their so called friends, Ray and Sissy? Perhaps it was only Sissy's dream.

As spring turned to summer, selling the co-op land turned out to be a real pain. There weren't a lot of prospective buyers wanting to move out to the middle of nowhere. It looked as if it would be a while before we could unload this piece of nirvana. All the members still legally owned the land and had to get rid of it soon. Meanwhile any one of us could drive out and spend time there.

The land itself was a paradise on a river, about a hundred acres of utopia, about an hour out of town. The fantasy of happy farmsteads with many joyful couples in overalls weeding lush garden beds, of children running in verdant meadows under arched rainbows, chasing monarch butterflies, of community dances and plays and suppers was never to be. Not this time, anyway.

It sounded good as a fantasy on paper but it takes exactly the right mix of folks to make it happen.

My feelings about the entire venture ebbed and flowed from a sense of deep loss to one of profound relief. Part of me still hoped someday Pete and I might hook up with the right people and try a co-operative thing again.

Sadly, "Someday never comes."

Jane stopped by unexpectedly and her visit ended with a tour of my emerging veggie patch, the black earth all dug up and partially planted.

"I love your peas," she said. "I can't have a garden this year with Bobby. He's so much bloody work."

She glanced over at the portable greenhouse which secretly housed our maturing weed plants, still in garden pots. And quickly looked away, a mysterious smile lit up her pale mouth.

We chatted for a bit before she finally waved goodbye with her thin, translucent hand and headed back to her run down house. Bobby stood under the willow tree in their back yard. He had been hitting the trunk with a large, knobby stick while Jane and I talked. Whack! Whack! Whack! His T-shirt was stained and unwashed. Stiff, corn yellow hair stood up on his large head. Bobby appeared totally zoned out.

Jane walked right past him, not saying a word. The old wooden screen door creaked and then slammed as she climbed the creaky steps to her back porch.

The Raven

He wears the hat of the desert, bleached ochre straw, wide brimmed, shading his glistening coal eyes. Western clothing—pale denim, faded pastels and a white cotton shirt contrast starkly with his long cobalt hair, which hangs down to a trim waist. Indian. He starts walking directly toward me.

I am halfway across the packed clay street. The flavour of a small Latino town, perhaps Mexico or Central America. Much too warm, a gritty breeze. Grains of sand are trapped in my teeth. Shades of coral streak across an enigmatic dusk sky. Barrel cactus, sagebrush and creosote bushes dot distant hills. Another land in another time. This is for certain.

As I walk past this desert man in the crosswalk his perfect shoulder brushes my own bare shoulder ever so gently, a light, caressing wind. Electric current runs through my body and almost knocks me down. It's exhilarating and pervasive. I am at once fully alive and my entire being: internal organs, muscles, hair, all the cells in my physical body are alive and prickling, tingling.

This being transforms in front of me, turning into a magnificent raven about the size of a small child. He flies gracefully to the top of an aging, weathered pole and stares directly back at me. His sharp eye reflects the eclipse of death and the endlessness of eternity.

Faceless beings on bustling streets below him mindlessly continue their business, walking quietly, carrying woven bags full of groceries and clutching purchases wrapped in plain brown paper, unaware of the magic that has occurred right in front of them.

Waking in a pool of sweat, cool, damp sheets cling to me. I open my eyes. The soft, early-morning haze welcomes me like an old, dear friend.

I'm glad to be alive for a change and remain positive and energized for the entire day. I see the raven while doing chores, in the clouds, in mud puddles after the rain, in shadows beneath the apple tree. I have to admit the dream raven looks very much like Vincent. I feel the old yearning return.

Treasures and Addictions

Mum asked for help clean up the ranch. She and Daddy Wes finally sold it and the new buyers have to move in immediately. She was in a tight spot and needed my help. All that went with moving stressed me out, but I have a hard time saying no to her. So I said yes, and drove over. And after twenty years of storing and saving stuff, there was so much crap to sort through, get rid of and clean up.

How do people accumulate so much junk? I wondered as we attempted to organize her priceless treasures. Rotting cardboard boxes full of fabrics, knick knacks and clothing, molding and stained, covered the floor of the old barn.

"What are you going to do with all this stuff?" I asked.

We had interrupted a brown field mouse attempting to nest in this most excellent location. He leapt out of the box and scurried away into a dark corner.

"Your Aunt Martha gave me these and who knows when a good pair of boots may come in handy?" Mum said. She pulled out a pair of short, scuffed black rubber boots, long past their prime. A rim of fake fur, covered in hoary cobwebs and stems of dried grass, adorned this treasure.

Why is she so sentimental, hanging onto all this old shit?

"Really? How about I take as much as I can in my truck to the thrift store? Someone may be able to use all these lovely things. I mean, how are you going to store all this at your new place?"

Mum would not budge. "We'll find a spot," she insisted. "There's a basement in my new place, you know! Let's just drag all this into the sunshine and we can sort it out there."

Her tiny, liver-spotted hands grabbed a large box and started hauling it outside. She was determined to hang onto this old shit.

Most of the day was spent loading old clothes into garbage bags and labelling them. I prayed I would never get like this. Come to think of it though, our shed at home was getting pretty full. What was in there anyway? It was simply full of things I had trouble letting go of: pre-teen diaries, Ethan's baby clothes, and hundreds of photographs.

At the end of the long day, after helping deliver three truckloads of sentimental what nots and rubbish to Mum's new digs, I revelled in a long, steaming soak in my deep tub to cleanse my body of all the grunge and dust from those ancient worn-out objects. Seeing them triggered fond memories as well as haunting, troubling memories, far too many to hang onto.

Later that week we got busy painting Ethan's room a soothing robin's egg blue. With a green hue. While facing the first painted wall, I was swept up in a beautiful, warm body of water. Afloat and at peace—who would have thought different colours had such a powerful affect? And of course it helped that I was stoned.

Was I addicted the herb? It wasn't an extremely potent strain of Mary Jane, being home grown . And the THC levels were very low. It was organic after all and certainly helped with all my aches and pains. And Pete had reassured me many times "a person could not get physically addicted to the ganga." *But then again, so what? So what if I'm addicted? We're all addicted to lots of things. I'm also addicted to air, water, food, love and music.*

I finished rolling the soothing colour onto the last wall. *Ultimately, what's the big deal if I have a toke once in a while? Whose business is it anyway? It makes me feel better. And besides, it's an exquisite, intelligent plant, a medicinal healing plant from the Creator.*

I spent a few minutes sitting on the cool floor, bathing in the glow of the pure blue-green vibration before gathering up my soiled paint rags and dirty brushes and closing the door on my way out.

Super Beings

As I washed out the paint brushes in the bathroom sink, milky blue topaz-water gurgled down the corroded drain. Rat-tat-tat at the back door. Spider and Stephen, two of our old friends surprised us with a visit.

We spent the entire night chatting around the kitchen table, drinking jasmine tea, munching on gingersnaps and roasted sunflower seeds. The four of us were excited about the new book we'd all recently finished reading, *The Center of the Cyclone*, by John C. Lilly.

"From my perspective," said Spider, starting the debate, "it appears Lilly is saying what we believe to be true becomes true, within certain limits. The body can only handle so much. We're super beings capable of superb intelligence, deep empathy and love for others, even for all of creation!" Spider tended to talk in long sentences since he was kind of a genius. "But we're all controlled by tape loops we've created in our minds from childhood trauma and cultural programming, so we endlessly repeat these negative patterns with our words and deeds. And especially in relationships! We continue on, year after year, carrying on blindly, until eventually we die from old age, unhappy and unconscious!" He threw up his hands in a gesture of despair.

This was all too much for Stephen, a hermit who lived in the woods. He was the more pragmatic one.

"Come on—super beings? This is all too airy-fairey for me! Isn't Lilly the dude who invented the isolation tank? And he did tons of acid in those tanks. What did you think was going to happen to his mind? Besides, he's a wealthy scientist. How can you trust anything he says?" He dunked his gingersnap into a large mug of steaming tea and smiled.

Spider ran his fingers through his hair then jumped up and started pacing. He nearly tripped on the hooked rug by the sink. "Yes, he's a scientist. But all of the experiments he conducted were on himself first, so he does have some scruples and isn't spending his life experimenting on helpless animals!"

Spider had recently become a vegan and couldn't take anyone being cruel to animals. Not ever. Not even for science. "And he has exercises you can do so you can become more aware, more conscious and not end up trapped in a life of mindlessness, constantly reacting, repeating those same tessellations over and over!"

Stephen was not impressed. "How is an isolation tank any different from meditation, like repeating a mantra with your eyes closed? I don't think I need to return to my mother's womb to become whole and happy on this earth!" It didn't take much for Stephen to feel content in his life: a warm shelter, food in the cupboard, hills to roam, and his home-grown pot to smoke. "Why not simply drop some acid or take a few mushrooms, and go sit in a dark closet?" he laughed manically.

We laughed along with him.

"Well, perhaps you could," Spider retorted, "but I for one can't! I am committed to my meditation group now and have to stay away from all mind altering substances. Didn't I tell you? I don't even smoke pot anymore. My state is too fragile. The layers between realities are already too thin." He sighed and sat back down. "I have to stay clean, to keep my energy clean."

Stephen patted him on his back, "It's OK, man. I get it. But you do meditate, right? You can go super deep by just meditating, eh? To get rid of all the old programming!"

The bantering went back and forth for a couple of hours. After they left I suggested trying an experiment, like Lily's.

"Aaahh. We have Ethan now, it may not be good timing," Pete said. "Why don't *you* try it? You could journey in the bathroom with all the lights off. It's pretty dark in there. We'll put the foamy down and I'll stay straight and be right here if you need me."

It sounded like a great idea. At the time.

Super Beings 2

The expression on the unshorn, bushy face in front of me, hoary from frozen days in darkness, constantly changes. A weak fire sputters in a rock pit at the entrance to a mountain cave. The countenance melts and transforms to take on the features of a regal prince with an Egyptian headdress, then into a handsome man with Roman features and curly locks. Then to a black man with wide nostrils, beautiful mustard brown skin and kind eyes. And lastly to a lean wizened East Indian monk with intense eyes who looks into me. And through me.

It is all the same face. A face who definitely sees me—the ever-changing face of the same man who now holds a cup of water for me to drink. First, it's the face of Pete. Slowly this facade dissolves and is replaced with an anonymous black-and-white mask, faceless and impersonal, hanging in a terracotta sky. Offering me water.

I do not drink the water. I close my eyes for a split second and go deeper.

I'm now curved and bound in a fetal position with only a few square feet of air to breathe. Cinder-brown soil surrounds and holds me in a world without resonance, only a muffled echo calling from far away. Blackness, obscurity. I reach out in all directions. A few sharp stones and roots stick into my legs and palms. An overpowering mineral smell of wet soil clogs my senses. I gasp for air. And panic.

"Get me out of here! Help me!"

Words spew out, muffled and garbled.

I kick and struggle but the more I push and thrash, the more soil and dust comes down on me. All my screaming and violent resistance is futile. I cannot escape it. This is my grave.

I think of my boy, Ethan. And of Pete and all the wonders of the earth and the tiny details of daily life I'll miss, the complex beauty of all creation. Salty tears run down my face and trickle into my mouth, in frustration, fear and hopelessness. Feet are numb. Hands are frozen.

Large, metallic arrow hands of a massive clock pulse away. My hands, icy and fragile. A second becomes an eternity. I have no choice. I must surrender to this situation, to my life. I have to accept all of it, not only the parts I like.

A brief moment of quiet, of peace, of total acceptance. I'm finally at the center of my cyclone, on the head of my needle.

Vertigo takes over. The body I'm leaving eases out of me. It seeps upward like heavy smoke through the soil and floats somewhere close by. A dusty field. I try to focus on where I am on the planet and can't. Can't get a reading.

A loud banging brings me back to my trapped body. Still underground. Open eyes. Blink. Close eyes. Can see without looking. Can see with eyes closed.

Perceiving a glimmer of light near my feet, a tiny shaft of heaven steadily widens as noises grow louder. Upside down. Let go and accept. Scraping, digging sounds and loudness of muttering voices increase. Let go and accept.

"Here. Here. I. Am. Here." I cry out and hear only a croak, like a subterranean frog.

Within seconds, cool air rushes into this tomb as earthen roof above opens. A strong hand reaches down, trying to grab me. Squirm. Upright. Grab it. Pulls gently. Can't see face. Tip head back and open gritty eyes. To see face. Need to see the face.

It is the face of my father, pulling me up.

Before blinking again, the face transforms first into Pete's, then into a rapid succession of familiar faces—all the faces I've ever known, ending in the most familiar one. My face. It slowly smiles back at me. A cheeky coal raven with a midnight-glass eye replaces this mirror.

One look at the raven and I'm gone, hearing only a forgiving voice explaining, as I lose all connection to reality. "It's all you. This is the dance of life. Every one reflects you. Everyone you meet is you. Everyone you have ever met is you. Everyone from your past. Everyone from your future.

There is only you. You, your creator and all of your helpers."

I wake in bed. Pete is sitting next to me frowning, eyes encircled in heavy bags. Dancing rainbow lights shimmer around him like auras. The grey light of early dawn around the edges of white drapes frames the square window.

"Are you all right?" he asks, taking my limp hand.

I turn my head. Ethan is asleep in his crib behind the rattan screen.

"Thank God you only did half," Pete says. "Did the meditation help?"

"Yeah, I guess. Wow, how long was I away?"

"All night! You were thrashing around and I carried you in here. I wasn't sure if I should call …"

I feel strangely energized. And reborn. My body is tired, but I feel much better in my skin. "You know, when I was a kid, we lived out in the country and used to play in caves created by the leaking water of big irrigation systems on the edges of potato fields. They were large caverns, close to five feet high sometimes. When my dad found out about them he freaked out, got his big steel shovel, stormed over to where they were, and destroyed them all! We were so mad at him. We didn't realize how dangerous they could have been. I was back in those caves. Damn."

Pete looks puzzled. I don't expect him to understand. This is for me to figure out. Closing my tired eyes, I sleep until the late afternoon.

Throughout the following weeks I continue to see Raven—a flash of black here, a penetrating eye there, piercing my heart. Reminding me life is simply energy, energy forming, energy flowing, energy shattering, dissipating and reforming.

Over and over and over.

And reminding me to be kind. To be kind to others.

For there is nothing to fear.

For everyone I meet is me. Everyone is me.

Ethan's Room

We finally move Ethan into his newly painted room. We'd hoped having more space may make everything so much easier for all three of us. But the poor tyke now cries at night, exactly as he did when he was newly born in the hospital and they wouldn't allow him to sleep with me. I have to drag myself out of bed at least three times a night and walk, half asleep, across the house and tend to him. I try to let the wailing go on for as long as I can, but his screeching slices into my womb.

My breasts ache. It doesn't feel right. What's a mother to do?"

He had become used to hearing us snoring and breathing close to him when we all slept together in the tiny bedroom. Mammal sleeping noises. It must have been reassuring for him to wake and know we were right there beside him. Now he's all alone.

We are animals, after all, with the same need for closeness and affection, and animals don't kick out their young until they're are ready to fly or survive or hunt on their own.

Now he's in a new room with creepy haunting phantoms and only his stuffed animals for company. It's a dark, scary world in his jail-like crib with the bars slicing up and down.

I wonder if we're making a mistake. *Is this supposed to be progress? More stuff, more rooms, and bigger rooms. Sometimes it seems that the further forward I go, the more backward I end up. Two steps forward and one step back.*

Nature Exploding

The spring weather continues to be super changeable, morphing from fierce winds to ominous clouds to hot sunshine, usually all in the same day. I'm feeling pretty level, a nice break from the usual state of affairs upstairs. Working in the garden keeps me going.

Being outside is the best. Nature explodes as fuzzy bees hum and purr around the stinky, pure white, sexy blossoms of the apricot tree. Cool breezes whisper magic verses in my eager ears, while the heady scent of decay and emerging life in the loamy, fertile earth keeps me grounded. For a few moments I'm in heaven. There is no denying it. I'm also addicted to gardening. It's in my blood. My head stays clear when I'm in the garden.

If only we could take this place and plunk it down beside a river in a secluded spot with trees and nature all around. But I've had a dream once before. I nearly had it all when I was with Karl, and look how long that lasted.

Well, I was too damn young. Besides, a lot of people don't stay married to the same person for an entire lifetime anymore. Times have changed.

What has not changed is me, and what I really want.

"I keep dreaming about him," I confess to Laura, a new friend, my sleepy voice almost a murmur. We're stretched out on a blanket on the patchy lawn, watching Ethan and Bobby playing in the sand pile. A genial spring sun slowly eases tight muscles. Laura has stopped by on her way to a tree-planting gig a couple of hundred miles to the north.

"Vincent *is* pretty cute," she says. "Not my type, though. But aren't you both married, or something? I mean to different people, not to each other."

"Well, yeah, of course. But I think they may be into the whole open-marriage thing. I don't know anything about it, but he mentioned it last time we were visiting there."

Laura turns on her side and peers at me through her thick glasses. She pushes her hands, strong and tanned from work in the bush, through her blonde mop of kinky hair. The curls spill through her fingers. She is not model-attractive but her intensity and intelligence are magnetic.

"What are your dreams about?" she asks.

"Nothing specific, simply thrashing around, fighting, in lots of different locations. With Vincent in them. In every dream we're working something out. Like getting through a lot of bullshit!"

"Damn!" She smiles and lies back. We each spend a few minutes in daydream time, in the middle of the day, stretched out on the plaid Woolrich blanket. Our toes point to the setting sun as the ground cools our backs. Almost summer.

One day in the middle of May the co-op has to do a land survey to prepare for the realtor's listing and we spend an entire high and beautiful day out on the property. A lot of members show up to help and it turns into a spontaneous picnic and short hike.

The energy of the place stays with me for hours after returning. I drag home pieces of driftwood and Rune-like stones and place them in special spots in the garden and on the floor in a corner of the bathroom dedicated to nature and beauty. A nature altar.

The most perfect art is found in nature, in the new petals of delicate wild flowers, the common snowberry, buttercups, and roses. In open meadows, where all wild creatures dwell and leave stealthy tracks. And in the mysterious, helix patterns perfectly imbedded in the weathered driftwood found on river shores.

I write:

> *Man's feeble attempts to create realistic, traditional paintings are crude in comparison to the original works which nature creates, things grounded in real matter. Paintings lack the depth, mystery and the power of light and energy and can rarely be faked on canvas.*

I draw an intricate spiral and colour it in with Ethan's crayons.

Vortex

Working quickly in the garden I dig deep holes for a dozen Beefsteak tomato plants, which are already far too tall and gangly and beyond ready for transplanting.

"Not before the end of May!" I've have been warned by the local Russian ladies. The danger of frost is real and can wipe out an entire spring crop. But I like to be ahead of schedule.

"Always be prepared, get it done as soon as possible. And there's way too much to do!" This is probably not true, and I don't know whose voice spoke those words, but they're deeply entrenched. *Another old tape loop.*

By early afternoon, the soil is warm. I enjoy the sensation of breaking up the clods in my palms and sifting the earth through my hands. A graceful, tranquil breeze caresses my cheek. Ethan is enjoying his time in the plastic-netted playpen. It keeps him out of my hair and he is good for about fifteen minutes at a time with his blocks, trucks and cloth books.

Only minutes later, opaque wet clouds roll in from outlying hills. Despite aching shoulders, I pick up my pace. Dig a hole, add manure tea, swish it around, plunk down the tomato plant, throw the dirt back in, tap it down, water. The gentle breeze returns, strengthens and starts to play with the strands of my long ponytail. This change is energizing, and I begin to relax into the work of digging the last few holes.

A tugging sensation in my chest alerts me and I glance up. A twenty foot high dust devil has appeared out of nowhere and whips ferociously through the fields of scrub across the road a few blocks away. As it swirls, it picks up all ungrounded objects in its path: tumbleweeds, sticks, and dried leaves. I flash to the twister in *The Wizard of Oz*. This is no whirlwind, this is a small tornado!

Please don't come this way!

The vortex ignores me and grows larger by the second. As if reading my mind, it furiously crosses the road and heads straight toward us.

Oh my God! Ethan!

He sits peacefully in the playpen, tapping out words in his storybook and chatting happily to himself. I drop my shovel and pushing through the strength of my terror, race over and grab him. My feet seem coated in heavy concrete blocks and a minute moves like a slow-motion movie as I drag us across the yard.

We hunch down behind the truck. The twister picks up the playpen as if it were a toy. Pieces of brightly coloured blocks and cloth books whirl above the ground and get sprayed over the yard. The cyclone whips and screams and corkscrews through the neighbourhood before heading east back the way it came, leaving a serious trail of debris and broken items behind it.

I stand up slowly holding my precious bundle close. My mouth is full of dirt. We're both shivering and chilled. Deep relief washes over me like a waterfall.

The next day, Pete and I head out to look for the missing playpen. We find it in a farmer's field two long blocks away, shattered and broken, like the bleached bones of a dinosaur relic.

Ethan and I narrowly escaped the destruction. The yard looks like a war zone. I manage to recover his books strewn throughout the back yard, tattered but still readable. Toy blocks lay scattered throughout the garden.

My tomato plants, newly planted on the edge of the spiral's wreckage, survive unscathed.

Thank you, thank you, thank you, I repeat over and over in my head, acknowledging the fragility of existence.

Deja Vu

I like Jess right away and find it refreshing to have a real conversation with someone my age about spiritual and philosophical topics. Most women in my life talk about boring stuff—all the domestic shit like childrearing, canning, what's new in fashion, food and on and on. Then they end up rapping about other people they personally know, discussing intimate details of private lives. Although part of me enjoys a bit of gossip, I've begun to wonder how I'd feel if the person they so casually criticized were me.

Today is different. Jess, a dark-haired beauty I met at Hannah's, introduces herself as an expat, a refugee from U.S. capitalism. I notice her accent as she confesses to leaving L.A. and all it has to offer. It feels like we've met before.

"Oh, it's so pristine here!" Jess raves. "Like, you have all these clean rivers and mountains, and there are barely any people. And the good vibes—I could feel it as soon as I crossed the border."

Jess has positive, upbeat energy.

"Good vibes? Here? Really?" I'm surprised. "It's a tiny mill town. Nothing much going on." I never imagined someone so sophisticated would find our small town to have good vibes.

"Yeah, I guess it does," I admit. "It's pretty laid back, and it is a beautiful valley. Other visitors say it, too. I probably take it for granted. Like the old saying, "you don't know what you've got 'till it's gone."

Give her a few months. She'll be begging to go back to California. Nothing here. So small you can read people's minds after only spending a few hours together.

"Perhaps I've been here before," she adds. "I've been having a lot of déjà vu since moving to the area." She smiles brightly and unties her colourful Indian scarf from around her wavy hair, rolls it up, and puts it into her geometrically patterned shoulder bag. "How about you? Do you ever have those experiences where you feel you've lived somewhere before?"

"Oh, definitely," I reply, admiring her natural ease. "Not as much here but quite often when I go to the coast, or even Nelson. It's like an old memory. I have all these feelings—intense emotions which seem to come out of nowhere. I'll be walking down the street, and then it'll happen …"

"And then," she interrupts, excitedly, "you're transported to another time and place. Sometimes it's only the smell of a flower, perhaps a wild rose in fresh bloom or the way the wind rustles the tall grass. I know! I can practically feel the kind of clothes I was wearing. Silken blouses and linen dresses. In another century or another time. You know?"

"And a sensation like something amazing is about to happen!" I add.

I'm overjoyed to be able to communicate with someone else on this level. It feels like Jess could be a member of a common tribe or a soul sister perhaps.

"Yeah, a lot of the time I feel like I could be living in the pioneer days," she says. Her voice trails off as her face turns up and looks west.

"Or on another planet!"

We both laugh and spend the next half hour discussing real things: *Autobiography of a Yogi*, current politics, the poetry of Kahlil Gibran, aliens, the Sufi faith, and various meditation techniques.

Before parting we exchange telephone numbers and swear emphatically we'll definitely be getting together in the near future for tea and more chats.

A few weeks later I hear from Hannah that Jess had met a hot tree planter from Nelson and moved away. I take it personally. *Why is it whenever I meet someone cool I can easily connect with they leave, usually for a better life?*

I fall into two days of depression, envious of Jess's freedom and her ability to go to a new place with a brand new boyfriend. My wanderlust bug kicks in, as it usually does in spring, and I mope around, resenting all my domestic duties. The day after I spend wrenched with guilt, wondering what the hell is wrong with me.

I should be grateful for all I have. But Jess's life is so much more exciting and interesting. She's so free. Beautiful and free. I only have tedious chores, responsibilities and heavy burdens.

Swimming

One early summer afternoon, after a couple of unusually scorching weeks, a handful of folks from the land co-op head down to the secret swimming hole near the black timber bridge a few miles up the west fork of the Kettle River. We scramble down the crumbly bank of loose boulders to a golden sand beach. Hannah brings a couple of joints and a large picnic basket full of cheese, crackers and fresh fruit to share. We enjoy this balmy day, swimming in the emerald green and clear cool waters and soaking up healing rays.

So far out of town no one has to worry about the nude police, so we don't stress. It's a luxury to spend the entire afternoon in the wild outdoors, slowly relaxing into all the free medicine nature has to offer. The gently healing, glacial river waters wash away all worries. Beach sand allows a body to sink into its own form and to rest. And the Sun, the true son of God, the Creator, the giver of all life in our world, burns away all darkness and heaviness from the previous long and cheerless winter.

But after returning home, after a tepid sun sets and after the blue hours of dusk settle into the cooling earth and when darkness hangs like a dense shroud, I contract again.

Ironically, after such a perfect day of connection to the grounding earth, a part of me is often called to the heavens. As I lie on my bed and try to sleep, a measure of myself, a very porous and lighter version of this self, yearns to be free.

I attempt to record the experience.

> *A 'me,' other than the one which normally resides in my physical body, becomes more of an observer. It's a strange sensation, not frightening, but like stepping out of my form, as if another body is pulling away.*

I see myself from above, my earthly body lying comfortably, on the verge of sleep. Who is looking at "me"? The porous essence is not malicious or terrifying, but the experience is troubling. I fear what would happen if this entity did not recede and I had to walk around with a psychic attachment for the rest of my life. Like a willful angel with sensuous, formidable wings, distracting me from my earthly joys and duties, continuing to pull me upwards and away from my body. Perhaps one day I wouldn't bother to return, choosing to live in the higher realms. Without this earthly form.

Wouldn't it be wonderful to be free of all the problems, aches and pains of having to care for this dense earthly form? Of having to feed it and water it and bathe it daily? After all, isn't our physical body simply the clothing, the cloth, the covering we wear that prevents us from seeing the real person, the real me, the real you, the naked soul. Hidden, but eternally so present?

Perhaps we all carry this earthly container around pretending this is the real person, when at the core, a true spirit or soul resides, invisible to most.

Every once in a while, as if by chance, we catch a glimpse of what's true, of something more, perhaps an accidental glance, a familiar profile, eyes that you have known for lifetimes, perhaps in a mind blowing synchronicity or in an experience that defies explanation.

I complain frequently about all my aches and pains, but I know I would miss this clumsy meat package if it were gone. I would miss the wind playing in my hair, the textures and feel of fabric, of fur, of water, of skin, of soil, of all I touch or come in contact with. I would miss every sound, from a robin's spring trill to the buzzing of lazy crickets, from the powerful bass in a rock concert to the cello and obo and haunting sounds in a string symphony.

I would miss all things I see, from the faces of those I love to the colours that reflect the vibrations of all things in my world. I would miss every smell, especially wet earth after a rain and desert sage and oranges.

I complain all the time, but if I lost this magic earthly body today, this evolving sensory machine designed especially for me by a creative force I don't understand, but definitely feel, I would surely miss it.

I would miss it like hell.

Why Bother

Everyone crashes early. As I drift off to sleep, the phone rings. Pete groans and rolls over, muttering, "Please get it. I'm beat."

I jump out of bed and race into the kitchen. The phone never rings this late at night. It could be bad news. Why else would anyone be calling at this hour?

"Hello?" I proceed to put on my housecoat, another old hand me down from my mother, but the sleeve is inside out and I struggle to turn it right side out.

"Hi, Sasha. It's Vincent."

My breathing stops. I haven't talked to him since the visit to the coast and am daily working on letting him go. I drop the sleeve of the robe and wrap the entire thing around me.

"Hey, there! What a surprise! I was almost asleep. So how are you, man?"

"I'm fine. I just got back from enjoying a beer at the pub and was thinking of you. Was wondering how you're doing?" He sounds bummed. "Are you sleeping better?" His voice is slurred yet still dreamy.

I'm suddenly much too hot and don't need the robe. It drops on the floor as my heart does a little kick.

"Yeah, I guess I'm sleeping better...no, actually, I'm not sleeping better. I have these strange experiences lately, kind of out-of-body stuff."

I hear him take a deep breath "Would you like to tell me about it?"

There's a tight band under my breasts, as if I'm wearing a push-up bra.

"Sure, I guess. Yeah, I'd love to tell you about it! This sounds kind of weird but sometimes as I'm about to fall asleep, I start to leave my body or some part of me starts to float above my body."

He takes another deep breath. "Hmm. . .you could be experiencing your astral body disconnecting from your earth body. It happens a lot in post-traumatic stress disorder, or even if your iron levels are low, like an anemia thing. Have you had your levels checked by your doctor? That might be it."

His voice is soothing and he seems to give a damn.

"I don't think my new doctor has checked my iron levels lately. The doctors here are such bloody know-it-alls! He suggested eating some meat! Yeah, not going to . . ." I start my fuck-the-doctors rant.

He cuts me off nicely. "Yeah, I have to agree. The regular establishment docs are so brainwashed. They're great if you need to get sewn up or even for a broken leg, or something. Possibly you need to get grounded. Mainly, all you need to do is to go barefoot more and spend more time outside. The earth is electromagnetic, of course. And we are electrical beings. So if you stand barefoot on the earth for a few minutes a day, that should help. It should help a lot."

"Okay. I'll try it. Sounds so easy. Thanks. Thanks for your advice."

"Anytime, my lady," he says. His deep, honey voice warms me down to my bare toes.

A sharp cry from the far bedroom brings me back to earth with a crash. "Oh, shit. I better go, it's Ethan. He's had a bit of a fever lately." The crying gets louder. "Thanks so much for calling, Vince. I appreciate it."

"Of course, no problem. Say hi to Pete!"

"Oh, sure, and say hi to Kath, too."

The end. I hold the receiver in my hand for a moment, still feeling the tenderness in his voice. The crying from the bedroom grows more insistent. I head in to comfort Ethan. Pete is sound asleep.

Strangely, Vincent had not suggested I was having a meaningful spiritual, out-of-body experience of some sort. Something mystical, helpful for the growth of my soul?

Maybe he doesn't know so much after all.

I push this thought away to where it can't cause me any more trouble or concern.

For the time being, anyway.

I do walk barefoot more and notice the difference right away. I feel more at home in my skin, less spacey and more grounded. That lasts about a week.

Lizzie comes by early and we spend an entire day doing normal domestic things, like cleaning out the sheds and tidying up. She takes charge and this doesn't bother me at all. I'm getting sick of permanently being the practical one, the one who gets things done.

"Let's get going," Lizzie says. "Is it all loaded up? Let's go unload this shit."

We climb into the old pickup and manage to all fit on the front seat. Baby Ethan sits between me and Lizzie. Jared squirms on her lap.

"Thank God it stopped raining," I say to get the conversation going.

"Yeah, it was way too much," Lizzie agrees. Jared is restless and jittering and she holds him tighter. "Sit still or I'll smack you." She raises her hand.

He settles down but looks a little hurt. Tears well up in his young, gentle eyes. Ethan snuggles in closer to me.

When we stop at the red light downtown, I start philosophizing. "I've been reading *Seth Speaks* lately. It talks about how if you imagine something clearly, with the right attitude, like internalizing it first, seeing it in great detail and clarity, it does manifest as something real. What do you think?"

She looks puzzled.

I try to explain. "This could be like the God, the creative force within us?"

She signs and digs in her purse for a cigarette. "Why do you think about all this shit? It's too bloody confusing. Just try to enjoy life. I think you think too much!"

Smoke fills the cab. I cough and roll down my squeaking window.

"Yeah, I guess you're right," I say. "I mean, you don't seem to be concerned or worried about all this stuff."

Lizzie rolls her eyes. "Why bother?"

We settle down for the last stretch of potholes on the dusty drive, crawling up winding roads and inching up the steep hillside to the dump. Dying and scruffy pine branches scratch the sides of the truck while unseen yet very present rattlers seek cover under piles of boulders on the road embankments.

"Whew!" I sigh, suddenly feeling hot and sweaty. Lizzie butts her cigarette on the side of the truck and throws it off into the bushes.

I stifle a comment about the dangers of starting a fire by throwing butts into summer dry brush.

Yeah, why do I even bother?

The next day all my aches and pains and stiffness and headaches return in full force. They seem twice as bad as before.

"You should see a chiropractor," Hannah recommends. "They help a lot of people, and it's covered by our medical plan."

"It's worth a try. What have I got to lose?"

It is certainly worth a try. I'm so tired of taking Aspirins. They help with the immediate pain but eventually tear up my stomach. In olden days, not so long ago—perhaps one hundred years ago—most women only lived into their late forties and I'm more than half way through. How I made it this far is a mystery.

I attempt a new technique. I'll ignore the pain and it will look for a new home. I'll refuse to let it be in control, whatever this illness is. If I chose to, I can be in absolute control of my vehicle.

Let's see if that works.

I pretend to be in control of my rusty body vehicle for a day or so but it's simply wishful thinking. A pounding headache returns in full force a few days later.

I make an appointment with the only chiropractor in Twin Forks.

* * *

During the week as I wait to get in to the chiropractor I try to keep my cool, but Pete and I squabble daily. We had driven out to Rock Creek to check out a highways road crew job but it still isn't looking good as far as employment is concerned. They did tell Pete there might be some work in the fall. We argued all the way home.

The next day he ignores me. I ask him at least three times to get started on refinishing the weathered window frames. He's in the middle of *The Monkey Wrench Gang* and isn't up for any work on the house. But the work needs to be done.

"They look fine," he says, turning a page.

"They're not fine," I stand firm, hands on hips. "They need to be sanded and painted. They'll rot otherwise!"

This motivation thing with Pete is so fucking frustrating. He doesn't seem to notice what needs to be done around the house. I have to push him to do anything. His pace is too slow for me and my pace is too fast for him. We never synchronize any more. It's aggravating and wearisome for both of us.

At this precise moment I'm concerned about the slowly rotting window frames and need him to understand it's important to keep them in good condition. My grandpa, old as he is, is a finishing carpenter and maintains his home, making sure to repaint and repair whatever starts to deteriorate. I learned at a young age how important it us to look after what you've got—even if it's not much.

"I know it doesn't feel like a big thing, but if we don't deal with it now we'll have to replace them all when they're worn out, and it will cost us big time!"

"Yeah, you're right. As usual," he fires back and drops his book on the floor. We walk outside together. He brings his red-handled hammer and taps lightly on the peeling paint. Uneven brows nearly meet in the center of a tanned forehead. His frown increases, wrinkling around brooding eyes.

"What the hell is the matter?" I ask. "Are you worried about getting the job? It's probably all for the best. I'm sure they'll call you soon. But forget about returning to Midtown. Their night shift is horrible!"

He throws down his claw hammer. It lands on the cement stoop with a hollow thud. "It's not about the bloody job! I've had jobs before and I'll have jobs again. I'm so sick of your bossiness! Leave me the fuck alone!"

He walks away, jumps into the truck and peels off in a cloud of spitting gravel and dust. I attempt to wave, hoping he'll stop, but my hand is too heavy and I go back into the house.

Jane is bent over in her front yard, weeding her overgrown irises. She looks over as I draw the kitchen curtains closed. *Fuck off! It's none of your damn business!*

I drag myself into the bathroom and slam the door. It's time for a soak to wash away the churning in my stomach and the ache in my heart.

Ethan bangs on the entrance to my refuge. He somehow knows when I'm upset. "Sasha? Sasha? Sasha? I want bath!"

I ignore him. I can't help it. *I'm sorry. I have nothing to give right now. I'll be out in a few minutes.*

The rushing water in the bathtub drowns out his persistent cries.

Headaches

"Thank God, some things are finally making some sense." I finally got in to see the chiropractor and had some X-rays taken. He called the next day to let me know there is an extra cervical rib in my neck area. C-7 or something.

"This could be why you keep getting headaches," he explains. "The discs could be quite squeezed in there and affecting the nerves. The spine is so important."

Who would have thought this was even possible? Wasn't it God in the Bible who took an extra rib from Adam to "make woman"? Well Eve I'm not! It all sounds bizarre, but this could possibly explain the headaches.

I look forward to my next appointment on Friday and am anxious to see what happens. I'm in such a good mood I manage to convince Pete we need to get out of town and spend a night on the co-op land. Gary and his dog, Boo, decide to come out with us. Gary brings his own wheels so he can get back to town before dark.

We plan to hike all the way to the north end, where a river forms the boundary, but spot a large black bear in the corner field and decide it's safer to head back and hang out at the cabin. Boo is a good dog, nevertheless dogs can be a problem around bears; it's generally best to stay out of their way.

At dusk Gary and his mutt head back into town but our little family stays. As the sun dips over the mountain ridge Pete gets a crackling fire going in the pot-bellied stove and we sit inside the rustic cabin on stools made of stumps and feel it get dark. Two large candles flicker and illuminate the tiny hut. We eat cheese and crackers and apples for supper. Simple, easy. At night I'm cleansed by the drizzle of light rain on the tin roof. The heart felt, throaty song of a lone frog a distance away warms my core. Peaceful and sublime.

In the early fresh morning we rinse our sooty faces in the icy stream as it trickles through the grove of alder only fifty feet away. Later, Daddy Wes and Mum arrive to cut down a cedar and load up the trucks before heading back into town. We'll split it for shakes and eventually use it to replace the roof on our shed. It takes quite a few hours. After all the sweating and effort, the rounds are loaded up and everyone gets ready to head back to town.

Daddy Wes, an Export-A butt hanging from his thin lips, rallies the troops to get going. "Get in here, mother!"

Mum, her newly cut and dyed strawberry blonde hair pulled back in a vibrant sixties turquoise-and-pink kerchief, hops into the truck and snuggles up to Daddy Wes. Although they're past middle aged, sometimes they act like a couple of teenagers on a permanent honeymoon. "There ain't no cure for love."

Perhaps those two will stay together forever, like two peas in a pod, and then pass on into eternity, like my bickering great-grandparents did. Then perhaps they won't. Life is so unpredictable.

I smile at Daddy Wes and get into our truck. "She's not your mother, you know!" I yell at him out the rolled down window.

He waves me off with a wide grin.

It's a little bewildering. *Why do some men call their wives 'Mother'? Maybe they all want a mother. Maybe everyone wants a mother, like everyone wants a wife, someone to care for them, wash their dirty undershorts and bake and darn and make heavenly meals, all with a gracious smile.*

Spending this day with the real mother, Mother Earth, with trees and open sky all around, is like being held in the hands of a creator. And I must admit it's thrilling to watch a tree being felled. The terribly loud drone and roar of the smoky chain saw, followed by the thunder clap of a falling giant smashing onto the forest floor sends deep vibrations rippling through a body.

I have to wonder though, if it's wrong to destroy such a marvelous thing as an eighty foot living, massive organism. We drive up in our large gas guzzlers, chop and saw it down, remove it from its primordial home. We slice its flesh to make our boards, build with it, hammer nails into it. Finally we burn it to create fierce, crackling fires to warm our weak, mostly hairless, fragile bodies. And usually not a word is said in honor of this grand being.

I know we need the wood but perhaps we could have said a word, a short blessing or given thanks at the very least!

No one here gets this concept; it seems kind of spiritually out there, so I keep quiet. Be quiet or get teased. I believe those are my only options.

Stop worrying so much. Stop trying to get people to see things your way. Stop trying to save the world! Words I've heard most of my life.

As the sun sets on another enchanted woodland day, the trucks head back to town, back to the modern world I don't actually miss, today. The world of chaotic noise and convenience, of logging trucks and trains howling in the distance, of light switches, refrigerators, televisions and flush toilets.

I'm still quite mellow from my night out on the land but am also a bit excited, a little anxious and can already feel my neck muscles tightening as I wait for the chiropractor.

Dr. M. enters briskly and sits down on his leather-topped stool. "So how are you this fine day?"

This is my first real adjustment appointment. He's the only game in town and I pray he's a decent guy. He appears to be middle aged yet fairly young, with enormous plastic-rimmed glasses slightly smudged on the bottom of the lenses. Average looking, and he didn't shave this morning. *All in all, a confident persona.*

"Well, things could be a little better," I say and hide my fear behind a giggle. My carnation pink hospital gown is open at the back, and I'm already feeling chilled.

"So, it's the neck. Yes. Let's have a look."

He opens his brown manila folder and pulls out an x-ray showing the head and shoulders of a tiny skeleton and hangs it on a wall mounted light board.

"Oh, my God, is that me?" I'm stunned at how strange and unrecognizable the X-Ray is—skeletal bones without muscle or skin.

"Yep, it's you, all right! And there appears to be an extra rib in the cervical region. It could be jamming up the joints in your neck, compressing nerve roots and possibly causing friction. And headaches. It's not very common, but some people are born like that. You're lucky, I guess."

After a lot of cracking and snapping and being twisted in all directions, I lie limp on the padded, blue plastic table. He gently covers me with a flannel sheet and reminds me to take it easy the rest of the day and to call him that evening.

"Take a minute here to rest and make sure to make another appointment for next week before you leave. See you then." He taps my shoulder and exits quietly.

The wet noodle effect and slight dizziness retreat as I get dressed mechanically. And yes, I do feel better. As if I'm in someone else's body.

Miraculously I don't end up with a headache the entire day. But Vincent calls and ruins my night. He lets Pete know he can't make it the next weekend. He had called a few days ago and swore he was coming out for a visit. I'm disappointed but not surprised. I refuse to mope around. I crash extra early.

The chiropractor calls right when I'm turning out the reading light.

"Wow! It's so wonderful to have a doctor, of sorts, actually give a damn. And to confirm something real is amiss," I say to Pete, coming back into the bedroom after hanging up the phone. But Pete's eyes are shut, he's already asleep, snoring his furry head off.

The Last Co-op Meeting

"And so it is done," says Gary, with Hannah on his arm. A closing statement. The final curtain call for the Wild Meadows Land Co-operative.

The four of us walk out of the rented Legion Hall where we attended the very last meeting. We stand around for a few minutes, all looking somewhat guilty. God knows all of us were ready to bail a long time ago.

"Well, almost done!" I remind them. "We still need to sell the land and it's not going to be easy. Two hundred acres for $120 thousand is a lot of freaking cash for wild land out of town. Even if it *is* all fenced and a near-utopia on the river.

They all nod in agreement. The property is listed with the town realtor. He'll have to talk it up with potential buyers in the area. And even with the cattle ranchers, which would break many hearts, as the cattle, those walking meat factories, can decimate pristine creek waters and muck up river edges.

Betty is obviously upset and teary throughout the meeting and doesn't talk to anyone on her way out. It goes to show it probably wouldn't have worked out anyway. Ray and Sissy didn't say a word and escaped by the back door. Hannah mentions that those two are looking into another co-op way up north, somewhere in moose country.

Well, good luck to them. But they did seem to be a little opportunistic.

Drapetomania

Ray and Sissy stop by our place a couple of weeks later. Rumor had it they were holed up on the mountain in their new makeshift cabin, figuring out what to do next with their lives.

I can hear them a block away—the muffler on their rusting wagon is shot and growls like a monster. I notice them drive up from my kitchen window and walk out to the back yard to greet them. Ethan is sleeping, Pete is in town, and I don't feel like entertaining company, especially these two.

Sissy carefully steps out from their scratched and faded brown panel wagon which is packed to the gills with cardboard boxes and yellowed bedding wrapped tightly in bundles with binder twine. She settles Zarya on her hip. He clings to her like a chimp. He hates to be left sitting on his own and she spoils him rotten, coming to his rescue whenever he falls down or makes the faintest squeak. Ray gets out, too. How he is able to drive is a mystery. The driver's side is stuffed with clothing (mostly filthy laundry), books (frayed and tattered encyclopedia Britannica, only half the set and various paperback cheap romance novels), grimy jars of apple cider (home made), and too many paper bags with mystery contents, mostly rotting compost and garbage, all this covering the floor and dusty dashboard.

"Hello, you two." I walk over and give each of them a tentative hug. More like a friendly pat on the back, since they both smell a little ripe. Patchouli does not mask days' (or several weeks) worth of sweat.

I lie and tell them Pete is working and Ethan is asleep. "Should we sit here for a bit?"

They look surprised, but we all sit down on the firewood rounds Pete and I retrieved from the co-op land. Sissy puts Zarya down gently. He looks over at me and whimpers. Sissy picks him up again, unbuttons her peasant blouse and pulls out a large healthy breast. He immediately latches on and starts suckling.

It would have been so good for Ethan to have been able to nurse. I only had small, swollen breasts and was too tense when he was born; the milk had not come. Or very little of it. This is what Betty, the midwife, told me anyway. She kept telling me to "just relax". Of course that didn't help. If only I had hung in there. But I was so tired and gave up easily. And it didn't help that all the hospital nurses also encouraged me to go ahead and buy some formula, constantly telling me how much easier it would be.

I come back to present time. "So where are you off to? You look like you're on the move."

Ray speaks up. He's usually the quiet one, but for some reason decides today he should be the one to share their plans. "Yes, we are. We're on the move. We desperately need some cash, though, so we're going to pick up a welfare cheque at the downtown office and then proceed north to the Chilcotin. I have a sister up there. She's ranching and farming with her husband. We may be able to stay with them a bit. Probably even get some work."

Sissy puts Zarya over her shoulder to burp him. "I hope to hell we make it," she says. "It's a fair ways, and I hate to leave this pretty valley, but we're so done here."

Ray looks amused. "Sissy has drapetomania," he says and smiles at me. "You know, the overwhelming urge to run away. She's had it for a while—comes and goes." He stands and stretches then walks over and gives her a kiss on the top of her head.

"Well, yes, I believe I could have drapetomania, and so what?" she laughs.

A jolt of envy sears me, watching them tease each other playfully for the next few minutes. *Who would have thought Ray was so playful and so smart? What do I know, anyway?*

Before leaving they ask if they can have their mail forwarded to our house, and offer me $10 to mail it on to their new address up north. Apparently Pete and I are "the most stable of all the ex-co-op members."

I take the crinkly bill, fold it, and stash it in my bellbottom jeans pocket. Ten bucks is ten bucks.

"Sure, no problem."

I feel used and kind of stupid after they leave, the tail end of their carriage spewing black, smoky oil. The stop sign at the corner flashes garnet in the sunlight as they turn off toward the highway and disappear. I'm left with a familiar, sick feeling in the pit of my stomach. Frustration eats away at my gut.

Why am I still stuck in this hole while they think nothing of loading up their car and hitting the road?

Many folks these days are able to pack up all their shit, throw it in a vehicle, and move to a whole new place. Gas is cheap and adventures are practically free. Some do this on a regular basis, not being weighed down by too many possessions, expensive mortgages, serious employment and needy family ties and obligations that can steal your youth and suck the life blood right out of you.

I mull this over as I pick up a twisted branch and whack the cut log I'd been sitting on. *She's such a taker, is Sissy. She does whatever the fuck she wants! And always looking for a free ride. Getting a fat welfare cheque and then moving on! That's not fair!*

Pete and I may have done the same in the distant past. But I've forgotten all this as I get caught up in my envy for Sissy and her perceived freedom.

Turning to go inside, I spy Bobby standing on his porch, staring with a glazed look in his despondent, child eyes. Pretending I don't see him, I stride back into the house, slamming the screen door.

Before bed, I talk to my man about the short visit and about the possibility I could also have drapetomania. He doesn't seem to hear me, so I continue on, "Old Sissy seems to be looking for a free ride. I didn't think she even liked me, yet she comes over here to ask me to send their mail on!"

Conveniently, I had forgotten to tell Pete about the ten dollars they gave me for stamps. It's more than enough, of course. The ten bucks is now hidden safely away in a matchbox in my linen drawer. He doesn't need to be bothered with such details.

He patiently listens to my rant then dumps all over me. "Sissy looking for a free ride, eh?" His voice gets shrill. "Yeah, maybe, but how about yourself? You know I pay the bills, even though you're raising our son and do a lot around here. Whenever you accuse someone of something negative, remember that finger points right back at you!" He points his crooked index finger at me and heads off for bed.

The harsh words shot off the end of his shaking digit spear my heart, as if a bullet has lodged there and real blood was pooling and would soon burst into a heavy stream, flooding all feeling.

I spend the rest of the sleepless night on the lumpy couch, fretting and uncomfortable. I finally admit to myself that perhaps he is right.

The remainder of the night is spent rehashing our fight and trying to make sense of it. *Pete's finger sure does seem to be pointing back at me lately. Sissy hasn't actually done anything to me, yet I always put her down. I'm not doing anything great with my life, either. Being a mother doesn't seem to count. It isn't enough for me, and it doesn't seem to be enough for Pete. I know he mostly appreciates what I do, but I rarely hear any praise.*

He was raised to "speak when you're spoken to" and "don't get too involved in women's concerns. Just make sure you pay the bills!"

He doesn't seem too worried about my concerns. He is not curious about me. Unless I make life hell for him. He doesn't ask what my true heart's desire is, but only complains. 'What's wrong with you? I don't know what the fuck you want!'

Perhaps Sissy, dear Sissy, has the right attitude about being a woman. She doesn't care whether being a mother or housewife may be all she'll ever be. Despite the fact I've always despised her and don't trust her, she seems to be so much happier than I've ever been. *Why can't I be more like her? Why can't I lighten up? Why do I have to be so intense? Life would be so much easier.*

Planting in the Woods

"Are you sure this is it?" Pete asks.

The two of us stumble along a matted trail close to the river. It's difficult to see the deer path through the tall, wet grasses of timothy, nodding oat grass and the decaying gnarly grey branches of dying cottonwood trees. Knotted white blossoming clover runs in patches here and there between rough fescue and milk vetch. We each carry a cardboard box of our special plants ready to be transplanted to a warm, sunny forest meadow, somewhere with easy access to the water. Off the grid. We'll check on them over the summer, every once in a while, to make sure they get enough moisture to thrive.

"He's supposed to be living out here somewhere in a shack," Pete says. He peers down the trail, looking for Stephen's rustic cabin.

I spot the hairy, shiny green foliage of poison ivy encroaching on the path and step around it warily, careful not to bruise the leaves.

"Shit, the mosquitoes are nasty down here." I swat a big sucker on my arm. Slap! "Got 'im!"

"Keep moving—we're almost there!" Pete urges.

Stephen's overgrown hovel is falling down at the corners. But it's sweet, a one room trapper's log cabin with a packed dirt floor. An overgrown herb garden in the front and outhouse in the back complete this squatter's paradise. We knock. No answer. Pete gently pulls open the barn board, leather-hinged entrance. No one home.

"Hello?" Pete yells, too loudly.

"There's no one here," I whisper.

"I know—I can see that!" Pete heads outside and walks around the back of the cabin. He returns, shaking his head. "Nope. No one here, I guess."

"We can't transplant these today if Stephen doesn't even know they're out here. I'd hate for him to get busted for plants that aren't even his! It wouldn't be right."

"Yeah, shit. It looks like we missed him by about a day or so." Pete checks the coals in the home-made tin stove. "Still a touch warm."

Stephen, or The Bushman, as we call him, survives on as little as possible by going through dumpsters for food and furniture, growing a few things and doing odd jobs. He doesn't want the typical house in the suburbs or a domestic life and is constantly on the move. At times he lives in tepees or tents when the weather is good. Or squats in remote, abandoned shacks and miner cabins, fixing them enough to make it through the hot summers or the snow and ice of winter. He must have his weed, though. It keeps him going. He always grows his own and tends it carefully in secret locations—under the radar, so to speak. He'd probably be OK with us planting our young ones at the edges of his meadow, but it isn't right to assume. At least this is one thing Pete and I agree on.

I am restless. "Let's go."

"What's the rush?" Pete asks. "How about we hang out for a bit."

He closes the rickety door and pulls out a thin reefer. We sit down and share a few tokes on the scruffy cot which is covered with a coarse, wool army blanket. It smells strongly of moth balls. He pulls me toward him.

"Hey, what are you doing?"

He unties my mop and runs his hand through my hairline, gently massaging and tugging on my ear lobe. He moves to kiss me.

I start to panic. "What are you doing, man? Chill out! Stephen could show up at any minute!"

"Yeah, I know. But he probably won't! Don't worry...shh...it'll be fine. Come here!" He falls backwards on the bed and pulls me down on top of him.

My heart races and I'm so damned anxious about someone coming in at any second. I feel so damn hot, and this is suddenly so exciting. I pull down Pete's frayed jeans. He undresses me, tearing open my loose cotton blouse and bringing his lips to my warming skin. I can smell mildew in the blanket and the wood coals from the stove. My arms are covered in goose bumps and I start to protest. Even though I'm burning hot, there's too much going on and I forget about it.

The old cot creaks loudly and rhythmically. My eyes keep looking back at the door, fearing anyone may enter. But no one interrupts our tryst, our long overdue sexual coupling.

We're more relaxed after the shared climax releases the recent tensions and fights, and we even cuddle for a few minutes before dressing in damp clothes and returning to the truck with our plants.

The next night, I plunk the healthy bushes in the greenhouse soil back home, which seems like the best option, considering the severe rain and wind we've had lately.

Something strange starts happening in the greenhouse though. Every morning when I go out to water or check on them, there is one less plant.

Are they being stolen or disappearing into another dimension? What the heck is going on?

Lo and behold, three days later, I discover mounds of fresh dirt outside the greenhouse and realize a local, friendly fat mole has been enjoying these morsels—the little rascal! I find his entrance hole a few feet away, turn on the garden hose and run the water full blast into his tunnels. I feel a twinge of remorse for possibly drowning the poor bugger. But I convince myself he'll dig his way out to the next field. Mainly I hope he never returns. He could wipe out what's left of our weed plants, all six of them, within only a matter of days.

Still, I have a cautious respect for and curiosity about, the little infiltrator.

And did our tasty cultured vegetation make him stoned?

Bad Things Come in Threes

The chiropractor treatments continue to work miracles on my headaches. I stop taking Aspirins. It's gratifying to know there is a physical reason for all those headaches. Once in a while I feel one coming on, but it rarely seems to manifest.

On June 15, Pete and I celebrate my twenty-second birthday. Most forget my special day, even my mother. I'm actually quite hurt but pretend it's no big deal. My chiropractor, Sam and Aunt Sally call to wish me a happy birthday.

Pete's gift for me this year is a used telephone-answering machine he picked up at a pawn shop downtown, as I complain about missing calls while I'm outside working in the yard and garden.

Even Vincent doesn't call. Shit.

I throw my phobia of dying at twenty-one out the kitchen window. For some reason I used to believe I would never make it past this year, in any of my lives.

Surprisingly, I'm still here.

As I finish sweeping up in the kitchen, I am feeling more optimistic about Pete and me as we haven't had a real fight this week. A little bickering here and there. It's tolerable. He sits in the rocker, reading an article in *Mother Earth News* about water turbines. Ethan has fallen asleep early.

"I checked out the newly painted thrift shop today. It looks like crap: Pepto Bismal pink, of all colours— yuck! Have you seen it?"

"No," he says, "I have not seen the new thrift store. Not on my list."

I pick up a tone in his voice. "What list?" I ask, and stop sweeping.

"You know, my list…oh, forget it!" He gets up and heads for the bedroom.

"What's going on?" I ask. "It's early, only 8:30, you crashing already?"

"Yeah, I'm a little tired." He rolls up his magazine. "Going to read in bed for a while."

"Tired? From doing what? Jesus! All you've done all day is sand the window frames and dig around in the garden for a few minutes."

"Oh, shut up! Not everyone is a workaholic like you!"

"A workaholic? What are you talking about? I don't even work anywhere!"

Why is he attacking me?

"Whatever! If you haven't noticed lately, you can never relax!" He doesn't look tired anymore. His eyes shine demon-like and his face is flushed.

Shit, what did I do wrong? Fine, if he wants a bloody fight, I'll give him a fight!

"Relax? What the hell? Yeah, I can't relax. But you, on the other hand, are a master of relaxation and are so fucking lethargic and lay around most of the time. I can't wait until you go back to work! This is ridiculous. You have no ambition for anything!"

He throws his magazine violently across the room.

"Fuck you! You know, times like these I wish I was single!"

Mother Earth lies on the floor like a beaten, dead animal.

"You're not the only one who'd love to be single. It would be great! Because living with you *is* exactly like having two children!" My throat is raw.

"Children?" Pete's eyes are blazing. "You don't know anything about children, that's for damn sure! You need to get some help with your mothering skills! You can be such a cold fish. You're not loving to Ethan much of the time, so worried about cleaning up any little mess he makes. You suck as a mother. It's all about you! You are so damned concerned about you! It's all about you! You, you, you! All you care about is how you're doing!"

"What the hell are you talking about?" My heart is pounding and my head feels like it's about to explode.

And so it goes, on and on, an all-nighter. Each of us blames the other and points out the other's defects. I finally run out of the house and sit under the apple tree, sobbing. Monsoon tears, held back for weeks over a long, dry season of hurt, overflow on the damp grass.

Pete eventually retrieves me and we make up as the house sparrows start their morning song. The dove- gray sky streaks to a peach orange, trying to welcome a new day. We're both sorry. We both say "sorry," anyway. I guess we're even, so to speak, even though it had been an exhausting battle.

I've learned a bit about myself. I'm getting to be a real bitch and if I want someone to truly love me, I'd better stop reacting so violently to Pete.

Perhaps he's right. Who really cares about things being perfect? Why am I obsessed with having everything so clean, and doing a "good job"?

❋ ❋ ❋

The words "bad things come in threes," another old superstition of my mother's, plays over and over in my head by the end of the day. Pete received our tax assessment in the mail. Seventy dollars! Where are we going to get this kind of money by the end of the month?

He rants non-stop all the way home. "Damn Bennett and his buddies, the old Socreds, they only care about their clan, the rich folks with the big bank accounts! They don't give a damn about us poor folks trying to scrape by. How people can be so stupid as to elect these imbeciles is beyond me!"

I pick up where he leaves off. "I know! And because they call themselves Social Credit doesn't mean they're social or socialists. On the contrary, they're such greedy capitalists— it's sickening!" Being Marxist leaning, if Pete and I agree upon one thing, it is politics.

Unfortunately, most of the taxes we pay are municipal and we don't even know who the current mayor is.

So that was bad thing number one.

Upon returning from town, I go into the shed to grab a bucket to water my tomatoes and discover with horror that a container of Rotenone, a natural insect repellent, had fallen off a rickety shelf and broken one of my favorite lush weed plants.

"Shit!" We had brought in a couple of the larger still- potted plants to feed them and left them in the shed overnight. This accident seems a little fishy to me and I'm immediately suspicious. *Why did that one specific can fall off the shelf on this day. And exactly when we were in town? Who would come in here, anyway? We do leave the shed door unlocked, so anyone can merely walk in.*

I glance over at the Bear residence, but it all looks quiet.

Although I have my suspicions, I can't go accusing people without any real evidence. Bad thing number two.

Incident number three: our well loses its prime and damn it, we have to ask Bear for his help. His behavior is so unpredictable and no one knows how dangerous he actually is. But we have no water. We can't live without water. He's good at fixing things and has those special tools in that creepy workshop of his. Pete walks over and chats him up and Bear comes over right away. Yep, Bear gets the old well going by the end of the day.

I drive downtown immediately after and buy him a case of Kokanee. We have to give him something, a compensation of sorts; otherwise, it would feel like we owed him, and I hate that feeling. It's like an unpaid debt that can catch up to you at the best or the worst of times.

And as everyone knows, there is nothing worse than unpaid debts.

Weeding Onions

"Hey, Missy! Wait up!" Patsy, the old boss lady shouts at me from a few yards away. "You have to pull out all the weeds. Not only the easy ones. Come back here!"

I started weeding early this morning; a grunt labor job on enormous onion fields owned by Rick Aberov, our most prosperous local farmer. He employs a lot of people. The wages are low, but he isn't fussy and he'll hire almost anyone. It's brutal, physical work, but I like it. No one bugs you and you can toil away at your own speed. I prefer working in the open fields to being stuck in the freezing, gloomy packing house. Suffocating and claustrophobic, that job requires standing inside all day while enormous belts continuously and noisily roll by, loaded with dusty onions or potatoes needing to be sorted and culled while weak overhead lights cast harsh furrows across grimy faces. A perfect horror-movie setting.

Patsy works six days a week. She's usually out here at the crack of dawn, joking and teasing the crew. She's friendly enough, but I get it: we don't have a lot in common. She's older, probably in her late forties. Her son owns the farm and the packing house and although she's the "boss" of the field crew, she treats everyone fairly and works as hard as the rest.

Her daily uniform consists of stained, baggy overalls and men's bleached white T-shirts that fit her stocky frame comfortably. A red, carefully tied bandana hangs neatly around her tanned, plump neck. A clean white hanky is always within reach, neatly folded in the front pocket of her coveralls.

"Don't bother me!" I yell back and playfully throw a small clump of grey clay back at her. It shatters on her leather work boot, creating a mini dust cloud.

The air is blistering hot and perpetually dusty and all anyone can see for miles are fields of weedy onions—row upon row of spikey green tops, sometimes submerged by lamb's quarter and alfalfa in bloom.

Patsy grunts, then smiles and holds up a long, limp clump of redroot pigweed. "Like I said, don't forget these, you can eat them, you know, but we still got to pull them out!"

Two older Doukhobour ladies, oversized woven straw hats shading their deeply creased, coffee- brown faces, start laughing and soon we're all teasing each other. It appears to be the only way to get through this kind of toil.

"Hey, what happened to you, anyway?" asks Patsy, as they catch up. "I remember you from when you were a little girl and you were so nice and cheerful. And helpful." She shakes her head. "Boy, have you ever changed!"

This comment is a surprise to me. She's probably only joking, but I instantly feel stung, and fire back. "Yeah, I smartened up, That's what happened."

Today I'm not afraid to talk back to these fellow workers, these women of the fields. It would be disrespectful in the Doukhobor culture to talk back to your elders. That culture has given me a deep connection to the earth, for which I'm only recently learning to feel grateful. Having long since abandoned going to sobranyas, the choir meetings, or following most superstitions, rituals or dogma that may still exist, respect and love for the earth and esteem for elders has somehow stuck. Toil and a peaceful life. Toil and a peaceful life. The peace part sounds good, but perhaps there is far too much toiling.

Patsy stands carefully and leans backward, planting her hands on wide hips, trying to ease her back pain. "Only an hour to go. And then it's time for cucumber kvass with lemon. And home, sweet home, to put my poor achin' feet up."

I can't wait to put my feet up, too. Imitating her movements, I try to get some relief for my taut neck and shoulders. Patsy enjoys being here. This is her life. But I also see how red, swollen, and stiffly arthritic her muddy fingers look by the end of her shift.

Is this how I want to end up at fifty, working the fields, dragging my body home at the end of each day with swollen fingers that can't bend, a sore back and all orifices full of black powdery dust?

I'm young compared to these gals but this field work is much like the working-in-the-mill trap. Next thing I know I'll be thirty then forty and then an old woman and still a slave. I fear ending up with no other way to survive and make a living except for this kind of body-breaking labour. I long for work which feeds my soul and is creative and nourishing, work which compensates me for my energy and contribution. I'm not sure what kind of work that is, but field work, it is not. Not today.

Today, aside from my sore neck, my main problem with this job is the stench. The smell of onions has leached into my skin, like the odour of a cheap perfume. I can't get it out even after a hot soak and a scrubbing. It may be stuck in my nostrils forever.

Even so, it feels great to come home when the day is finished, dusty and tired and sweaty, but with a bit of my own hard earned-cash in my pocket.

I earned these pennies through my own efforts, by the sweat of my brow. Perhaps I can support myself if I have to.

Knowing this sits comfortably in the back of my mind like a soft cushion, a soft place to land. Or like a colourful book marker showing me where I need to look when I need to remind myself of my own small power.

Meditation actually does help with premenstrual crankiness and headaches. Unfortunately, I don't seem to have the willpower to sit still. I need to be doing something.

Even weeding onions can be a meditation. As long as I remain in the "here and now," the work is easy and smooth. As soon as I try to get finished faster, or to catch up to someone, it becomes difficult. Sometimes I even get mad at the weeds.

As the summer heats up, there are days when it's already scorching hot at only nine o'clock in the morning, reaching 90° F in the shade, so it's even a challenge to get through the first few hours and survive until noon. The ground turns to packed clay and eventually dries solid as concrete. While toiling, I pray for a good cool shower to drench and soften the earth.

And with the physical stress on my back and neck from this kind of labour, bent over all the time and straining to pull every weed, my headaches return with a vengeance.

Gifts and Callings

"You're crazy." I hold a crisp, brown $100 bill. Queen Elizabeth The Second stares back at me, her expression distant and unreadable. "I can't take this!"

Mum hangs her clean dishtowel on the stove handle. "You will take it, and when it's all done, you'll get more. You'll receive more when all the paperwork goes through. You two girls have helped me when we lived on the ranch and you should get something now it's sold! I love Daddy Wes, and we have our new family now, but it makes me feel good to give you all something. So take it, and shut up! I know you need it. Lizzie had no trouble taking her share. And I forgot your birthday this year! Now what kind of mother is that?"

Her lip sticks out, drawing a tired mouth down, a face of regret.

We finish up our Red Rose tea and walk out to look at the new garden. Mum and Wes don't have as much land here in their more modern home in town. It's much smaller than the ranch. But one must have a vegetable garden, no matter how big the yard. Not to have a vegetable garden would be sacrilege.

This addiction to gardening wears us both down in years to come. A blessing and a curse, the constant work in nurturing and growing things is so beneficial for body and soul. But after years and years of digging and pruning and pulling weeds, it can also tear rotator cuffs, destroy weak backs and wear an aging body out.

At dusk I swallow my still lingering feelings of rejection and hurt from our last visit and call Vincent in Vancouver to let him know about a job for a school counsellor recently posted in the local rag. He is a psychologist after all, more than qualified and has often said both Kathy and he would love to leave the big city and get back to the land, possibly set up a small hobby farm or a retreat center. The co-op is totally done, yet I continue to hope he'd still like to move to Twin Forks.

"How did you hear about this job, Sasha?" he asks.

"Oh, I noticed it in the Valley Voice while copying out a recipe from the Foods Page and ..." I suddenly feel awkward.

He doesn't press for more details "Well, thank you so much, Sash. I won't forget this. I'll send them a resumé right away! And I may be seeing you sooner than you think."

Hours later, I'm still flushed from talking with him. I swear he can see right through me—sometimes I think he can read my mind. He says all the right things.

It may be a total waste of time to think of him and yearn to be closer to him, but I can't help myself. It's beyond me—out of my control. Maybe it is an addiction.

Who knows what may come of all my yearnings, but I must be true to myself. I must follow this summons, this plea from my soul.

This calling.

❋ ❋ ❋

My grandparents invite Pete and me to Sunday dinner to meet Gregoire, a visiting and quite distant Russian relative. Shortly after arriving and exchanging a few words, it's obvious he's a total redneck. He's dressed like a mafia character and acts like one, too. His black hair is slicked back; grey polyester plaid pants and a mottled print on his stiff shirt complete the outfit. He's as straight-laced as they come and snickers at Pete's long hair. He makes rude comments in Russian, calling Pete a girl, a dyevoshka, and tells him he needs to get his hair cut, get a job, and act like a man.

When Pete finally answers politely, trying to make conversation, Gregoire says, "What? What?" and pretends he doesn't understand.

I have a short fuse for mean people and am ready to leave after only ten minutes. "Let's go," I tug on Pete's sleeve.

"It's OK," he says. "We'll stay for dinner and then head out." He's not being diplomatic; he's a sucker for my Baba's borscht and her vegetable tarts, and he missed out on the last batch because of the fight we had months before. He doesn't understand most of what the thug is saying. I attempt to translate for him, carefully skipping the snide, nasty remarks.

The smell of cheap aftershave and Brylcreem still linger in the kitchen after Gregoire and Grandpa head out to the workshop to partake in appetizers: shots of vodka and puffs of Belomorkanal, those fetid Russian cigarettes. Neither invite Pete to join them.

Dyeda looked a little embarrassed as he walked past us, his balding head hanging down, drooping eyes peering at his worn slippers. Baba booted them out only a minute before, right after Gregoire lit up at the table. No one smokes in her house, especially in her kitchen.

I give a silent cheer. Pete and I share "the look" and decide to spare ourselves an evening of discomfort. We thank Baba for inviting us over and then lie, telling her we're both not feeling well and have to go home. She asks no questions and quickly wraps up a dozen bean, pea, and potato tarts in a clean flour-sack dishtowel and stuffs them into a yellowing Cheerios box pulled from the crowded pantry. My grandma, the original recycler.

The treats are still warm from the oven, and we'll have them at home, in peace, topped with melted butter, sour cream and homemade sauerkraut.

We give her a big hug and make our getaway, waving goodbye to the old boys who stand by the back door of Grandpa's workshop, sipping their booze. They are chatting away and appear totally lost and preoccupied in their conversation and don't even notice our departure.

Or pretend not to.

And the world doesn't end this evening as was predicted by a psychic in Vancouver. Shit. I'm actually curious as to what would happen next. It could be a whole new adventure.

After our delicious meal, I stand in the kitchen and look out the window, facing the setting sun at exactly six o'clock and give thanks for all the life around me.

It could all still come to an end at any second. A comet could crash into this paradise, a solar flare could send the magnetic poles off balance and it would be the end of civilization as we know it. Anything could happen. But today I feel blessed to have this complex and beautiful setting in which to learn my life lessons. Perhaps in another reality or plane of existence the world does end. But on this day, Pete and I and Ethan, and the entire group of people in my reality, we're all still alive.

Leonard Cohen lyrics run through my head. "They laughed and laughed and said, 'Well child, are your lessons done? Are your lessons done?'"

No, my friend, never done. Never done.

❋ ❋ ❋

We finally get around to finishing sanding and fixing the front window frames and painting the bedroom one. Am I materialistic because I like to be surrounded by nice things? By nice I mean good vibrations, clean, peaceful, beautiful and aesthetically pleasing. For me, perhaps that is normal.

As I work beside Pete, scraping and painting the old wood, I experience an intense flash: *One day I won't be here. Like in ninety, or a hundred or a thousand years. My body of flesh won't be here, this is for certain. So then, where will I be? The "I" who is me?*

I desperately want to carry on, somehow, somewhere, as a self-conscious entity or at least a being conscious of itself in some way. Is this simply narcissism? Or a large ego, afraid of being totally extinguished? As I scrape off the flaky pieces of decomposing wood and they fall onto the ground like dried flower petals I try to imagine Nothingness.

Zero presence. Absolutely nothing.

It doesn't work. Try as I might, I cannot comprehend non-existence.

Lizzie gets another job and asks me to babysit. Again. Recently, this babysitting has become a regular thing with way too many overnighters. She's started slinging beer at the Five to One Inn, a foul-smelling, smoky pub on the edge of town. Her housekeeping job at the motel doesn't pay enough. I know she needs the money, but can't understand how she can work in a bar.

I don't mind helping out but more than half the time she doesn't pick him up until late afternoon of the next day. She has a serious problem with booze. Like so many people in Twin Forks, poor Lizzie suffers from too many twenty-four hour hangovers.

Am I being too judgmental? I check the clock. Already past nine. Jared had been over since nine o'clock this morning. *Perhaps I am, but aren't most people judging everything and everyone all the time?*

As I am about to turn out the lights, I hear an unexpected knock at the back door.

Take the Back Road

Half an hour later, Daddy Wes sits slumped in a kitchen chair. He slurs his words. "Are you sure I'll still be able to drive home?" He's had a few too many drinks before stopping by. His widely spaced eyes are heavy lidded and I feel a flash of doubt, fearing the worst. *He could drive off the road and crash into a tree, or…*

Pete jumps in. Surprisingly he woke up and jumped out of bed as soon as Wes showed up. "Of course you'll be able to drive! Having a toke or two does not affect your driving in any way!" he swears emphatically. "In fact, you'll probably feel a lot better than you do now!"

Pete gets up to roll one. I haven't seen him this excited in weeks.

The last thing I expected was for Daddy Wes to show up on our doorstep on a Saturday night and ask us to smoke a joint with him. "A lot of the guys at work have been talking about it," he admits. "I want to see what it's like! Do you have any? Can I buy one?"

"Where is Mum?" I ask, refusing the five-dollar bill he waves at me. "Does she want to try it?"

"Your mother has a headache. She's probably in bed already!" He taps his cigarette on the tin ashtray. Much like Lizzie, I have trouble saying no to him when he wants to smoke in the house. I open the kitchen window a crack.

Pete lights up a fattie of leaf and sucks back a big one then passes it to Daddy Wes. Who looks terrified but takes it gingerly and attempts to imitate Pete's method. The coughing fit lasts a good three minutes. He slowly settles down, his eyes soften and his shoulders drop. He looks relaxed and leans back.

"Yeah, this is nice," he says. "All right. Cool. Actually I feel pretty good." He has a silly grin on his face, which is now flushed and a little sweaty. "Should I have some more?"

I glare at Pete and shake my head.

"How about I give you one for the road? Or you can have a few puffs when you get home. Just remember to hold it in for a few seconds." Pete pulls out his stash from the back of a kitchen drawer. A plum-coloured velveteen bag holds the treasure.

"I know, I know. Wow, I feel way more laid back! Thanks, you guys."

Daddy Wesl stands up and starts to put on his work jacket. He appears more relaxed yet still troubled. A secret storm brews behind those coffee brown eyes.

"Well, at least we can celebrate tonight!" Pete says. "We got some tax money back from the Feds—can you believe it? Overpaid our income taxes! Now that's a bloody first!"

"Nooooooo! What the hell is happening? I've never received any extra money from the government!" Daddy Wes starts laughing then tries to stop snickering and clamps his hand over his mouth. His shoulders shake up and down as he silently chuckles to himself. We join in the merriment with belly laughs and giggles.

I hear a clatter and Jared runs in from the living room where he's supposed to be sleeping. "Grandpa, Grandpa!" He climbs onto Daddy Wes's lap and they snuggle. Those two have a special heart connection.

D. Wes soon passes a clinging Jared over to me. "I better head home or I'll be in big trouble with Mother!" The same dark look.

Despite Jared's whimpering I manage to pry him away. We both give old Wes a warm hug and remind him to drive carefully.

"Take the back road! The cemetery way, you'll be safer." I pat his arm. "Say hi to Mum."

He smiles. "Yep!" and heads out the door.

Pete walks him out to his truck while I tuck Jared back into his makeshift bed on the couch, rubbing his small back to sooth his little troubled soul. He keeps asking for his mother. All I can say is, "She'll be here soon; it's OK." But it isn't OK at all.

I check on Ethan in his room before turning in. The moonlight falls gently on his soft baby cheek. I pull up the covers.

The phone rings alarmingly in the middle of the night but when I finally crawl out of bed and pick it up, no one is there. Only a distant humming and a buzzing in the earpiece.

The next morning, Mum calls me out of the blue. "What the hell did you do to my old man? He came home last night from your place around ten thirty. He turned on all the outdoor lights and stayed in the yard, digging holes and singing old Charlie Pride songs until way past midnight! He told me he was putting in the new wooden fence posts. And he seemed so damned pleased with himself when he came inside."

I can hear her rinsing the dishes as she chats. Mum's craned neck is probably trying to hold the phone on her shoulder as she works. "I was wondering what the hell was going on! He had this shit-eating grin on his face all night. But we had a truly enjoyable evening, playing crib and drinking coffee with shots of Bailey's, of all things! He never drinks Baileys!"

A laugh escapes before I can stifle it.

"Ha, you can laugh, Sasha, but when we got up this morning and looked out the window, all the friggin' posts were crooked and out of line!"

Mum and I then share a chuckle. She knows.

No more is said.

The Bite

During the weeks that I try to bring in some cash with my babysitting and field work, Ethan becomes more and more needy. I understand he probably feels abandoned, but it's a real pain. The other day he sat down by the bolted bathroom door and called my name over and over until I emerged. It broke my heart to lock him out, but sometimes a girl needs her privacy.

The rain brings a much needed break, thank the gods. The soil is still much too compacted to work in the fields so I'm home, trying to catch up on my backed up housework. Am overwhelmed and irritable. Ethan is bored and irked, wanting to be tearing around outside with that misfit Bobby from next door. "Please, outside?" he repeats. I ignore him.

"Sasha, look!" he says loudly.

"What?" I'm bent over and right in the middle of darning the heels of Pete's worn woolen socks. My neck is really kinked and feeling sore. "One minute!"

He clamps his chubby arms around my thighs and dangles from my leg while I sit. Darning, darning, darning. Trying to get my attention, he starts jumping up and down. "Look!" he says. "I made a tractor!" He points at the floor.

I glance up. His toys are scattered everywhere, covering every square inch. He's pleading, but I only have a few stitches left.

A shot of pain hits me in the calf. I look down. His mouth is next to my leg. *Shit! He bit me!* In one slow-moving instant I lash out, a survival mechanism at best, a pure reaction at worst and smack him right across his cheek.

He looks shocked, his eyes wide and alarmed, and he starts screaming. His cheek turns a fiery red. Horrified, I shake my leg and run into the bathroom to rinse a washcloth in cold water. His tiny teeth haven't punctured my skin. The pain in my heart is so much worse. I almost throw up then rush back and grab him. He is sobbing and we sit down on the floor. I rock him back and forth until all is settled down and nearly back to normal. But it doesn't feel normal. *What the hell is wrong with me? I must be losing it.*

I apologize repeatedly. "I am sorry, my baby. I'm sorry I hit you. But it is not OK to bite Mommy. To bite Sasha. To bite anyone! OK? OK?"

He shakes his little head up and down as if he understands and soon nods out. His cheeks are flushed from crying. I carry him to his crib and cover him.

Pete is right. I suck as a mother.

After rinsing the bite with iodine, I cover it with a large Band-Aid. It's already turning a pale eggplant colour. I decide not to tell Pete a thing.

After tidying up my yarn and needles from the darning job and before I can change my mind, I pick up Pete's socks from the floor and chuck them into the overflowing garbage can under the kitchen sink. I pull out the garbage bag, tie it off and heave it onto the back porch.

I've done enough mending for a while.

Pete can bloody well darn his own fucking socks from now on.

Tune In, Tune Out

Our old boob tube died months ago. So with the extra moola from our tax return Pete and I check out a used TV at the Holy Sisters Thrift Store. The clerks, two seriously senior ladies with permed, pale violet hair, turn it on for us and adjust the rabbit ears to pick up ABC. The black and white picture tunes in crystal clear and I imagine us all cuddled up, watching late-night movies with a big bowl of popcorn, smothered in flax oil or melted butter and nutritional yeast.

"Are you sure we should get it?" I ask. "Just because we have an extra couple of hundred doesn't mean we have to spend it!"

I have to admit watching TV is so damned addictive. Before our old one died, I was beginning to love watching TV more than I loved eating, reading or possibly even sex.

"Shit, yeah!" says Pete. "It's a great picture. It's good for Ethan, too. He doesn't have many kids to play with. Sesame Street is great for teaching kids. Let's get it!" He turns the dial to NBC. "We'll get three stations because of the transmitter up on Gentle Mountain." His eyes are gleaming like he's high on something.

"OK, man." I give in and laugh. "*But* I'm going to try and keep it turned off as much as possible. Way too much crap on that stupid tube. It's such a subtle trap and so bloody easy to turn it on and sit back mindlessly while it entertains you. I don't want to simply numb out!"

Pete replies in his corny mobster voice, "Don't worry, babe! You're a quite a long ways from numbing out!"

I feel insulted, but let it go. "I don't want it to become like a sitter for us. It's just as bad as hanging out in the stinky bar every weekend because you're bored, as if there's nothing better to do."

"Hey, chill out, why don't you? It's done!"

He grins, counts out four blue, crisp fives and slams them down on the counter by the antique cash register.

Evening finds us comatose in front of our new purchase. We sit mesmerized, amazed at the complex life out there in the big, bad world: news and entertainment stories coming at us through the brown Pandora's box with the spindly rabbit ears. The metal probes point to the sacred repeater on the hillside, receiving countless images and voices from the skies and transmitting it all back to us on this surreal, magic screen.

It'll be up to each of us, as the years slip by, to remember it is just a screen. And those images which are so easily manipulated and distorted benefit a very few at the top, billionaire wizards pulling invisible strings behind dark curtains.

But for now, it's a wonderful and easy escape into stories, fantasies, and imaginings, a reprieve from all the daily hassles and stresses and pain. A little escape has to be a good thing. I decide not judge this escape. Not today. Today I make more popcorn and settle in for a break from my busy brain, enjoying the stories on the boob tube, even the commercials, until my eyes are dry and sore and everyone else has fallen asleep.

I hear the disapproving words buzzing in the back of my mind, "But this…but you shouldn't…" I decide to ignore the voices today. I won't judge this secret, short break from reality, this mini-retreat. I'll save all that self-judgment for the future.

There will soon be plenty of it to go around.

❃ ❃ ❃

After bingeing on popcorn and butter, it's time for a food fast. Toxins must have accumulated over the years and I'm feeling the need for some sort of purification to wash away all the crap. For three days, I drink only real juices, apple cider vinegar and honey with water. Even with the muggy weather, I end up working in the garden. It makes me feel naturally stoned and totally connected to all the plants.

Plants which grow to feed us. Now that is a miracle.

Pete hangs out with Ethan most of the time. They watch an insane amount of t.v. Mostly Wizard of Oz, Sesame Street, news items and cartoons. *It's all right. It's only for a few days, too humid and miserable outside, anyway.*

Later that week the weather clears and I let Ethan out on his own for a bit so I can get some work done. I hate to do this as he sometimes ends up in terrifying situations.

I glance out the kitchen window after running to the toilet. I was only gone five minutes. Damn! I can't see him anywhere.

And then…my God, I nearly have a heart attack. He's standing proudly on the rickety roof of the shed, looking down on the yard like a king surveying his kingdom. He has climbed the wooden ladder we left leaning on the side. He probably thought it would be pretty cool to climb up there—to explore and expand his world view.

I run out and slowly and carefully make it to the roof, placing one trembling hand over another, rung by rung. At the top, I plead and try to coax him down. He's on the far side and firmly refuses.

"No! No!" He stubbornly crosses his arms.

Bobby shows up and tries to get Ethan's attention by calling him and throwing stones at him.

"Go home!" I yell at Bobby. He runs around in circles, laughing and ignoring me. And then disappears.

I finally bribe Ethan down with cookies and more TV. And a ride to town when his dad gets home. He confidently walks over to where I stand and climbs back down the rungs.

I immediately stash the ladder and bolt the shed door.

I say nothing to Pete when he returns from town.

Lizzie has decided to rent a suite on her own in the Rusty Addition, a pretty rough part of town, but it's not a bad apartment and it's cheap. We help her move on July 4th. Later, all of us meet up with Sam at the Jackrabbit Hotel Pub to celebrate with our anonymous American neighbours fifty miles to the south. Those two are definitely split up, but everyone, even Lizzie, still likes Sam and the four of us may as well have fun and get along.

Amazingly, I get asked for ID, which is a little weird, because when I was only seventeen and underage, I used to go to this very same pub on a regular basis and they never asked me once. I'm having a good day and take it as a compliment.

Perhaps I'm getting younger as I age. I must be doing something right. Far out.

I run into Hannah in town and she tells me the co-op finally has an offer on the land.

"How much?" I'm hopeful it may be sold.

She looks disappointed. "One hundred thousand big dollars." She shakes her head. "It's something, but not enough! We need $110 simply to break even! My god, it's over two hundred acres. Gary says we'll counter with $115 thousand and hope for the best."

We stand on the street corner in front of the Credit Union by the traffic light for fifteen minutes and catch up on the latest gossip then chat about the evils and pros and cons of land ownership. During the drive home, I debate the entire concept of buying and selling land. The co-op members all realize they'll have to play the wicked real- estate game until our piece of land is finally sold. Wicked, because it is a game. The seller tries to get as close to the asking price as possible and the buyer negotiates to pay as little as possible. Wicked because there's an exchange of large sums of money which enable one group of persons to live in a house (a home?) or on a piece of property and then make a profit when they "sell" it to the next buyer.

The entire concept of land ownership is so intangible. No one actually "owns" the land, yet humans have devised a way to somehow make a profit on a chunk of earth, sometimes on our common grounds. And with it all the air and water and plant and animal life. All of these elements are crucial for human life to survive and for the survival of other beings we share the planet with. How long could any one person live without land? Not long. Unless you lived in a spaceship.

Is it possible to live on land without owning it? Without having to trade it for useless beads or dollars shuffled through greedy hands? Without destroying it with gold mined from open pits scarred with cyanide, or decimate entire wetlands with dirty oil pulled from its depths, or pollute drinking water with agricultural waste from cattle, hogs and pesticides.

Do we actually own the land?

Can we take it with us when we die?

Do we actually own anything? Can we take it with us when we die?

Everything is simply on loan.

If anything, the land owns us.

Aunt Sally

Aunt Sally arrived around noon yesterday for her yearly summer visit. She came with way too many outfits, all perfectly folded into her upscale luggage.

Two large suitcases already stand unpacked and empty by the back door. I'll have to haul those out to the shed to make more room for us people. She also dragged in a picnic basket filled with too many shoes, including three pairs of Birkenstocks and a pair of shiny black high heels that she always brings but never wears. All this takes up space we don't have. Usually we enjoy her visits, but this year it's a big adjustment.

She swooshed in reeking of jasmine incense. Shoulder length, brunette hair recently trimmed in a page boy style, wrists loaded with dime-store bracelets and a sheer, bright scarf around her thinning turkey neck completed her look. (Pete picked her up from the bus depot and a day later he still appears flustered.)

After unloading, unpacking and organizing, Aunt Sally now helps me clean the house from top to bottom. Kathy and Vincent are also on their way; Pete got the call a few days ago. It will be a full house. Winter dust and cobwebs hide in corners no one can reach; we stand on chairs and drag the mop along the edges of the ceiling. Large, dead flies get wiped off the window sills and chucked into the overflowing compost bucket. The scouring and cleaning is a nice distraction and a breath of fresh air.

Kathy and Vincent plan on sleeping in their canvas tent which will be set up on an empty lot across the street, with their girls—at least until they figure out their long-term plans. Vincent finally got laid off and they're making the big move. Pete borrowed a tiny cot from Hannah. Aunt Sally can bunk in with Ethan.

I'm determined not to give up my space. The bedroom has become my new sanctuary, as there probably will be lineups for the bathroom. I burn sandlewood in a little corner of the room where I've placed a small Buddha statue, a stout beeswax candle, bleached white beach stones and my meditation cushion.

My singing heart races and soars as I prepare. I am ready.

THE GREAT AWAKENER

Arrivals and Premonitions

We celebrate Ethan's and Aunt Sally's party two days later. They both have birthdays on the same day. Almost twins.

God, how time flies! And what a what a precocious and delightful person he is. But as I ice the cake and get the party stuff ready, I suddenly feel blue. Wave upon wave of sorrow washes over me. I wonder whether it's hormones, maybe I'm only getting my period. But it turns out to be a real premonition.

That afternoon as Ethan and Aunt Sally blow out their birthday candles and all the cheers die down from the well- wishing crowd of neighbours, friends and relatives and right before Pete cuts the cake, we hear a soft rumbling on the gravel road outside.

They're finally here. They said they were coming, but I never believed it until this moment. My heart starts to race.

We're in the middle of a busy party. *Why do important things all happen at the same time?* Utter chaos ensues for a good twenty minutes. This works in my favour, because before I know it, Vincent and family are inside the house and milling about. There's no time even for sweaty hugs or the usual awkwardness and chit-chat.

After the party finally breaks up, the fab four—Pete, Vincent, Kathy and I head to the bar for a few drinks while Aunt Sally babysits. She actually volunteers, saying she's too tired anyway.

"Let's go," I say. "It's time to have some fun!"

And we do. And the electricity between Vincent and me is still there. It's a powerful pulling energy drawing me to his side time and again. We talk, drink and dance and don't get home until the wee hours.

The next morning as we stumble out of bed, parched and hung over, Aunt Sally is already dressed and standing by her packed suitcases, apparently waiting for the town's only taxi.

"What's wrong?" Pete asks, rushing over to her.

"What's wrong? Are you kidding? I didn't come here to babysit all the kids and clean your bloody house!" She's furious. "It's one thing to go out for a couple of beers but quite another to leave me here alone all night until the bars close. I'm going to a hotel and then back home!"

She's immovable, standing in the porch doorway, arms crossed, legs firmly planted, facing the exit. "I come out here every year to see you guys and you don't seem to appreciate it! Every time you get together with Vincent, you treat me like shit! I know he's your friend, but he's trouble." She wags her finger at me. "Mark my words; he's more trouble than he's worth!" She sighs and starts to sniffle. "Oh, never mind. Don't pretend to give a damn! I'd love to go out too and have some fun, but I don't know anyone here!"

She fidgets with her black leather purse, opening and closing the imitation gold snap. Then the waterworks start and she slumps down onto a chair and wails. Briny tears and wet mascara stream down her ruddy cheeks.

"Forgive us, Aunt Sally," Pete says. "We'll try and include you. No more babysitting! Please stay with us. We'll do something fun this afternoon." His words soothe a troubled heart, she stops sniffling and shuddering. She then holds his hands and looks down at the floor.

"I'm sorry," she says, her voice trembling. "I know they're more your age. And I am an old widow. Yes, yes, I am. After your uncle died…never mind… and I'm sorry for my outburst. It's the change. I can't help it sometimes. It's like I'm possessed. By a demon, or something. I'm sorry Pete…and Sasha."

She shoots a quick glance at me; I walk over and lightly pat her cushioned shoulder.

"I'm sorry too, Aunt Sally. We're so self-centered at times."

We all agree it's going to be fine. Not perfect, but fine. All folks fight, even if they genuinely like each other. It happens.

And isn't a fight better to deal with at the beginning of a visit than at the end?

"I'm so sappy. I'll be OK. But I'll miss you guys!" Aunt Sally is finally heading home.

She gives Ethan a peck on his glowing, pink cheek, then hugs Pete—a big, friendly hug. His grey eyes grow moist. We load her on the Greyhound and wave goodbye until our arms are tired and the grimy bus has wound its way through our sleepy town and down the long highway.

Two parched summer weeks have passed. There's a ton of weeding to catch up on. The garden is overgrown and I need to see the chiropractor; only two visits left on my medical card.

"Guilt sorrow" pecks at my heart strings but relief plays a softer tune. We're too different and are from different generations. We can't go skinny-dipping or smoke pot with her, now can we? Of course we enjoy her company and she's such a big help. We did explore the area and had fun, but I always have to be someone else when Aunt Sally visits. And lately I'm not even sure who this someone is.

Not for Fun

After Aunt Sally leaves, Pete and I start to spend a lot of time with Vince and Kathy. Strangely, it's not as much fun or quite as exciting as imagined.

I try to figure it out one afternoon after we had spent a few hours together. We seem to clash about most things. *Why is Vincent constantly trying to be one up on me as if I weren't his equal? He's such a know-it-all, but if I disagree with him, I practically have to produce a master's degree before he takes my opinion seriously. He treats Kathy the same way, but she deals with it by smiling her perfect smile and walking away. Sometimes she tosses him a flippant remark over her shoulder. I stay for the fight. I think he respects that—maybe he's intrigued.*

The bickering and the sizzling conversations ramp up as the hot summer days fly by.

Vincent and Kathy have rented Ray and Sally's old place. It's totally primitive. Honestly, it's a shack. There's no running water. Kathy also likes to have a batch of healthy cookies on hand for the girls, so my oven has been getting a lot of use. They usually end up crashing in their tent, all four of them, and then joining us for breakfast and showers. Most of the time, I don't mind. It's like having a close, extended family.

Tonight the moon is ripe and full, stale air in the small house hangs heavy and tense. A small, metal fan in the kitchen blows that hot air around at floor level, trying its best to cool things down.

Kathy burnt a batch of granola earlier and reacted with lots of cursing. She blamed the oven, calling it a fucking piece of shit. But the truth is I've made buckets of granola in that oven and it always turned out perfectly fine.

All four of us have finished watching an old Bonanza episode from 1972 entitled "Forever." Little Joe finds true love in Alice Harper, but Alice meets a tragic end. Poor Little Joe. As the credits roll, Kathy starts up.

"So, what do you feel?" she asks. She's sitting cross-legged on the floor, knitting a sweater vest for Vincent—rich, warm colours for the coming fall. "Come on, out with it. It is obvious there's something going on with you two. You can't stop bickering!" She tosses her long golden white hair over her shoulder and glares at Vincent. She's feisty tonight. Maybe she's getting her period. I say nothing.

She's right, though. Vincent and I have been clashing a lot lately, badgering and nipping at each other. She appeared not to notice until this evening Tonight, it looks like she wants all of us to lay our playing cards on the table.

"What's going on between you two?"

"Well ..." Vincent is spread out on the floor, his head held up by a stuffed pillow. His large hands, bronzed and muscular, hold up his neck. "It's true. I may have some feelings for Sasha."

He flushes then sits up, charcoal hair falling into those eyes. I hold my breath, my heart stops. I'm suddenly dizzy. But not surprised.

Pete scowls at me, throwing blades of confusion. This passes quickly and he looks amused, like he's watching a couple of kids in a tug of war.

Kathy doesn't miss a beat and stares at me, demanding a response. "And what about you, Missy? How do you feel about Vincent? Be honest now!"

She likes to call me Missy lately. I can't tell if it's an insult or not.

She continues with her knitting. Click, click, click. It's as if this is normal stuff—her husband falling in love with a friend.

I swallow and take a deep breath. "I don't know what to say. I don't want to hurt anyone, you or Pete, but yeah, I guess I feel something. It could be love of some kind—at this time, anyway." I blow all the air out of my lungs. Everything can change with a few wrong words. My face itches and I feel a familiar stress rash igniting on my cheeks. My heart races like I'm running a marathon. Terror lies under the surface, bobbing like a message in a bottle, but I ignore it and smile, all the while feeling a little foolish. My words don't sound exactly right.

Vincent steals a peek at me, and nods.

Kathy lays into the both of us. "What are you going to do about these feelings? Are you going to continue to drive us crazy with all this wrangling?"

She wants something to happen. That's obvious.

But I don't actually care what Kathy wants to have happen. I only care about what I want to have happen.

"When will you two end up in the sack?" She fires the question at me. "This is what I'd like to know. Get it over with! What are you waiting for?"

I take another deep breath. "Whoa! This is moving way too fast. I don't know what's supposed to happen here. I'm not sure how to proceed. Pete? Please talk to me. What's going on with you?"

He still looks tickled and somewhat superior. "What's going on with me?"

Pete has finally woken up. His volume increases, as if he's had a coffee, which makes him way too hyper. "You're your own person, God knows and I can't stop you from loving someone else. Whether you want to go the distance where you end up sleeping together is another story! But again it's up to you! What can I say? 'No, you're mine and no one else can have feelings for you!'? Shit, I don't know what I'm supposed to do. I'm not a fucking psychologist!" He laughs his fake , exaggerated laugh and gets up and goes into the kitchen to make a pot of tea and roll a joint.

Vincent leans back and almost touches my knee with his hand, then sets it down. I haven't been able to stop thinking about this man who drives me crazy with the attention. And constant pestering. I am pulled into his vortex. *It's not only me—other women feel it too. I've watched them in bars. It's some kind of voodoo he has.*

My entire being is yelling *yes!* Except for my brain cells, my brain is telling me perhaps I should think about this for a minute. Or two.

Fuck it. I don't want to think about it. I want to lie beside him and hold him and feel what he's made of. I want to feel all this energy, to follow through on this desire to melt and to merge.

It's as if I'm desperately thirsty and he's the cooling oasis, a bottomless, clear pool of perfect clear water.

Kathy icily sums it up. "Oh, you two, what bullshit! You're both so damn repressed! It's 1976, for God's sake! You're not going to get beheaded or burnt at the stake for sleeping with my husband. Those days are gone. What's wrong with expressing how you feel about each other? We all have the right!"

"Yes, but…but wouldn't it be easier for everyone if we kept this on a no touch level?" I ask. "It could get pretty complicated otherwise."

A roller coaster takes a short but intense ride in my queasy gut. *I need the honesty. I need to know where I stand.*

Meanwhile, Vincent doesn't say a damn thing. Pete looks at Kathy in a funny way, somewhat like he's appraising her. He passes a joint to Vincent. We've all forgotten about the tea.

"I think people should have the right to express whatever it is they feel about each other," Pete says. "I'll be fine."

Kathy starts sewing pieces of her knitting together. She squints and her eyes look forlorn and fatigued, but she's not backing down. "I think you both should get on with it," she says. "I don't feel threatened by you, Missy. At all. It's fine, as Pete says."

"Now, Kath," says Vincent, at last. "Let's not rush these guys. Yes, I would like to connect with Sasha. But I'm not sure they're ready for this. I do not want to jeopardize our friendship. Let's just leave things as they are and remain friends."

Vincent expresses himself so well.

"You mean the friendship where you two are constantly badgering and snapping at each other? That friendship?" asks Kathy.

She can be so sarcastic! A skill worth developing.

"Ouch!" she shrieks. She's poked herself with a sharp needle. Her finger is oozing blood. She sucks on it.

"Are you OK?" everyone chimes in.

Kathy nods and continues her stitching. I raise my arms and lean forward to stretch my back, doing a child's pose, trying to get some perspective. All I want is to retreat into a darkened, self-created cave at this moment. But before I can disappear into my own world, Pete comes over and rubs my back.

"Why don't we all go outside and cool down and work this out," he says. "No one has to jump into the sack. Let's all just chill? We're all friends, aren't we?"

I steal a glance at Vincent. His face is totally blank.

We all sit in a rough circle. We've found a nice area in the side yard next to the thick cedar hedge, under the stars, away from all prying eyes, to sit together and figure this out. A small kerosene lantern, its wick turned down, sputters in the center on an old pie plate. A coyote howls and yips in the distant hills. Thrilling and haunting.

Pete reaches out and holds Kathy's hand. I hold hands with Kathy and Vincent. The electricity between all of us is intense. Shivers run over my body.

Vincent barely looks at me. I don't need him to. I know. It's obvious. We have a current. Powerful and terrifying.

Maybe we don't need to consummate this, but we do need to hold each other and connect physically. For me it will probably be enough.

Or will it?

It's late. Or much too early. We end up back inside after ferocious mosquitoes descend on us. The conversation continues in the living room. Kathy stretches out on the mat and covers herself with her long poncho. Her abandoned knitting lies in the corner. A small lamp illuminates the wicker bag with its precious contents, like an oil painting from another time--ochre light on natural weave.

"I'm tired," Pete says, and lies down beside Kathy on the mat as if it's the most natural thing in the world. They both pass out within minutes.

I sit up from my stretched out resting place. With a mischievous gleam in his eye, Vincent looks directly at me. "Well then." he says. He stands and walks off. Into my bedroom.

I follow immediately, tiptoeing in, not even looking back at Pete. I gently close the bedroom door. The light of a steely grey dawn peeks through the narrow vertical crack between closed curtains.

Nervously, I remove my cotton nightie and join his smooth, naked body. The sheets are already warm from his heat. I smell cedar and a hint of patchouli. My soul has come home. I have come home.

This feels so good. This is magic, mystical. We're both here, on this island, the two of us, and I feel loved. I feel completely loved.

"This is for real, you know," Vincent whispers. "This is not only for fun."

He strokes my entire body, every square inch is examined, kissed, every mysterious corner and every damp curve is appreciated and loved.

I stretch up toward his touch. I'm in heaven and don't even care if I make it to the promised land. I am wet and so ready, but he seems reluctant to go further. He leaves me hanging.

I convince myself I don't care.

Today, I don't care. Today, I'll take what I can get.

Aftershock

Pete does not take this new development well and mopes around like a whipped puppy. He refuses to speak to me and ignores me when I try and talk to him. I repeatedly tell him, "I still love you." And try to be especially nice. I even make him pancakes on Sunday. But it doesn't help. It doesn't help a bit. I don't understand. He said it was all right with him at the time, and now he's a total mess.

But of course if it were reversed I'd feel the same. Or would I? Poor Pete. How could I be so heartless?

Heavy guilt starts to kick in. What were my true motives? Did I simply need to know someone else could love me? Anyone else. I tell myself I didn't need to have a physical thing with Vincent. The ultimate ego boost is for someone to say they love you. I certainly didn't want this thing between Vincent and me to be about my friggin' ego.

Journaling:

> Am I so insecure? I don't really need Vincent's physical love but could simply appreciate the divine connection between us. Maybe his friendship and affection is all I need. I could be free.

Or so I tell myself.

Why can't Pete see that I still love him?

Aren't there different kinds of love, for different people? There has to be, otherwise nothing makes any sense.

In a short amount of time, this whole love thing had become so damned confusing. So much more confusing than any other of life's mysteries.

Walking It Out

A week after our special night, Vincent and I take an afternoon trip out of town to talk out the concerns in my head. We walk all the way to the river and back through a heavy rain.

"Kathy says she doesn't resent you loving someone else at the same time you love her," I tell him. "Should I believe her?" At this point I don't. "I think she does resent it! And maybe she would be more sexually satisfied if you were only with her?"

"Well, Kathy has had problems in that area. I don't think it has anything to do with me. She's been with lots of other guys, you know!" He frowns, looking quite ruffled.

"Of course I know. And she did say something about you two being into that open marriage thing! For a long time now." I hadn't wanted to bring it up, but there it was.

"Yeah, well let's not talk about that today," he says.

"Yeah, OK."

We walk on, shoes getting soaked as we plough through the wet grass. Neither of us can find the trail that supposedly cuts through this wide meadow. A summer breeze rustles toothed, pale green leaves of the proud white-skinned paper birch trees which outline the edge of deep green.

"I still do feel something for you," I say, "but I think it must be infatuation."

"Yeah, I'm not sure either," he answers. "But I do care about you."

Rain drips off his perfect, straight nose, rivulets run down his long trench coat. His tangled black hair is damp and matted under his hoodie. We walk on.

"I really don't know you," I say.

"Well, I sure know you!" He laughs and teasingly pokes me in the ribs. I smile but mostly ignore the jab.

Aspects of him definitely turn me off. Some days it's obvious he is too much of a city dude. Like when he almost sliced his finger off while shaving kindling. He is also obsessed with keeping his fingernails clean, always scraping the dirt out with his tiny Swiss army knife.

He pretends to like the finer things and reads a lot of philosophical and mystical books, especially stories about pain and hardship. They're usually about people with troubled lives, like Dostoevsky's *Crime and Punishment.* A favourite of his. *Shit. That's depressing.*

He finally sums things up. "Well, Sasha, let's see how things go. I certainly like hanging out with you and miss you when I don't see you for a while. What can it mean?"

I don't know what it means, so I don't answer. Instead, we chat about the trees and the stones on the river bank and try to enjoy the rest of the walk, each lost in private thoughts. And big doubts.

As long as everything is fine with me, he's so pleasant to be around, nice and cheery. But if I'm upset for any reason he simply leaves, fading out the picture as if there's nothing that can be done, like it's out of his beautiful hands. *This is when someone needs to be comforted, or at least given a warm hug.*

I keep all this to myself, mulling it over as we walk back. We get back to his car and crawl inside, wet and scruffy, two drowning rats.

I feel somewhat blue and am not sure why as we silently drive home.

I got what I wanted, didn't I?

Dreary rain falls unabated the whole way back. Windshield wipers whip back and forth on full speed, and the grinding heater runs full blast, doing its best to dry us out.

Shallow

Vincent finally convinces Pete it would be alright to have a fun evening out. Pete sure needed some lightening up, so off we go to the bar. Besides, it was Sam's birthday. Halfway through the night, Vincent stands before me and bows, as if to royalty. "May I have this dance, madam?"

He's certainly enjoying himself tonight, flirting with all the women. It doesn't seem to bother me. I feel honored to be asked and immediately stand. He takes my hand and leads me out to the dance area, which is empty except for a totally loaded couple dressed in rancher boots and gaudy country and western clothing, their black shirt pockets outlined with intricate gold filigree. They teeter and wobble, barely able to stand. I look away. As usual, the beat up hardwood floor is sticky with spilled drinks.

I stand only a foot away from Vincent as we start. He pulls me close. I don't resist. I don't resist at all. In fact I allow myself to melt into his welcoming arms. I smell his slightly oniony sweat and the oil in his hair. I lay my head on his wide shoulder and allow myself to relax and let him lead. I'm tired of pretending, of trying to be good and nice. Of having to do the right thing. *Please, yes please, lead me to a new place, a place of adventure and magic and beauty. It's all I ask.*

A slow, sensuous waltz. His hands are warm and comforting on my shoulders and upper back. I start to perspire.

The tune ends too soon. I raise my head and birthday-boy Sam is standing behind Vince, smiling. A Cheshire cat smile.

"It's my turn," Sam winks.

Vincent smirks, gives me a gentle kiss on the forehead and heads back to our vacant table now covered in half-empty glasses of stale beer and ash trays overflowing with Sam's butts. *Where are Pete and Kathy?*

I look around. Laura has met us here and is leaning over the counter, glued to a tall bar stool, tittering and sharing a drink with a heavily tattooed biker.

Sam plugs the ancient juke box with a handful of quarters. A popular CCR tune about "a bad moon rising" blasts out from the crackly speakers. The bass pounds and voices are muffled and croaking. The quality of sound is horrible, but it gets us moving. Within a minute most of the bar is up and dancing to the beat, bumping and grinding, including me. Sam gets close, but it's all in fun and I bump into him, hip to hip. I haven't felt so good in ages.

Pete and Kathy enter from outside as the song is ending, both looking a little guilty. The heavy oak door slams shut. A cool night breeze slipped in unnoticed and now meanders through a thick haze. They must have slipped out to smoke a reefer. I'm ticked off but forget about it almost right away.

When the dancing ends, all five of us get dressed and head outside. I'm still in an upbeat mood and hop into the front seat of Sam's car. The others squeeze into the back. Their prickly, hot stares poke my neck, like sharp stilettos, but I ignore it.

So this is what it's like to have fun. It's not so bad.

Damn, it appears I can actually be quite shallow after all.

After the gang comes in for a midnight toke and the babysitter is paid and leaves, Pete is grumpy and in a rage, accusing me of being "much too friendly" with Vince and "too comfortable" with Sam. I guess he means

I was much too physically close to both of them, bumping into them while dancing and slow-waltzing with them.

"How was I to know?" I ask. "You never used to get jealous! Ever!"

I stand in the kitchen, feeling shaken and overly chastised. *Fuck it.* In a flurry, I grab my denim jacket.

"I'm going for a damn walk!" I head off alone for a walk to the marshes.

Through copious tears I follow a well used deer trail to the edge of the cemetery. Out of nowhere a ghostly apparition appears, marking a newer grave. It takes a minute to realize this is a marble angel. An angel lit from deep within by a heavenly glow. I realize someone must be resting here, but feel drawn to her and collapse on a gravel patch near the cool, dense, welcoming marble.

For some reason I believe this spirit statue can hear me and I confide in the seraph through hot tears. "Why is Pete so damned angry at me? He's so bloody laid back about most things. He doesn't usually give a shit about what I do! Maybe I *was* flirting. But what's wrong with flirting? He does it all the time. It was fun! Why should he care? And why do *I* have to be so serious anyway? Why can't I relax and have mindless fun like most other people?" I peer up at the glowing angel to make sure she's listening. The angel smiles her knowing smile. But not a word escapes her icy mouth.

"You know, Kath and Pete went outside together and smoked a joint but didn't include me! Did I raise hell over it? No, I did not! What a fucking bastard! I'm so sick of him. I'm sick of him and sick of men and I want to die."

I collapse on the gravel and lie there.

"Poor girl, poor girl, no one ever gets you," is all the angel whispers.

So true—no one.

Except before too long this gets quite boring. And uncomfortably chilly, lying here wallowing in my sorrows. I scramble to my feet, brush off the litter and head back to the house.

It's time to make up with Pete.

Getting close to the back yard, I spy a tiny flickering orange light attached to a familiar human outline standing by the back porch. Sam is having a smoke. Player's—I can smell it a block away.

"So girl, how are you?" he asks as I come closer. He holds out his hand.

"Oh shit. Not good!" I connect with his outstretched arm and then collapse onto his chest.

He strokes my head gently then carefully combs out the ends of my rusty hair, much like a mother would. Copper coils. He draws his hand up and lifts my chin. As I look into his face, his eyes glow. Too much. I look down and back away.

"If only I'd known how excruciating this thing with Vincent would be, I'd have made different choices. Probably. I guess I'm not quite so evolved." I manage a smile and take another step back. Sam looks different tonight: more open, more caring. Perhaps I could trust him. "Is Pete still upset?"

"No. You should be OK now."

"And Vince? Is he still here? I don't see his van." *Of course Vince isn't here.*

"No, he's not here."

"Damn! When there's trouble, Vince seems to vanish!" I wave my arms. Sam lights two cigarettes and offers me one. I puff once or twice on the vile stick then extinguish the flame in the dirt. I spit into the lilac bushes. *I can't get hooked on this crap again.*

We stand together for a few minutes, enjoying the vast view of the star clusters above. The Milky Way stretches like a thick, lacy band around the cosmic basin. I smell the slightly acrid garden soil and sense the crawling tendrils and thirsty roots of all the garden plants and vegetable crops exploring and seeking nourishment and growing, a few feet away.

Sam abruptly reaches out, gives me a quick hug and then soldier-like, salutes his goodbye. He crawls into his rattletrap of a car and slams the door. It starts up and rumbles; a small, dense cloud of burning oil spews forth and he's gone.

* * *

I go back into the house. Quietly. I don't want to stir up the recent hornet's nest of jealousy. Pete appears fine when I tiptoe into the bedroom. He's in bed, reading the latest *Rolling Stone.* I feel relieved and say hi then tiptoe out to put on my special nightie—the newer, flimsy one that makes my thin frame look more robust and sexy. I figure he deserves it. *Maybe he's not getting enough lately.*

I get dressed in the can and then slink into the dimly lit room. Only the small reading lamp is lit. I crawl onto the bed and lay close to him, drawing my thigh across his lean hips. His hair smells like the pub.

He looks up from his reading, but instead of an eager expression on his face at the prospect of some passion and play, he appears angry and aloof.

"No, sorry, not tonight. I'm not up for it. Too tired." He drops the magazine on the floor and clicks off the lamp.

"What? What's going on? Do you mean it?"

"Go to sleep. Jeez! It must be two o'clock in the morning!"

"Great, just great! It's obvious you aren't attracted to me anymore! Why do I even bother? Fuck!"

I shake him. Nothing.

"Leave me alone, I'm trying to sleep!"

My body is hot and confused, yet the hollowness in my heart aches the most. I try to be logical and think it all through.

I can't count on Vincent and Pete is sick of me. Vincent talks a big talk but isn't there for me when the shit hits the fan. And he has his own family to think of. Do I still love Pete? Perhaps, but he doesn't give a damn about my feelings anymore. Maybe he never did.

I turn away from the drunken sawing and stare at the wall and into the darkness, praying for the sleep of oblivion, for the blackness and the calm emptiness of an elusive void.

As I start to drift off I remember that I forgot to call my mother on her birthday, the day before.

So, I am my mother's daughter. I'll have to call her tomorrow. Damn.

The Bear Returns

The gang is over and we sit around the table sharing a large pot of oat straw tea. Have heard it's good for frayed nerves. And it's cheap. Underlying tension hangs in the sour night air, like silt. I'm hoping the tea might help. The old slate blue Formica table sits under the kitchen window and looks down onto the porch steps. I love to see the garden at night and have not drawn the curtains closed. It's the usual chatter. Despite the obvious strain, all of us appear to be getting along. No one seems to be specifically upset with anyone at that exact moment. I happen to look up.

Framed in the window is Bear's fflushed face, bloodshot eyes bulging. An image straight from hell. I scream. He starts banging on the glass with his huge fist, as if trying to break through.

"Oh, my God!" *How long has he been there, listening? And what has he heard?*

Everyone jumps up like startled gazelles about to be decimated by a lion on the prowl. Pete swings the back door open and steps outside. Drunken spit flies as the Bear beast waves his puffy fist in front of Pete's face.

"You fucking bastard, you act like you're my friend, but all this time you or your buddy here have been hitting my boy," he snarls. He glares right at Vincent, now cowering behind Kathy. And points his finger and starts yelling, "Don't lie and tell me you didn't hit Bobby. I know you did! Fuck! Bobby is having nightmares because of you! He wakes up screaming and says...do you know what he says? He says: 'No, don't hit me!' He cries over and over: 'Bad man, don't hit me!" Bear strides forward and swings and almost lands a punch on Pete's shocked face.

I stand trembling in the kitchen in bare feet. The back door is now wide open. Sam picks up his leather jacket and gently wraps it around my shoulders. A large moth beats its powdery wings against the tansy-yellow porch light. Vincent and Kathy have snuck back into the living room and peer around the doorway.

Pete's face is stark white. "Hey, man," he pleads. "No one would hit your boy! No one here would!" He steps back from Bear and shakes his head.

I'm stunned. Pete wouldn't hit Bobby. And Vince? No, it can't be. Although I've seen him smack his girls. At least once. We try not to hit Ethan, although he may have gotten a smack or two on his bottom when he acted out or when my temper was short.

Sam is tall and wiry, not a big guy, but he's scrappy as hell and his father was a raging alcoholic. So he knows about this shit. He steps right in front of Bear.

"I know you're upset, man,“ he says in a calm voice, "but how about you go home and sleep it off, and tomorrow you can come over for coffee and we can talk about, eh? Now Pete and Vince were wrong if they hit your boy. And I'm not saying they ever did. But I'm sure they'll apologize and things can be made right." Sam looks right into Bear's eyes. His voice gets calm and low. "OK, man? Head home now and we'll talk tomorrow. It's gonna be alright."

Bear teeters on the edge of the sidewalk and nearly falls over. It's obvious he's outnumbered.

Sam wraps his arm around Bear, who lurches like a falling sack of potatoes, then steers him home, which is only half a block away. Their windows are dim but I can't imagine Jane is asleep with a drunken monster in the house.

Vincent and Kathy and the girls quickly throw their stuff into their vehicle and head back to their shack in the mountains. No time to even ask Vincent about the hitting. I load up our backpacks with essentials, grab the foamie, and throw it all into our pickup. We drive across town and spend the night at Sam's place.

No one sleeps a wink, tossing and turning on the floor, trying not to think of what to do the next morning. Did Pete or Vincent hit Bobby? I sure hope not. I want to believe them.

One thing is for certain: Sam is turning out to be a really good friend.

In the morning, as we pull into the driveway I notice the precious beauty of our garden, lit up with dew crystals and early summer light. My heart sinks. I'm never going to feel comfortable in this home ever again.

As we unload the pickup, I glance over at Bear's house. A curtain falls back behind the streaky window.

How many times has he sat outside our house and listened to our conversations?

My stomach churns and I nearly lose my breakfast.

So my night terrors were based in something real after all.

We haul our shit inside.

Bear does not return to our place. I never want to see him again. I watch them come and go. I keep my curtains drawn and my door bolted. One afternoon when they're not in their yard I go outside to water plants and to dump the compost but leave Ethan inside. There is no way to explain to him it's not safe anymore. How can you tell a child things are normal, but aren't? He cries as I close the door. As I quickly do my chores Bobby steps outside of his house, walks over and sits down in our dirt driveway. He looks over at me then peers woefully at our back steps. Ethan continues banging his little fist on the back door.

"I want to go outside!"

At night I turn off the bedside lamp and lay back on my pillow.

"We have to find another place to live. We could rent, if we have to."

Pete has already fallen asleep. Or is pretending to.

Throughout the night I continue to feel Bear's slimy energy outside the walls, sucking any sense of safety and security out of my aching bones.

A couple of weeks later, around mid-morning, I hear a light rap on the back door.

"Can Ethan play with Bobby?" Jane asks through the torn screen.

Her eyes are bagged and heavy and full of shame.

"Yeah, OK."

After I take Ethan outside and the young ones reunite and run gleefully down the road, we stand around awkwardly, talking about the nice weather. We don't discuss Bear's recent meltdown. We don't discuss anything real.

We'll probably be gone soon anyway.

Coffee with Sam

My pace slows as I approach the Pine Woods Cafe. Slowly, I reach up to chest height and grab the cool, steel handle. I take a deep, purposeful breath before pulling open the heavy, thickly painted blue door. As I step up into the dimly lit foyer it creaks loudly, like a groan from a bridge troll. Then slams shut. *Those hinges need oiling.*

Peering into the darkened interior, my eyes slowly adjust to the murky light. The smoky room is lit by dusty and fading plastic shell sconces and is only half full of customers. Ruby red, distressed and, worn vinyl booths line the sides and middle area. After blinking a couple of times, I spy Sam in the far corner, engrossed in a paperback thriller. He doesn't see me and starts on a piece of apple pie, silver fork piercing the dense crust. He appears preoccupied. Without first checking to see if anyone else I know might be in the café, I walk over to the dingy booth and plunck down. Sam looks up, his thick eyebrows rising in alarm.

"Hey, man!" I say. "Don't look so surprised! I made it."

He flashes a quick smile.

I hate coffee shops and restaurants—in this town anyway. They're usually filled with nosey people with nothing better to do than to listen in on everyone's conversations, then gossip about them as soon as they leave. I know, because I've done it myself.

"All right, you're here!" he says.

He appears pleased, lightly touches my hand and calls the waitress over as I unbutton my wool pea coat and lay it on the grubby seat. The plastic bench is covered in crumbs and greasy streaks of unknown origin. I brush off the crumbs with my navy knit hat. *Another reason I hate greasy spoons. I usually feel like having a bath afterwards.*

Against my better judgement, I order a weak coffee and a small bowl of borscht, which today ends up being more like a salty, lukewarm tomato-cabbage broth heavily spiced with salt and too much dill. We settle in to chat about Lizzie and Sam's troubles. They have stopped seeing each other, for good apparently. He appears relieved. Lighter.

Sam can be somewhat of a chauvinist at times, but he has been kind to me. He listens to all my concerns and asks how I'm doing whenever I happen to see him.

Lizzie is off my radar. She's never around anymore and has stopped calling or stopping by. She has not returned any of my calls. Her answering machine doesn't even kick in when I try to leave a message. I tried to track her down last week at the stinky bar where she works but the owners said she only comes in on weekends now. I used to worry about Lizzie. Today, I'm almost ready to give up on her. She is a big girl, after all, and has to grow up sometime. She'll be fine.

I ask about Jared.

And then, "Is she drinking a lot lately? I have to know.

He shrugs. "I don't know. Honestly, we try to stay away from each other. We're both happier that way."

I attempt to pry details of their separation out of Sam. "Where is she living now? Is she still in the Rusty Addition? Did she go back to cleaning rooms at that sleazy hotel? How long have you two been apart now?"

Sam appears reluctant to talk and only mentions he hasn't seen her in weeks. He pushes his half-eaten pie aside and lights another smoke. For some reason, it doesn't bother me when he smokes compared to most other puffers. It's like his cigarettes are part of him now, like clothing or accessories, and maybe the association is one of comfort, rather than of stench and headaches. I actually still like the smell of Player's. Reminds me of the good old days when I was young. And free.

I'm still working on my lukewarm, orange borscht when he glances toward the far window by the entrance, pulls back the cuff of his shirtsleeve and stares at a shiny new Timex wristwatch. He makes a face.

"Shit, I totally forgot. I have to meet someone at two-thirty! I'm so sorry, but I'm going to have to run, Sash. Don't worry about the bill. I'll grab it on my way out. I'll call you soon!"

He grabs his jacket and bolts, stopping only long enough to pay the waitress, who appears far too curious. She glares at me, and then stares at my half empty bowl.

I ignore the glances of two older white-haired ladies on the other side of the room as I put down my spoon and put on my coat. They've been slyly watching Sam and me, pretending they're focused on random people on the street, all the while leaning toward us, attempting to hear what we're chatting about. They look down as I exit. I wave a timid bye to the waitress and step outside, almost tripping on the crumbling concrete step.

"Oops, I forgot my hat," I mumble to no one in particular and head back in to retrieve it. The waitress stands beside the booth. Her arm is outstretched and her long white fingers, embellished with bright red nail polish, are pinched, holding both my hat and Sam's scarf away from her body as if they're contaminated. She must have read the article in the local rag yesterday about there being an epidemic of crabs and lice at the commune down by the river.

She holds the stuff out to me. "Your friend forgot his scarf too."

The way she says "friend" sounds gross. I grab our nearly-lost pieces and rush out, hissing, "Thanks!"

I rush to Sam's place to drop off his crimson and gold, paisley-silk scarf. *He's probably not home— will just tie it to the doorknob on his front door.*

I leave the truck parked on the main drag and climb the dozen steps to Sam's apartment and knock. When there is no answer, I tie the scarf to the door knob. It looks ominous hanging there, like a small warning flag or a hidden message. I rush down the steep stairs. It's getting late and Pete may be wondering where I am.

Bear and I crash into each other as I turn the corner to walk the last block back to the truck. His dragon breath reeks and his shoes are mud-spattered. I look up at his ruddy face and angry red eyes.

"Hey, Missy, what are you doing here?" he slurs.

"What are *you* doing here?" Bear definitely doesn't belong here, right outside Sam's apartment.

He smiles cunningly. "I'm going up to visit Sam. My old buddy, Sam, you know. We're going to talk about things."

"He's not home! I saw him in town. He's got an appointment." I need to get as far away from this fucker as possible.

"An appointment? Yeah, he has an appointment. With me!" He points his thick finger back at his barrel chest. "He has some good stuff."

My gut does a flip. "Stuff? You mean pot? Is Sam selling pot to you?"

"Pot? No, not pot! Pot is for babies. I'm talking about the good stuff. The pain killers. You know, perka…perka sets. Yeah. And the other good stuff. The stuff like Codeine. You know, vica, something… hell, it helps with all my old busted-up bones and aches and pains. But you wouldn't know about such things, being a young girly girl!" He smiles crookedly.

Without saying goodbye, I turn and run back to the pickup .The image of Bear's horrifying peeping-tom face in our kitchen window flashes in my memory. *Fuck! And now he's friends with Sam?*

It's a challenging drive home. I'm so bloody confused. *All this time, I thought Sam was a nice, normal kind of guy. Our good old friend Sam, writing James Bond stories and working at the mill. Well, I thought he was a friend, anyway. But a friend of Bear's is not a friend of mine. Shit!*

As I turn left off the main drag I spy a familiar truck parked in the driveway of a new neighbour. What the hell is Daddy Wes doing at Barbara's place? She moved here just a few weeks ago. So out of place and so damned unexpected. I've definitely fallen through a distorted and fragmented looking-glass of confusion. Sharp edges of a fragmenting reality tear at my overworked brain. And pull at my over broken heart.

The rabbit hole is dark and deep.

I fall and fall and fall.

Where I'll land is anyone's guess.

Hassles Continue

Closeness cannot grow without honesty, and Vincent and Pete continue having trouble relating. I ask Pete if I should leave and he says no, but it's obvious he doesn't enjoy spending time with me. Or with Vincent. Although they've known each other for over fifteen years, they've never been close friends or confided in each other. It's a superficial relationship—basically pool playing, dope-smoking buddies. They have to start from scratch and neither of them knows how to be the sort of friend they seem to be expecting to come out of this grand experiment.

It's more important the four of us get along as friends than Vincent and I get along as lovers or whatever the hell it is we are.

I still believe Vincent likes to be alone with me. And I like to be alone with him. It isn't a passionate, burning desire; we simply don't communicate as well with other people around. We need to spend quality time together, without distractions or worrying about other's issues.

Summer's end is right around the corner. The days are shorter, the nights cooler. The kettle has finished boiling; steam rises like mist against the white porcelain stove. We had planned on going to the hoedown at Towne Park after the Fall Faire Parade but the admission was three dollars each. With Ethan, this was way too expensive, only to run around after him in the Parade Circle, so we went home.

Initially I was extremely disappointed, but my mood is lifting now as I pour hot water into the teapot with the dried yarrow and mint. It will be ready in only a few minutes.

Vince and I sit on the low, wooden steps trying to catch the last direct glances of the setting western warmth. We both experience a few minutes of feeling safe, parked on the stoop, our knees almost touching. Pete has taken Ethan to town to run errands.

"She slept with Sam," he says, shattering the peaceful space. "My God, I wasn't expecting that!"

"What? You're fucking kidding! With Sam?"

He picks up a scabby willow stick left by Bobby and scrapes the bare ground.

"Kathy does what she wants," he says. "She's always has. She's the one who got us started on this whole open-marriage thing, you know."

We sit for a good five minutes. I'm covered in stale sweat. Toxic, fear-based sweat.

Finally I venture a few words to try and ease the discomfort. "Shit. I can't believe it. Maybe she's feeling insecure or threatened by me. Maybe she needs more of your attention!"

He only shakes his head.

"You must be mad as hell!" I am mad as hell.

He shakes his head again. "Nah, what's the point? What'll that do? Shit—I guess they were both really drunk at the time."

He rubs his tense neck muscles and stretches his legs out until the toes of his dusty leather city boots point skyward.

I stand up, feeling cramping in both calves. "So this makes it OK? If you're drunk you can do anything you like? At least they could have been honest and talked to you first. You know, like we did."

He laughs. "Yeah, like we did! It's made all the difference, eh?

"What are you saying? Jeez, are you saying it's the same? I thought we had a special relationship!" A dark hole opens up in front of me. "How can you trust her after this? I thought the whole idea of your open marriage was you talk about everything out in the open and people are honest with each other."

He stares at the ground. His face is blank.

"I don't get you! I don't get you and I don't get her!" I kick clods of dirt. "And I risked my relationship for you. For what I felt for you. And you think it's the same as what Kathy does? Just spreads her legs for someone 'cause she's drunk? And what about my sister, does she know? How do you think she must feel? I know they're not together now, but this is low!"

He doesn't answer but pushes up off the steps, stands stiffly and walks briskly toward his car. He mutters, "I have to go home now, supper time."

I yell at his retreating back. "Supper time? What the hell is going on?" I panic and then start to plead. "Please come back. I'm sorry."

He turns to me. In this one second, there are only two of us in the world, in pain, staring at each other. He grimaces and pulls that beautiful, ebony hair back out of his eyes, combing it with his fingers. "I'll see you later, man."

"Man?"

He doesn't answer. He gets into his van and starts the engine.

"I'm not a man" I whisper as he backs out.

Fuck! More great timing! Bear's family is returning from a trip to hell knows where. Vincent nearly backs into them. Then hits our red wheelbarrow and knocks it over. He peels away.

They all look surprised. Jane's ghoul-like eyes meet mine.

The last thing I need!

I run inside.

❊ ❊ ❊

As I pin the last few towels from the laundry basket onto the back yard clothes line and while Ethan finishes creating his miniature village in the sand pile, Kathy and Vince pull up. Out of nowhere. Am immediately flustered. My tangled hair is unwashed. Worn jeans, covered in garden soil are also stained with vinegar from this morning's window cleaning.

Within moments they are all in the back yard. The girls proceed to "play" with Ethan, which means they start to destroy his handiwork, bombing his bridges and mud roads with small rocks.

Khapoo! Khapoo! Khapoo!

I hold my tongue. Kathy grabs a couple of towels and a handful of clothespins and starts to help me hang what's left.

"Isn't it a little too late to be putting out the laundry, Missy? It looks like rain on the horizon!" Her tone is condescending and sassy, more insolent than usual.

She wags her finger at me. "The early bird gets the worm, you know! We managed to get an early start today, and we're off on an adventure! Right, girls?" The girls ignore her, continuing with their decimation of Ethan's architecture, now a pile of dirt and sticks. He has joined in and is helping to level the village, throwing more clods of earth on the pile.

Kathy chucks an extra clothespin into the basket. "OK," she declares. "We're done." She claps her hands together as if scoring a point. "So, Missy, we're off to Nelson, land of fairy-tales and enchanted creatures. It's definitely time to get out of this hell-hole. I so need a break. Know what I mean?"

I feel the thick tension between her and Vince as he lifts the engine hood and pretends to check the oil in their vehicle. He ignores me and does not say a word. I say nothing. Two minutes of awkward silence pass as I adjust the wet laundry on the line.

"Tea before you hit the road?" I ask.

"Yeah," Kathy says, "let's have a cup of tea first! Girls, get on in here. You need a snack before taking off. Neither of you had any breakfast to speak of. And we aren't stopping for French fries today."

She rustles her children into the kitchen. They complain but run into the sunny room and plunk down on chairs around the table.

"So what do you have in your cookie jar today, Sash?"

Kath has always been a little too comfortable in my kitchen. Without waiting for an answer, she starts opening and closing all my treat containers. A dozen homemade oatmeal raisin cookies fill the bottom of a large gallon jar. Kath unscrews the lid and starts to pull out a handful.

"It's OK if they have one or two each, right?" Without waiting for the answer, she hands each of her girls two, and keeps two for herself. As they munch away, I fill the kettle and set it on the stove. A sudden screech. I swivel in time to see Carson trying to pull Ethan's favourite Tonka truck out of his hands, which are now red and swollen from the effort of hanging on.

Before I have a chance to intervene, Kathy walks over and snaps at them. "Give it to me! Right now!"

Ethan passes it to her, his hands shaky.

"If you can't share, none of you can play with it!" She takes the truck, walks to the screen door, pushes it open and with great force throws it out onto the stone pathway in the yard. Even from inside the kitchen, I hear a horrible crashing sound.

Hell!

The kettle whistles loudly on the stove. I quickly turn it off. Clack. All of the children are sniffling, including Ethan. I pick him up.

"And no more fighting on this trip!" Kathy shrieks. She smacks both girls across the face. They immediately wail and run out to the van, slamming the screen door behind them. Kathy decisively leans forward against the counter, her arms locked tightly in front of her, knuckles bleached. She stares out the window at Vincent, who is now pretending to clean out their vehicle, anxiously sweeping out imaginary debris with a hand-held whisk broom.

The girls have climbed into the back and now sit quietly. Teary, rigid and mournful, waiting for their adventure to start.

"How about I take one more cookie each for the road?" Kathy asks, her face blotchy. She takes out a handful, wraps them all in a pink handkerchief she pulls out of her purse and stashes them in her tote bag. "We all have to learn to share, right Sash?"

I turn to the cupboard to pull out dried mint for tea and croak, "Of course, yeah. But I...I was hoping to save some for Pete and Ethan."

"Save them all you want, we're out of here. I think we'll skip the tea today." she says. "Later!"

She hustles out and jumps in the car. All the doors slam shut, bam, bam, bam. And in an instant, they're gone.

I hold Ethan on my hip and stand still, looking out the window. Both of us are shaken. Ethan's eyes are wide, his pupils dilated. We watch as the rectangular monster roars off in a cloud of yard dust that slowly and gently descends on my once perfectly clean, once perfectly white sheets and towels.

Sam calls the next day and begs me to let him come by for tea. For some reason I can't stay mad at him for sleeping with Kathy. Or for selling drugs to Bear. He says he was helping Lizzie out and they both needed the cash. I choose to believe him.

"She's definitely not the same Kathy who told me it was fine to sleep with Vincent—she swore she wouldn't feel at all threatened." I explain.

"Yeah well, I do feel bad that we screwed, but she kind of threw herself on me! I'm a sucker for blondes, what can I say?" he looks down and picks at a thread on his shirt.

I don't know whether to believe him or not. But today I need to believe someone. And so need a friend.

"She seems to be reassessing herself lately," I say, "like she's insecure about her relationship. Oh damn, I don't know what the hell is going on with her." I stir more honey into my tea. "She's acting weird lately, anyway. She scares me." I exhale deeply and get up to check on the batch of granola in the oven, stirring it with an old wooden spoon.

"Give it some time," says Sam. "I'm sure you all can be friends again. There's nothing more complex than the bloody human heart."

"Yeah, I guess." I sigh.

Sam says all the right things at exactly the right time.

SHEDDING OLD SKINS

The Break

Pete and I are nearly finished preparing a batch of Saskatoon berry and apple fruit leather. The wall phone rings. I jump. There's a subtle buzzing in my head; I know who it is, even before Pete picks up the earpiece.

I can't stop what I'm doing, though. The natural sugars will instantly stick like glue to the bottom of the pot and all will be wasted. I keep stirring.

Pete turns away, walks into the living room, dragging the phone cord. "You guys back already?"

"Who is it?" I ask. I already know who it is. But I must keep stirring. The thickening magenta berries, loaded with beige specks, remind me of the intestines of squashed birds on the roadway: drying crimson and burgundy flesh among broken feathers and tiny beaks.

Pete ignores me and now gazes toward a distant corner of the kitchen "Oh yeah? How was it?"

What's going on? My temper flares. "Pete, who the hell is it?"

He spins around. "It's Kath," he says, spitting out the words.

"Oh, hmm. Yeah, I get it. Yeah. No problem. Okay." He continues.

"Can I talk to her?" I whine, stirring the thick mess.

He brusquely shakes his head.

"Have they returned from their adventure? Will they be coming over for dinner soon?"

He still won't look at me and shakes his head again.

"Yeah, for sure, I understand. I'll tell her," he says before hanging up the receiver. Sorrowful eyes avoid mine, yet there's a smile at the corner of his mouth.

"So..." Stirring, stirring, stirring. "What?"

He stares at me with a blank look.

"What the hell is going on?" I turn off the burner and stand with hands on hips, ready for a face-off.

"Christ! Settle down—it was Kath. They're back. She called from town."

"And? And?"

"And both Vincent and Kathy have decided they don't want to continue their friendship with us. She said...it wasn't worth it. It's way too complicated and they have their own problems to work out."

"What the heck? Of course they have their problems to work out! They always have and they always will! But not being our friends anymore? It doesn't seem right!"

I feel dizzy and sit down. They needed to get away for a while, to get some perspective, take a pause from the crumbling of their marriage and the breakdown of our friendship. But I never expected them to totally bail.

I look over at Pete. "What do you think about all this? You don't even look sad! You should have let me talk to her! Damn it, should I call her back? Where is she?"

"I think her mind is made up!" He looks to the heavens and sighs, then drops the metal sheets on the table. The loud bang echoes through the small room. His fists are clenched as he strides toward the door.

"You know, to be honest," he says, "I'm actually feeling good about this news. Maybe this is all for the best! This thing, whatever the fuck it is... this friendship...Is it friendship? It's all become too much for me! I don't know who the hell I am anymore, never mind what I want. And you, well, I definitely don't know who you are! One thing is certain: it'll be way more peaceful around here!"

With that he kicks the screen door on his way out, leaving a black smudge on the wooden bottom. I feel it in my gut. I watch him leave. He drives east toward town for who knows what and who knows where.

A break from me. A break from all our bickering, all our fights about Vincent, about money, our future plans. Well, go on then. I've stopped worrying about where you go, and have even stopped worrying that one day you may never return!

Of course the argument and the clamor of the metal sheets awakens Ethan from his nap. I have to keep an eye on him while spreading out the fruit leather onto the cookie sheets then carrying the patties outside to dry in the autumn sun. I manage to drop an old flat door stored in the shed onto two sawhorses to act as a table. The thick, syrupy fruit mash must be quickly and completely covered with fine cheesecloth to keep off the clusters of flies. A few overly large, pesky horse-flies appear. They are swatted. One is accidentally stepped on in the soft dirt. I have no patience for small irritations and nuisance bugs at this moment.

When the work is done, Ethan and I go for a half hour walk down the road. I put one leaden foot in front of the other. It's all I can manage. Vincent and Kathy are not the people I thought they were. They constantly talk about being free and having the freedom to love whomever they want, but they can't even practice what they preach.

After a block or two of shuffling along, it's obvious I'm sleepwalking or out of touch with my physical body. With sizzling clarity I know this new development is probably all for the best.

For everyone concerned. For now, anyway. Pete is right. Our lives will be so much more peaceful.

I experience these few shreds of reason and focus, as if someone had opened an opaque drape in my mind and a luminous beam of awareness has burst through. *All will be fine.*

All the Time in the World

During the break, which ultimately turned to days and became two full weeks, I keep super busy. The busier, the better. Some days, when Pete is home with Ethan, I go for long solitary walks to the cemetery or to the marshes, if only to shake out the emptiness in my heart. Hoping to exhaust myself, I toil for longer hours in the yard and the vegetable garden, fingernails black and hands sore with calluses. By the end of each day I pass out long before Pete comes to bed. He accepts it and leaves me alone.

The August evenings are now a little cooler. A little softer. But as the harsh daylight transitions to a muted grey and when a violet sky forms a perfect backdrop for the silhouettes of diving barn swallows, I start to feel a deep yearning to connect with Vincent's presence and long to see him again. Some days, it's all I can do not to drive over to their cabin and confront him, but I let it be. I know it's best to wait this one out and let him return to me. It's going to take a while, and for a change I'm not worried. Today I can accept all that is and know it will eventually work out for the best, no matter my course of action.

At the two-week point, I realize I don't have to do anything. I can spend the entire day with Ethan playing in the yard. So we do. We harvest the squash, the small pumpkins we grew. We sit on the earth together, snacking on overripe tomatoes and watching dancing butterflies: cabbage whites and a few painted ladies, all the while cocky robins dig for worms and the occasional raven snitches tidbits from the ever-rotting compost pile.

I can wait and I can be. And do what I do. And wait some more. There is no reason to panic. There is no hurry. In the end, all works out for the best. All I need will come to me. There is no beginning and no end. Even the human clock starts at midnight, ends at midnight, and starts again.

I have all the time in the world.

* * *

My wait is worth it. Vincent picks us up after inviting us to dinner at their place and drives us to his home on the mountain. Pete, Ethan and I follow him down a dirt path winding along the edge of a meadow, along a narrow stream, facing south.

The setting of the old home site is quaint. An old timber bench has been set up. It leans against the cedar-shake walls of the cabin; a cozy place to sit, to watch the sun glimmer through distant birch and quacking aspen. Fading yarrow, field daises and cinquefoil dance in an early autumn breeze.

I carry Ethan inside, my stomach anxious and twisted in knots. Pete brings in a salad I made earlier loaded with late summer greens from our garden. The air is strained, thick with old sorrows and a hint of fresh irritations.

This is Kathy's space and she takes control like a queen in her castle, albeit a small, musty castle.

"Kids, head outside and play with Ethan now!" her harsh tone commands. Vincent takes the girls outside. Shaken, I turn to her and attempt to offer support and cheerfulness. "It all smells great, Kath. Can I help?"

My effort is met with the energy of a wet dishrag: rotting, clammy and rank. "No thanks, I'm good," she snaps. "Sit down at the table and dinner will be ready soon." Her mouth is set in a firm line. It's obvious she's doing this supper thing for Vincent.

"I'll wait outside." I make my exit, leaving Pete and Kathy. Vincent sits on the bench and pulls a small baggie out of his jeans pocket. His eyes light up when he sees me.

"Are you sure this is all right?" I ask. "Maybe we should do this dinner thing another time."

"It'll be fine," he says. "She's having a bad day—a sore back or something. We have to haul all our water here, you know!" He lights up a joint and takes a puff. I take it from him slowly, feeling the energy of his fingers.

"Bad days are going around."

He lightens up and smiles. "No kidding."

We share the joint, joking back and forth. I start to relax in the warmth of the failing sun. It's only minutes however, before a silhouette darkens our bench. Two steps out the door and there stands Kathy, hands on curvaceous hips. She is steaming.

"I haul the water and make the supper and you two sit out here enjoying yourselves? What the fuck, am I some kind of slave? Give me the joint, you jerk!" She tugs it out of Vincent's hand, sucks it in, holds it and exhales like a dragon, then hands it back.

"Supper is ready!" she announces.

A film covers Vincent's eyes. We both stand; he puts his arm around my shoulders and softly nudges me through the front entrance.

I stumble in and quietly sit down at the dilapidated table, hoping to get through the meal without being sick. Kathy opens a bottle of cheap wine.

"So, Pete, did you guys find another place to live yet?" she asks as she pours us a drink into pint-sized canning jars. "*I* wouldn't feel safe leaving my woman and child alone there after what happened. Has Bear returned?" She stares at Pete and continues to speak only to him, totally ignoring Vincent and me. Sweat trickles down my back. The room feels stifling from Kathy's lasagna baking. A tiny window in the sleeping area of the loft is open a crack.

I somehow get through the meal. After dinner, Kathy starts clearing off the table, again refusing any help.

I finally speak up. "I need to go home." I look at Vincent. "Now!"

"Why?" Vincent asks, a whisper.

"I don't feel comfortable." I touch his hand lightly.

He ignores it and stands up. "Fine, let's go," he says loudly. He stomps out the door. I walk outside without saying a word and pick up Ethan who'd finished his supper and is now stacking rocks by the bench with the girls. Pete looks puzzled but follows me out and down the trail.

Kathy catches up to us as we're ready to open the car doors. She is breathless but looks happier and appears friendlier as she leans into Pete. "What, I don't get a goodbye hug or anything?" She runs her hands through his thick hair. "I think you need a haircut! Come back this week and I'll do it. You're getting a little shaggy." She pinches his cheek as if in jest then winks at me. It's awkward. We leave.

Vincent does not speak as we bump along down the mountain road. Pete doesn't say a word and stares out the window. Ethan nods out in his lap.

"Would you like to come in for a cup of tea?" I ask Vince when we get home. I pick at the reddish peeling paint on the car door with my fingertips.

"No, thank you!" Vincent replies. He looks straight ahead then quickly puts the vehicle into gear. The grinding sound sends this piece of rusty metal right to my insides.

Tires squeal as he makes his get away.

More drama continues to present itself day after painful day. I begin to wonder if this is karma for all my wrong actions regarding Vincent. Pete ends up going to bed with Kathy one night as I walk home with Vincent from town. Sam was also there. He had been feeling depressed lately. His reasons were it took his mind off his bummed-out space and it was enjoyable at the time.

Holy shit, this is getting a little cracked. A threesome? How did they share her? I don't want to think about it. *Acceptance of the good with the bad. That is real love, isn't it?*

After hearing about it, I lock myself in my bedroom and stay there for the rest of the day.

Pete takes Ethan and they are gone for hours.

I am totally numb.

Pete and Kathy continue to act out whenever the four of us are together. Sometimes they both disappear and Vince and I have no idea where they go. One night while driving home, Pete interrogates me.

"How're you feeling?" he asks.

"Not too much."

"Do you love Vincent?"

"I think so, yes. But I love you too."

Pete freaks out. He drops Ethan and me off. And is gone until the next day, then refuses to say where he's been. I am cornered. If I take a step one way, I may fall off this narrow ledge. But if I step back, I'll have defeated all I was aiming for. Perhaps the only kind of authentic, true life, one that's realistic is some form of communal living.

I find my journal and scratch words across the page.

> *When you live with a person for any length of time, there is a tendency to become possessive of that person's affection, time, and sexuality. In an ideal situation, every person would have their own room or space. First and foremost they could be their own person. Then whatever happens with others is totally voluntary. A person could be monagomous or polyamorous. Or celibite for that matter. No heavy judgments. People who wanted their freedom wouldn't have to feel guilty or ashamed.*

There is so much confusion about commitment and freedom. Why does it have to be commitment or freedom? Why does it have to be one or the other?

Why must I choose? Why?

Lately, I've been picking up something heavy in the air, a pressure, as before a storm, like a dynamite stick sizzling right before something volatile explodes and blows everything to smithereens.

Still Looking

Despite all our relationship problems, Pete and I continue to look for a nice chunk of land— handy to town, but not too close—a location where we can have privacy, be surrounded by uninhabited nature, and still be able to get to town or work, or the occasional movie or dance. It's a challenge. Both of us feel totally unsettled and aren't sure we even want to stay in the valley. At least I`m not sure.

We drive out to look at a few of acres on the edge of town and meet up with Garth Stephens, who owns land throughout the Southern Interior. Gary recommended him, saying he was a straight shooter, which means he doesn't bullshit folks.

As we pull up, a tall, lanky gentleman in blue jeans stands by a new black Ford pickup.

"Hello there!"

We wave and crawl out of our Chevy beater into a large, flat meadow with beckoning pathways leading into the surrounding forest. Pete lets Ethan run loose.

The seller strides over. "Garth Stephens," he says, introducing himself. We each shake his hand. Warm and firm. He looks like a cowboy. His wide-brimmed felt hat, a gleam in his eye, and the toothpick in his mouth instantly puts me at ease. He smells like a healthy farm: fresh hay and livestock. I`ve heard from Hannah he rescues horses and goats.

"How much land is there with this piece?" Pete asks.

They start chatting and I head down the trail which circles this opening in the forest, following Ethan, who runs toward the woods as fast as his little legs can carry him.

I settle into the land right away. My body feels at home here. Grounded and at peace. The matted grasses entice, a soft mattress.

I grab Ethan and we fall down, laughing, then sit up and chill for a few minutes, soaking up the colours and sounds. Disturbed by our presence, Angelwings, getting ready for the coming winter hibernation, swarm and flutter, their golden butterfly hues reflecting the sun. One late helicopter iridescent dragonfly along with a mass of tiny hoverflies, creates a gentle symphony of flickering resonance.

I would love to lie down and sleep for a long, long time, in this meadow surrounded by only wild, growing things. This place offers oblivion. It offers to soak up all my pain and fears. The damp earth calls for new beginnings. *Didn't we all emerge long ago from such soil to struggle in our awkward and clumsy human form—this inelegant, often graceless, often stumbling human form?*

But first we were earth.

Somehow I know this. I know this well.

Ethan jumps up and gets going again and I follow him for a while along the edge of the forest.

After walking the perimeters and exploring the three acres, Pete and Garth meet up with us at the brook. It's about three feet across and bubbling musically in kaleidoscopic colours over sandy patches, smooth stones and gravel, even now, in late fall.

Garth picks up a short balsam poplar branch from the side of the path and starts poking the edges of the stream. "Lots of water here," he says. "Shouldn't be a problem for you. Wouldn't take much to put in a well and drain some of this creek, if you need to."

He flashes perfectly spaced, gleaming teeth. Younger than I thought.

Pete nods. Ethan picks up pebbles the size of marbles and starts chucking them into the water. They each create a tiny splash and ringlets.

I think of all that could go wrong. "What about in the spring? Does the area flood? It must, if it's this low! It looks like the river is only a few hundred feet away."

Mr. Stephens flushes and looks a little surprised I would even ask.

"Well, ma'am, yes, it might flood a bit in the lower areas, but if you build on the other side there...you might be OK." He looks back the way we came, pulls his hat down to cover his eyes from the afternoon sun and continues chewing on a toothpick. "Yeah, it should be OK."

I think out loud. "I've heard flooding could be a problem if you build near a river. So it could be a real downer if someone worked hard to homestead this land, and then had it flood!"

Mr. Cowboy nods, agreeing it could be a difficulty. We all continue walking along the creek. Pete says nothing.

But now I'm emboldened. "What about the mosquitoes—they must be freakin' bad here in the spring."

And on I go, pointing out all the conceivable complications, as in reality there could be many. I still don't trust this cowboy gentleman, even though he appears sincere enough. I do love it here, though. It's private and quiet and peaceful. I also have to question whether Pete and I are ready to dig a well and throw a cabin up before winter. It's already the end of September. *Time's a wastin'.*

Honestly, the mere thought of us having to work together, hour after hour, day after day, week after week, terrifies me. To my core. To have to actually dig a well terrifies me. Then to have to put in a foundation and build a cabin, with Pete as a workmate, makes me horribly anxious. Perhaps I am a worry wart, but I know we're so different in our energy levels. I have my health problems. And Pete his sleeping sickness. So buying an acreage like this would be asking for a hell of a lot of trouble.

We continue to debate the pros and cons of the land and spend the next couple of hours exploring and soaking up the beauty and healing energy of the property. I feel re-energized when it's finally time to leave.

We let Garth know before we head off home that we're interested. Even with all my serious concerns, we make him an offer of $4,000. It all depends on the co-operative money coming back to us once that land is finally sold, which could take a while. We'll be lucky to get a cheque by Halloween.

Pete is distant and preoccupied and doesn't say much on the drive home, I try to be positive and engage him.

"It's so beautiful there, I know we could do it—we could make it work! But it sure would take a lot of backbreaking labour to drill a well and build a house. Are we up for this?"

I continue trying to create some enthusiasm. It doesn't seem to be working, but I can't imagine continuing with our life in the little house in town.

He shuts me down. "Come on, girl, get real!"

I feel slapped.

"We could be looking at a lot of problems, Sash! I know you don't like our place now. You never have. Come to think of it, you don't seem to ever like wherever you are. Aside from the problems with Bear right now, there's really nothing wrong with our little place!"

I glare at him. The evening sun has warmed the driver's side of the truck, and casts an unnatural light on half his face, which looks sunken and skeletal. The screwdriver and other small tools in the glove compartment rattle loudly. I kick it with my foot. It stings. *Shit.*

It doesn't stop the noise. It doesn't help a bit.

"You continuously complain about every little thing," he says, "wherever we've lived. It's never going to be perfect for you! Don't you see? You could probably be happy in our little house! I think you have a severely chronic case of wanderlust, or the grass-is-always- greener-on-the-other-side thing." He pounds the steering wheel with his palm. "I know your people and your culture were like nomads or something, but really, can't you settle down? Can't you just be normal for a change?"

My heart stops beating. But only seconds later, my blood is boiling. "What the hell are you talking about? My people? Damn you, Pete! If it was up to you, we'd still be living at the side of the highway in a tent! And what the hell is normal? I do not want to be "normal", I may never be normal! Damn it. Stop the damn truck! Stop it now!

He pulls over. We're only a mile from home. He doesn't seem to care I'm upset. I'm not surprised he doesn't care. He looks straight ahead, his square jaw set. I open the passenger door and jump down.

"Please feed Ethan when you get home! I'll see you later!"

Ethan has woken from his car nap and looks confused. I slam the door and walk off as Pete speeds away in a cloud of pea gravel.

I watch them leave then turn away, suddenly guilty for leaving my boy in the truck and angry at Pete for taking a sharp staff to my heart.

Could he be right? I am *guilty of always wanting more. And maybe I* am *a gypsy. But what's wrong with that?*

I walk in the opposite direction until I see shelter and crawl down to a grove of hawthorn bushes at the side of the road. The branches of undergrowth scratch me with their sharp needles, but I must have cover, so I push through a small opening in the bramble and sit down on a pillow of flattened and entangled dried grass. Weavings of purplish-black twigs form my cathedral ceiling. I have a good long cry and wonder again whether Pete is right.

Why can't I be happy with what I have? Why can't I accept my life just as it is and be grateful? Why must I always be searching? Searching for the right man, the right people. Searching for a place where it feels exactly right. I've tried to squelch this seeking, this constant yearning for something more.

Somewhere this exist; I just don`t know where. Forever beckoning, calling me endlessly, like a melody drifting over ethers, promising a safe refuge, a joyful life, full of my people, love and healing and acceptance.

I'm stubborn. *So what?*

It may take a lifetime for me to find this. *So what?*

I can't give up now. I must keep searching.

A feisty magpie, dressed in his Sunday best black-and-white tuxedo, lands in the thicket and squawks at me. Crawwwwk, crawwk, crawwwk.

As I clamber out and scramble up the dusty bank a large thorn catches my sleeve and tugs on it, scratching me. Blood droplets well up from a tiny cut on the back on my hand. I gently pat it dry with my shirt sleeve.

Cowboy Encounter

After brushing myself off from the mini retreat under the hawthorn bushes, I turn homeward and spot a black truck heading straight toward me. It slows down and pulls over.

A tinted window rolls down and the driver smiles broadly. "Hi! What a coincidence, seeing you on the side of the road of all places."

Garth winks at me.

And surprisingly, I feel a tiny bit better. "Yeah well, married life, you know," I confess while looking downward and scratching in the dirt with my toe. "Disagreements, etc. I needed some down time. I guess." I feel a little stupid, an abandoned pup at the side of the road. Messy hair covered in pieces of leaf litter, my tear-streaked face is certainly dirty. But I feel safe. And this light exchange feels like a friendly chat.

"Well, I wouldn't know about such things today, having been divorced twice myself. Better to be single, I think. It's easier." He smiles sadly and looks away toward a peach tone sunset streaking across the western edge of the valley basin. "Hey," he says lightening, "I was just going for a quick bite. Want to join me? I'll buy you a milkshake or a Coke or something. To drown your sorrows."

He grins again. The sparkling teeth.

Part of me is pulled to go home, tuck Ethan in, try to make up with Pete, and go to bed early. But right now I could use some casual time with a friendly face, someone accepting and cheerful.

"Yeah, sure," I say. "Sounds good. I'm assuming the chores are taken care of at home and this is probably exactly what I need right now."

I hop in the passenger side. *Jeez, the upholstery is immaculate. A soft cotton blanket for me to sit on. And newish. Surprising for a cowboy dude.* A familiar tune dances from his eight track, “take it easy, take it eeeasy...” He pulls a tidily rolled joint out of his shirt pocket and after expertly lighting it with his slick Zippo lighter, hands it to me. The light scent of butane and bud fills the cab.

Nice. I take it gently when he passes it over. “I thought cowboys only drank beer. Wow, this really blows my mind!” I laugh.

Somehow I developed the belief over time that only a certain kind of person got stoned, smoked pot, or took mind-altering drugs to experience another reality, or simply relax. That people of different lifestyles and values might have something in common with a socialist, tree hugging, vegetarian hippie is news to me. I thought ranch hands and cowboys were rednecks, not very intelligent or sensitive. Where I got this idea from is a mystery. It could be true, but it could also be old tape loops. Outdated programming.

He laughs lightly, the sound like fresh water gurgling down a drain-pipe. “No, not this cowboy, and not in this part of the world! I’m a bit of a Bolshevik. And this is so much nicer. I’m pretty much done with the booze.”

He pats my thigh, lightly, respectfully “It’s all going to be OK.”

I look out the window and smile. “I sure hope so.”

It’s after nine o’clock. I remove my ankle boots outside and carry them in after quietly turning the key in the lock and opening the back door softly.

My new friend Garth kindly turned off his headlights and his engine as he coasted into the driveway and parked behind Pete’s truck. I explained clearly to him it wasn’t necessary. And contrary to popular opinion in this town, I'm not a loose woman. Or a teenager. And that I don't have to sneak around at night afraid of getting caught.

He frowned, "Good night," with a trace of something lost in those kind eyes. "I'll pick you up next Wednesday at seven o'clock. If you change your mind, call me."

I carefully shut the door of his truck and waved, "Bye."

Inside the house, I tiptoe around, checking to make sure all is well. All lights are out. But there's a heavy smell of stale fags. Where is it coming from? Sniffing my jacket doesn't solve the mystery and I continue to Ethan's room. He's perfectly tucked in and seems at peace in his dreamland with a stuffed Pooh Bear under his arm. A recent gift which came by mail from Aunt Sally. Still skulking about, I creep into the bedroom where the smell of stale butts is much stronger. Pete is dead asleep.

I pick up his plaid shirt. *Whew!* It smells like a pub. I'm perplexed and immediately suspicious but am far too weary to care tonight. I'm too tired and it's not worth it.

Pete wakes as I undress. "Are you all right?" he asks. Not waiting for my answer, he turns over. "Don't worry," he mumbles. And falls back asleep. Or fakes it.

In the morning he's heading out the door as I walk into the kitchen still in my flannel nightie. "Hi, what's happening, man?" I feel like I'm prying, much like an old spinster aunt or nosy mother.

"Ah…" He stops in his tracks. "Heading into town. Need anything?" He looks down, picks up his jacket, and opens the back door. It scrapes.

"No, nothing, I guess. Well, maybe some salted butter. We're out." I sit down.

"Yeah, sure. Oh, and Eth is fed and watered. He's with a book in his bedroom See you later, I guess." He bolts.

I continue sitting for a few minutes, staring out the far window, not sure how to proceed. I stand up carefully, check on my boy then head into the bathroom to wash and get dressed.

In the afternoon, after Pete returns, we have a short talk about the land we looked at the day before.

"It's pretty nice," he admits. "But, honestly, we're quite unsettled. And we don't have the cash. How about we stay put for now? It's better for Ethan and probably easier for all concerned. Let's see what happens in the spring."

I have to agree. Today, my world feels shaky. It's clear the walls of this world with Pete are slowly crumbling, and I can't hold them up any longer. My arms and shoulders are sore and tired from holding up too much for too long. Whatever has to fall, will fall.

Sometimes, when it's time for something to crumble, we have to let it crumble.

Before bed, I dig a crinkly but neatly folded slip of paper out of my jeans pocket. It's the prayer that Garth, the group, and I shared at an AA meeting the night before—the meeting for alcoholics and "survivors" of alcoholics. I learned last night any addiction is fair game for the twelve steps, including love addiction, about which one unhappy twelve-stepper shared painful stories.

Who would have thought? Such a bizarre concept. But Garth told me after the meeting, as the group stood around outside chain-smoking and chatting, this kind of addiction is a real thing. People can get hooked on the rush of infatuation.

It was uncomfortable to sit through a meeting with a room full of old drunks trying to get sober. Along with a lot of co-dependent relatives and spouses of such ex-drunks. So many stories, so many pained and tortured souls.

But a lot of it stuck. A lot of it made sense. I could relate. I wasn't addicted to booze or pot, but I was addicted to unhealthy love. Or an idea of love. The kind that initially leaves you breathless and high, but eventually broken.

I'm going to need some help. *It may take a while to kick this. Real love should not be painful.*

God grant me the serenity to accept the things I cannot change, the courage to change the things I can and the wisdom to know the difference.

I leave the Serenity Prayer out on the counter beside the granola jar.

In the morning the prayer is on the kitchen table, flipped over. I had hoped it would give Pete some comfort, too. Oh, well—I'm not pushing any more. How much serenity can one person muster? Some serenity would be nice. Can I accept the things I can't change? I struggle with the acceptance part. And for sure I don't seem to have the wisdom to know the difference. Yet.

I tidy up around the prayer on the table but leave it there under a small, turquoise glass jar that holds a tiny pale sunflower head, the last one that year. Its cadmium-yellow petals drop off softly, one perfect petal at a time.

ONE HUNDRED AND EIGHTY DEGREES

A Decision

A decision must be made. I must figure *something* out. Leave town, stay with Pete, run off with Vincent? If he'll have me? Just run? My eyes don't cry anymore, but my heart weeps.

I've stopped going to the CODA and AA meetings and notice how my life suffers. But I have a great list of excuses for not going. My head aches, I'm too tired, I have to bake bread. I have to take care of Ethan.

Pete recently told me, "I'm still trying to make this work, but I feel extremely uncomfortable when Vincent and you are alone together. Even if you're not having sex anymore."

Mum called me yesterday. "I've been hearing stories," she said, her tone sharp and disapproving.

Falling right back into victim mode, I write:

> *What a screwed-up world. As long as I'm a good little girl and do what's expected of me then all is fine, but if decide to be real and follow my calling, then people disown me!"*

I admit this mess was my doing and I need to end this thing with Vincent. From going to a few meetings with Garth, I've figured out I have some kind of problem with men. But I can't—I've tried, but can't. I can't say goodbye to Vincent.

I want to still love Pete, but the future looks bleak for us. Some arrogant, rebellious part of me believes I should have the right to express some feelings for Vincent.

We have a special spiritual bond.

"Or do we?"

Happy Halloween

Vincent as "Ghost" makes his way towards me through the darkened room full of shaking and quivering bodies and deafening music at Gary and Hannah's Halloween Costume Ball. Bales of messy straw and oversized pumpkins litter the corners of the shadowy living room. Ghouls, devils, pirates, Cher and Richard Nixon lookalikes groove to the pounding beat. Many of the old land co-operative friends are here celebrating the sale of the land with a rip roaring bash. It's finally sold! And we got what we asked for it! Close to $120 thousand. The co-op is so damned relieved.

"Where is she?" he asks.

"What? I can't hear you?' I gently lean into Vincent, trying not to appear too intimate. Anyone could be watching.

"What's going on? And where the hell is Pete?" he asks. "I can't find him either."

I adjust the sheer gauze covering my Middle-Eastern princess costume. Or perhaps it's a Persian costume. Or old Russian. Definitely exotic. I feel feminine tonight, for a change, and can't wait to start dancing. I jingle the tiny bells attached to a plaited belt, trying to play. Vincent doesn't bite and looks away.

"She's disappeared," he mutters.

"Who?" *Whoever is he worried about? I'm right here.*

"Kathy, damn it!" his face flushes. "I can't see her anywhere!"

Oh! "Let's have a look outside." We make our way through the heated crowd and out the back door. Then stand for a moment on the cool earth, under the stars. A waxing, gibbous half moon lights up the sheds scattered on the edges of the property. Tall prairie grasses form a spikey silhouette against the outlying hills.

A light is on in an old pottery studio on the edge of the property. I point it out and we walk over. Seeking warmth I hold his hand. It is cool and clammy, but reassuring somehow.

Peering into a small grimy window, we spy a small mattress on the wooden-plank floor. On the mattress lie two bodies closely entwined. I stop breathing.

Vincent leans against the door and tries to open it. It resists and he pushes forcefully. Finally it squeals loudly and creaks open. His face turns crimson and sweaty. Two startled faces look up. Our hermit friend, Stephen. And Kathy, yes Vincent's Kathy look up at us at exactly the same instant. You could hear a pin drop.

"What the hell? What the hell are you doing?" Vincent steps forward, fists clenched, then hesitates and shrivels back. He can't yell at her like this. Besides, she has the right to sleep with Stephen if she wants. *Doesn't she?*

Well, doesn't she?

Kathy and Stephen sit up slowly, not at all concerned they are naked and exposed.

"Hey, Vince. Meet Stephen. Stephen, Vince!" Kathy laughs her deep belly laugh and lies back down, relishing all the attention.

Vince storms out, slamming his clenched fist against the weathered door as he struts away into the darkness. I don't see him for the rest of the night, which is fine with me! I am so done with that bastard! *This is perfect karma. Kath falling in love with Stephen. The social butterfly and the recluse! A perfect match. I hope they're happy together. And fuck Vincent. Fuck him!*

I spend the entire night drinking way too much vodka and dancing my socks off.

I start off slow, enjoying the beat in my loosened body. Eventually I relax and get into each song and allow it take me where I need to go. To the edges of not feeling my pain, to the place of not remembering, the place of no borders, no embarrassment, no shame, the place of freedom. My loose dress swirls clockwise in the spinning of this new found ecstasy, faster and faster in spirals that take me to hopeful new beginnings and to releasing tangled and messy endings.

I weave through the room, dancing with all my fellow travelers, soaking up the loving energy in that space and absorbing all the laughter and warmth and joy of the celebration. It is a night to remember. And I make it count. For I am free.

The next day I don't remember all the drinking. Or most of the party. Or my pain.

I don't even remember that Pete was gone most of the night and returned only in the wee hours of the morn to drive me home.

But I do remember the freedom of the dance. The freedom of movement. My body remembers. Some long lost part of me is finally returning home.

Conclusions

Laura called me a couple of days later and mentioned she heard "through the grapevine" that Vincent is sleeping with someone he met while at the Halloween party. *Damn him, I'm so completely done with the scumbag! I've said it before but this time is for sure.*

I record a few lifesaving conclusions:

Never fall in love with another woman's man, no matter how many times she says it's all right.

Vincent and Kathy are both not ready for a giving and sharing relationship with each other *or* with any other people.

Poor Laura, who I introduced to those two, is fast becoming a "Vincent fan," and Kathy is accepting her as a good friend mainly because at this time she isn't any kind of a threat. I fear she'll be the next victim, like a helpless insect caught in their intricate web.

I've been such a stupid fool.

It usually goes like this:

Vincent becomes involved or interested in another woman, or is not giving Kathy the attention she requires. Kathy reacts by ignoring him for a while and pursues many outside friendships and interests. If there is a man around who pays Kathy a sufficient amount of attention, Vincent gets worried he'll lose her and she becomes desirable to him again. For a short while they do this twisted dance and go through all their back-and-forth hassles and crises. In the end, they both forgive each other and continue their relationship as if they've simply had a refreshing dip in the pond.

I've witnessed this three times already over the last few months and am not interested in seeing it ever again. Ever.

I am done. Cured.

❋ ❋ ❋

For weeks after Halloween, I fall into a deep blue funk. My own self created personal depression. I know I'm in withdrawal from Vincent but it doesn't make it any easier. Garth has left messages on my machine, but I don't have the energy to return his calls.

I was prescribed iron pills from my new doc and should be taking them but can't be bothered. I take them once in a while. He told me it was important as my iron levels were dangerously low. I hate taking these pills. They constipate me. I finally told my doctor off, right in his office, which felt great at the time, but now, months later I'm too embarrassed to make an appointment. So there's no one to check my iron levels.

I'm so damned tired. Sometimes I stay in bed for days. My energy gets lost in day-to-day maintenance. Showering, eating and taking care of Ethan.

And sleeping, my new escape which I now love almost as much as Pete used to. But now, whenever I see him, he seems super energetic and cheerful. This which drives me crazy. He told me yesterday he's starting back to work at the mill in a couple of weeks.

"Great. Have fun!" I said and went back to bed.

It's as if I'm floating. Perhaps I'm becoming transparent. It's easier to move between dimensions.

I'm becoming so sheer and so light one day I may entirely disappear. Maybe this is what happens to all those people who vanish. 'Woman disappears without a trace.' They become so porous that they transition right into another dimension.

Will I ever be healthy again? I pray to be stronger. I pray because there doesn't seem to be anything else left to do.

I'm not afraid of death, only of a painful dying.

I'm here for now—it's all I know.

The mid-November freeze sets in, reflecting my inner coldness: crisp ice and a scattering of snow.

I no longer believe it's possible to have a lover or a "best" friend. Not being special to anyone anymore, I feel alone. I know I can no longer look for security in some other person. My empty heart yearns for a real love, perhaps a love for God, or for whatever is true. At least for being able to experience a real truth.

A truth which does not leave me frozen.

But even a truth offers no real security.

No warm fuzzy feeling. No safety in a person, place, or thing.

There is no security. Anywhere. It's all a myth.

Most of the time, I can't feel a damned thing.

Change of Plans

One dark morning in mid-November, right before the heavy snows are supposed to hit, I wake with another headache after a sleepless night of wrestling with Bear demons. Demons who leave inexplicable claw marks on my white thigh: four curved scratches mysteriously appear overnight. I actually admire and respect wild bears but suspect the hairless one next door is far more dangerous than the ones who live in the woods.

As I cook up porridge for breakfast, I start thinking. *He knows all about my life and the affair thing with Vincent. He knows I used to smoke a lot of pot and that Pete and I are on the verge of breaking up. And I only know a few things about him. Like the fact he's an alcoholic, buys street painkillers off a supposed friend of ours, he's sly and sneaky and has hidden outside our house at night and listened to our conversations. There is a huge imbalance. And we still live here— next door to a monster.*

Despite my terror, I need to walk over to his slum haven and have a heart-to-heart with old Bear. There's no getting out of it. I can't live like this any longer. Pete is almost never home anymore. And I still wonder—who the hell killed our poor Felix? We still don't know. Did Bear do it?

I'm thinking he did it.

I am so sick of all this. Sick of feeling sick. Sick of being afraid. Sick of my life. Sick of all my fears. Am I going to live out the rest of my days as a frightened mouse, scurrying around in dark corners and hiding quietly in the walls? Stealing little scraps of food, having to gnaw through heavy cardboard to get at a few bits of real nourishment?

This is something I can deal with today. What's the worst that could happen? I need to face this reality and try to deal with it head on instead of cowering in my dark corner. This could be a start. So, I need to have a talk with Bear.

I scrub my face and cheeks with a scratchy facecloth, "And the talk has to happen today!" I growl at the reflection in the mirror.

After bundling up, I let Pete know I'm heading next door to have a word with Jane. He looks puzzled, but says "Sure, go ahead."

Minutes later, Jane stands on her doorstep after opening the door. Rotting weather stripping falls away around the edges of the frame. She's still in her frayed housecoat and I can smell something like burnt eggs wafting out from the stove area. Surprisingly, the house looks clean. Worn out, but clean. It's the first time I've ventured this far onto Bear's property.

"Hello, Sasha, what's happening?" Jane asks. "Sorry, I was up late with Bobby. He had a high fever. Not dressed yet." She's pale, as usual, and her wispy hair is not yet brushed. It floats above her like burnished ivy tendrils, seeking the light.

"Oh, don't apologize, Jane. I know it's only 8:00 a.m., but I wanted to talk to Bear before he left for work…"

"Talk to Bear?" Her silvery armor flashes. "What about?"

She folds her thin arms protectively over her fragile chest. I take a step back.

We aren't actually friends, but the last thing I need is for Jane to be mad at me.

"Oh, nothing too serious …" I struggle to find the right words which won't offend yet could get to the heart of the matter. "Ahh…well, we lost our cat a while ago. He disappeared, he simply vanished, and …" I shift in my boots. Their walkway is slippery. "I was just wondering if Bear. Or you, might know anything about this. Remember old Felix?"

She softens a bit. "Felix? Yeah. I remember Felix."

"Well, I know Bear really loves his Buddy cat. Perhaps he's seen something?" I clear my throat. "The truth is we found Felix's dead body last spring. His head was smashed in and …"

Jane's face turns ashen white. I hear a scuffling sound from the back of the house and Bear walks out of the bathroom wiping his face with a clean baby blue towel. His hair is slicked back and oily. I smell cheap shampoo or aftershave. *So he does preen.*

"Hey, Missy, what's going on here?" he asks. "Got another problem with your well? Sorry, can't help you today. Have to go to a grunt job in Green River." He limps over and stands next to Jane and rests his huge paw on her right shoulder. His nails still look dirty, his cuticles ragged. Jane appears more pallid than usual. She teeters and looks like she's about to fall over.

I lean forward instinctively. I may need to catch her in case she collapses.

"No, no, our well is fine today!" I reply. "Actually, I was wondering if you know what happened to our cat. Remember our cat Felix? We found him dead behind the shed months ago. I'm not accusing anyone here, but…Do you know anything about this?"

My fear is churning inside me, like clothes in a top loader, but it's also agitating and transforming and slowly turning to anger. Out of nowhere I lose patience and am ready to torch this son-of-a-bitch. I'm on the verge of screaming at him. "So, do you?"

Both Bear and Jane appear stunned, their eyes wide and glassy. I hear a faint whimper from the back room.

"We don't know anything about your damn cat," Bear says. "Settle down. I may be a drunk and a loser, but I do *not* kill cats!" He's shouting now, his enormous fists are clenched and hanging at his sides. "Get a grip and go on home. I'm sure your old man is waiting for you! Maybe you should stay at home more instead of ..." He's suddenly smirking and has a twisted smile on his puffy face. I take another backward step. He's ready to smack me, I'm sure of it.

Jane steps in front of him and with all her sprightly weight pushes, then pulls him back into the kitchen and slams the door shut behind her. I hear them arguing loudly before I head back home, shaken but grateful.

Thanks Jane. She may have prevented a nasty, dangerous incident right there on her back doorstep. *Who'd have thought she had the strength?*

Still, this is not the end of this matter. I must keep going until I get to the bottom of it! Instead of heading back inside, where I can hear Ethan screaming and Pete trying to comfort him, I walk past my home and head down the dirt road to the river. I need to sit for a few minutes beside the frigid murmuring waters, the smooth grounding stones. And try to get my head straight.

This world is closing in on me. It's time to find clarity, to make a positive move for myself and my family.

I hike to the river and walk and walk and finally settle down on a sunlit boulder. I sit alone with my troubled thoughts. I watch them come and go. I don't actually have to believe any of them. The crisp air sharpens my focus. A couple of grinding hours collapse into this time warp as the minutes flow by like the icy chunks in the azure waters of that shallow river.

I need to get home. The sun is already disappearing quickly over the remote horizon.

When I get back, I'm feeling much clearer. I open the front door quite cheerfully. Part of me is hoping that my relationship *can* be rescued or restored. We're simply going through a bad patch. Pete and I could get some counselling, either buy that piece of land in the country or move to the city for a change of pace. It would be great to go back to school at some point and find meaningful work. We could enjoy cultural events, art galleries, and music concerts. I imagine a busy city life full of intellectual friends, creative pursuits and loving people.

As soon as I step inside it is obvious something is amiss. The electric heat has been turned down. It's much too cool. I glance out the window. I hadn't even noticed the truck isn't in the driveway. A large cardboard box with graphics of the Jolly Green Giant on the outside sits in the corner. I look inside and find Pete's sweaters, worn shoes and books. My heart flips a couple of times like a large fish trapped behind the cage of my chest. A note lies on the kitchen table with letters scrawled clumsily across it. I pick it up with trembling hands.

> Sasha, I've taken Ethan with me to town. We should be home later. I can't take it anymore and need to move on. I'll move out tomorrow. Sam said I could stay with him for now. I'm sorry, but it's time for a fresh start. Kinda love you but can't live with you, Pete.

I hear a groan, but it isn't me. The sounds are coming out of my mouth. Dry lips are moving but it isn't me. "What? No! We can work this out, Pete! No!"

Sliding downward I land with a thump on the nearest kitchen chair. The floor is littered with unmatched socks and wooden blocks and toys not put away. It needs a good sweep and a wash. Cookie crumbs and mud tracks create a messy pattern leading to the braided rug in front of the scratched, chipped sink. Light fairy dust coats windowsills and counters and dances gleefully in a sunbeam streaming in from a disappearing glow. A tacky, browning flycatcher hangs in the corner. Half a dozen winged victims who survived the chilly autumn but now find themselves doomed, wave tiny stick legs and struggle hopelessly to free themselves.

I sit for hours, it seems, in a daze, then realize I need to find Pete. And Ethan. He's my baby, and I don't trust Pete to take care of a child on his own. *What is he thinking?* I have to get dressed warmly and hike downtown and find them. Right now!

Maybe they're at Sam's? I'll check there first.

The phone rings as I'm preparing to leave. Perhaps it's Pete. No, it's Mum. She wants me to come over right away. I tell her it's not a good time, but she insists. "Come over, it's important."

"How about later? I have to take care of something first."

"Yeah, OK. Get here as soon as you can." She hangs up without explaining further.

I eat a tiny cheese-and-apple sandwich, chewing small bites. I'm not hungry but know I'll lose steam if I don't feed myself. I pack a small knapsack with a hat and mitts and fill a small jar with tap water for the hike. It's only a twenty-minute walk to town and then to Mum's house. I am so naked. Not the naked of nude sunbathing on the river, but a terrifying, vulnerable nakedness of the soul. Naked without any emotional armor or defense. I need something to cover me; a tough, turtle-like shell would be best, a bit of protection on my back. But all I have is a ragged knapsack. It'll have to do.

The walk is rejuvenating and brisk. But with each footstep my heart twists and tightens. When I get to the edge of the town proper, I hustle through shady back alleys and side roads, noticing every piece of tarnished tin foil and every brown, decomposing candy wrapper.

Following the path of least resistance, I look everywhere for Pete's truck, or his slouched figure, carrying my boy. *He has to be here somewhere.*

The Lie

Heading toward Sam's apartment, I turn the corner on the main drag and see two familiar faces framed behind a window in the Pine Woods Café. Pete and Lizzie sit across from each other at the window seat and appear immersed in a conversation while sharing a smoke. *A smoke? Sharing a smoke?* Pete doesn't smoke! As I get closer, I see the dreamy, intense way they look into each other's eyes.

As I pull the heavy door open and walk in, they both look up. Surprise and guilt are written on both faces.

Ethan sits in a filthy restaurant high chair, a few ketchup-stained fries in front of him. "Hi, Sasha," he says, smiling widely. I reach in and pick him up. He squiggles, trying to sit back down. "No, no, I want my fries! Mum, mum!" I hang on tighter.

On Pete's plate lie the remains of a hamburger. *A hamburger?*

"What the hell is going on here?"

"Chill out, girl. Pete and I are sharing a late lunch. Don't shit your pants over it!" Lizzie says, defending Pete. Her face is grey, her eyes sunken, and her makeup is smudged as usual. But she looks happy, content even.

Pete butts his smoke into a slice of stale pickle on his plate and leans back, his face also pasty looking. He doesn't say a word but peers out the window, ignoring me.

I shift Ethan to my other hip and drill into both of them. "What the hell is going on? Where is Jared?"

Lizzie rolls her eyes. "I left him in the snowbank—ha, ha!" She rolls her eyes again. "He's with Sam. What's your problem?"

It's obvious. I freak.

"Are you two sleeping together? It sure looks that way? How could you? Man!"

They both look guilty but neither says a word.

Finally Lizzie blasts me. "Get a grip, Sash! You're one to talk!" She jumps up, grabs her purse, and runs out the door.

Pete glares at me. "I didn't, Sash. I did not have sex with Lizzie. We're simply really, really, good friends." His mouth twists, he looks down, then over at another table full of elderly diners, who pretend to be eating their fried chicken. He shrinks back, expecting the worst.

And he gets it. "You're lying, you bastard. Why should I believe you?"

He shrugs. "Your choice."

The waitress walks over right then, casually drops the bill on the table, and whispers to Pete. "Take your time, honey." She winks at him and saunters away, ignoring me.

He looks so damned guilty. I probably can't prove anything, but I know it deep in my gut. Pete is sleeping with Lizzie and probably has been for a while. *Oh, my God!*

I grab Ethan's coat off the high chair and walk towards the groaning door. Pete throws ten dollars from his wallet onto the table and nods to the waitress whose big hips sway as she wipes the table next to him. He follows me out and we start to argue on the sidewalk before I tell him we had better have this out at home.

"I can't believe you!" I say through clenched teeth.

"Oh, shut up. Like Liz says, you're one to talk."

Ethan leans out from my hip toward his father and I let him go into Pete's arms. I'm not going to fight here on the street about who Ethan wants to be with.

At this moment, anyway.

"Damn you, Pete!" We both stand there on the street corner, looking down at our boots. Ethan chews on his coat sleeve while we throw invisible hate daggers at each other.

I'm chilled, I need to move. "Shit, I promised Mum I'd stop in for a minute. She says it's important! Damn it, I'll walk over there. See you at home later. We have to talk!" I'm shaking and can't stand being in Pete's presence.

"Yeah, sure, whatever, man!" He walks toward the truck parked only a few feet away.

Ethan turns his head to me and yells in his sweet voice, over Pete's shoulder. "Bye, Sasha."

I blow him a kiss. "See you soon, Eth!"

And then I see it: I am losing him. I see it so damned clearly. I have been such a fucking idiot. Everything has been about me. I have been such a self centered, narcisstic fool. Although I try my best to be a good domestic caretaker, a practical, caretaker mother, I have missed too much of the joy of simply hanging out with Ethan. Of playing with and watching him grow. *Oh my god.*

I must get my Mom's damned errand done and I must get Ethan back before it's too late.

And knowing Pete, I could be in for the fight of my life.

I turn quickly and head towards Mum's house.

My heart is shattering into a zillion little pieces.

Spilling the Beans

A familiar car is parked behind Mum's vehicle. I can't place the owner, but know I've seen it somewhere. I knock a few times on the aluminium screen door. No answer.

Following what feels like a frigid eternity, Mum opens the door, tired eyelids pink and greying reddish hair wrapped in blue foam rollers. A pallid mouth set in a tight line.

"Well, you finally made it," she says. "Come on in, I'll put more coffee on."

"Yeah, well Pete has the truck and I walked. It takes a while…Is Daddy Wes at work?"

Mum's eyes tear up and she shakes her head. "We'll talk later."

She turns abruptly and heads into the kitchen. Her home smells like garden tomatoes stewing, laundry soap and stale cigarettes. I kick off my boots and follow. A pile of speckled pinto beans lies on the checkered linoleum near the pantry, covering a square foot or so. I gingerly step over them.

"Watch out for the beans I spilled," she says. "I still have to sweep them up. I was going to make a pot of soup."

Entering the kitchen, I am frozen at the sight of… Jane. Jane? Yes, Jane, sitting comfortably at the table, counting out holes, moving a peg in the cribbage board then skillfully shuffling a deck of worn Vegas cards. A cup of coffee sits in front of her and she holds a cigarette between stained fingers, her feet up on the wooden stool.

Mum blinks nervously and politely introduces the mystery woman. "You remember Jane, don't you? Your neighbour? We're finishing our game here. Have a seat. You need to sit."

I stand frozen. "Yes, I know Jane," I mutter. " Hello again."

Jane and my mother had been friends since the days before both of them remarried. Still, she's the last person I expect to see in my mother's kitchen having coffee and smoking a Cigarello. She looks totally comfortable and at ease. Not at all like the wispy, ghost-like figure from next door, constantly ill, looking like she's on the verge of death and fearing for her safety. And not at all like the wife of a violent and unpredictable alcoholic.

Mum pours fresh water into the coffee maker.

"I don't think I should have coffee," I tell her. "It sometimes upsets my tummy and makes me too hyper."

"I know, sweetie, you can't drink coffee, but today you might need it."

She grabs a mug, my favourite, the one with lily-of-the-valley flowers on it, and plunks it down on the table. With a weak smile she pours a few tablespoons of Bailey's into my cup. "Jane needs to tell you something."

I sit down in the kitchen chair. *A dream. This must be a dream.*

Jane's slate-grey eyes mist over as she stands and folds her arms over her thin torso. She peers out the window as if searching for something.

After a deep breath, she stares down at the floor. "I'm sorry," she says. "I should have had the courage to tell you this before, but I was so ill for a while and couldn't do it. I felt too exhausted. I nearly told you earlier today, but Bear was there and…well, Bobby… well… Bobby is a good boy. He lashes out sometimes, and I know he does have some behavioural problems, but…"

I'm mystified. "Bobby? What does Bobby have to do with anything?"

"Well…your cat, Sasha. Felix. He was over one day and Bobby was goofing around, you know, just being a kid. He probably teased him too much. And I guess Felix must have scratched him, and so Bobby must have lashed out and accidently, well accidently…killed him."

I watch as she descends into her chair. "Damn it. Damn it! Bobby killed your cat. Yes, he killed Felix! There, I've finally said it! He took a heavy board that was lying in the garage and whacked your poor kitty over the head. I'm sorry, I'm so sorry, I know it must be quite sad for you, but he's only a little boy and may end up on medication…" She pulls a delicate white hankie out of her purse and dabs her eyes.

Mum pours coffee into my cup with the liquor and I manage a big gulp. It burns going down, but in only a few seconds, I feel a tiny measure of relief.

"Jeez!" I say. "Oh, my God, who would have thought?" I stare into my coffee cup, watching the creamy spiral.

"Yes, well, I thought it only fair to let you know," Jane says. "And I know you must have found him later, because I checked behind the shed where I left him, and he was gone. I was so confused for a while, but now it's all so clear since you've told me about finding him there and…well, hopefully, he's at peace now in kitty heaven."

She adjusts herself in the chair and looks out the window again, this time to gaze at the distant mountaintops.

I stare at her as if she's from another dimension as she gets up to leave. I barely hear her say, "And so now, because I know you worry, like me, now you don't have to worry about there being a killer out there doing away with all the problem cats in the neighbourhood. It wasn't Bear. Of course not. Bear's a dear. He wouldn't hurt a fly."

She stands and walks over and lightly touches my shoulder. "Well, I'd better go now. It is getting on, and I must pick Bobby up from his grandma's." She glances at Mum, who looks oddly at peace. And smiles understandingly at Jane.

"I know it must be difficult for you Jane, keeping this secret for so long," Mum offers. "But sometimes you have to protect your kids, you know. You would do anything for them." Her eyes tear up. "Right?"

Jane nods slowly and dons her overcoat, "Yes—anything." She picks up her purse and walks toward the back door, then looks back. "OK. 'bye Sash." She tiptoes past the pile of beans on the floor. "See you next week, then?" she says to Mum.

"OK. I'll let you know what day next week." Mum slips into her slippers and walks Jane to her car.

I watch through the window as Mum waves goodbye to her new best friend then pour myself another shot of Baileys.

"Well, isn't life fucking bloody strange?" I say to the ceramic owl cookie jar which sits comfortably on the countertop, his round eyes enormous and unflinching. He looks as alarmed and perplexed as I feel.

"Who would have thought?" I ask.

"Indeed." Owl answers. "Who? Who? Who?"

THE UNKNOWABLE

Opening the Door

On the frosty walk home, cerulean twilight wavers overhead as the wide valley darkens. A sliver of a white moon crests the horizon, gently caressing carbon silhouettes of ponderosa pines. I miss Ethan terribly. I want to miss Pete, but he has hurt and betrayed me. I can never trust him. And Mum mentioned that Lizzy has secretly been seeing Pete for months. I'm so disappointed, but I'll work towards forgiveness and want to wish them the best. And move on. Of course I am not blameless. Despite my sincere attempts at honesty and the pursuit of an authentic life, I know I've hurt Pete too. It's been over between us for a very long time.

Walking is so necessary, so beneficial right now. Put one foot in front of the other. Walk and breathe. So simple. So simple. Walk and breathe. Repeat. As these footsteps carry me forward, I'm more all right with the world.

I've learned a lot over the past year. Before I can truly love another, I must learn to love myself. It has cost me dearly but I'm learning to be more of my true self. Not so afraid of my anger and not needing to be perfect or play a role. I'm a person, a woman, a daughter, a mother, a seeker, a friend, and so much more. I have a positive side yet also a dark, negative side which needs to come to light. Old, ugly issues resurface for healing over and over—much like a spiral. Or layers of an onion. As we peel it, sharp and stringent juices make us weep.

Blaming does not help, I tell myself. It all starts with me and ends with me, with my own self-awareness, the choices I make, and my desire for greater consciousness. And to live with a compassionate heart. I create and destroy, over and over and over.

With the help of a main creator, higher power, angels, God or whatever positive force I choose, my life will be all right as long as I continue learning and growing. As long as I don't shut down.

As I get closer to the tiny house that was home, panic sets in again, the old anxiety over being stuck here washes over me.

The kitchen lights are on. I see a flicker of movement behind amber curtains. Pete and Ethan are home. The truck is in the driveway. I stand frozen outside the back door. Jane's car is home, too. A moisture halo vibrates against a bright street light a block away. The first star twinkles, teasing me. *I wish I may …*

It all looks so normal. Another cute house in a small town. But I can't go back to this life, back to being the housewife, back to being a version of my mom, bless her dear heart. I can't. Nothing looks different on the outside, but everything has changed.

Everything has *completely* changed.

Have I changed? Have I changed enough?

Am I ready for the next good thing?

I take a full, deep breath.

I open the door and step inside.

Acknowledgements

Thanks to my supporters, beta readers, and writers groups, especially Allessandra, Brian, Paul, Tao and then Lorna, Brenda, Kamala, and Cathy. You cheered me on and encouraged me to finish. Thanks Harold Rhenish for the mentoring/editing and for making me dig deeper. Also the folks at Freisen Press for hooking me up with an editor who "got it". And Tellwell for their professional services and support. Thanks my dear Rigel. And Liv. And thank you Larry for being my rock, and for believing in me. And finally thank you to all those seekers of truth who refuse to shut down, who retain their compassion and authenticity and continue to work towards creating a better world.

About the Author

Alexandra Baresova was raised in the wild and stunning mountain valleys of southern British Columbia. She has explored many diverse professions and passions too numerous to mention, from community theatre and environmental activism to the visual arts and energy healing. She currently lives on Vancouver Island with her husband and a super intelligent cat called Azia. This is her first novel.